NOW YOU SEE HER

NOW YOU SEE HER

Eileen Dewhurst

This first world edition published in Great Britain 1995 by
SEVERN HOUSE PUBLISHERS LTD of
9–15 High Street, Sutton, Surrey SM1 1DF.
First published in the USA 1995 by
SEVERN HOUSE PUBLISHERS INC of
425 Park Avenue, New York, NY 10022.

British Library Cataloguing in Publication Data
Dewhurst, Eileen
  Now You See Her
  I. Title
  823.914 [F]

  ISBN 0-7278-4733-3

Typeset by Hewer Text Composition Services, Edinburgh.
Printed and bound in Great Britain by
Hartnolls Ltd, Bodmin, Cornwall.

For Mike and Sylvia

Chapter One

Mrs MacPherson saw the couple next door from her bedroom window as they walked down their garden.

She hadn't been looking out for them. She had, in fact, been hoping not to see them, but when she did she found herself grabbing a jersey and struggling into it while she hurried downstairs as fast as her short legs could manage and out across her own neat lawn, catching up with them halfway down and being relieved by the murmured normality of their conversation. Father and daughter, she anxiously reassured herself, strolling in their garden in the autumn sunshine, the father commenting on the trees and shrubs as they passed them, the daughter no doubt staring into space in that unnerving way of hers.

"The hawthorn's going to have a lot of berries this winter, Judith."

"Uh-huh."

"I think it's an old wives' tale, saying it means a hard winter. We had good blossom this spring, it's more likely to be the result of that."

"Could be."

Between the two gardens at the spot both parties had now reached was a lattice of branches, which Mrs MacPherson decided might give her a view of her quarry while being thick enough to keep her safe from discovery.

"I love the way the roses linger. October . . . Oh God, Judith!"

"Daddy! Please, Daddy!"

Mrs MacPherson found her space too late to see what had happened to change the tone and nature of the conversation with such dramatic suddenness, but when she peered through she could see that it had left them both trembling and distraught, standing stock-still and staring – glaring – at one another. Making her painfully glad she hadn't seen them that minute earlier . . .

Mrs MacPherson's unsuitably shod feet slid from under her on the slippery soil of her border flower-bed, and she fell with a thud against the boundary fence.

She lay motionless where she had fallen, not because she was hurt beyond a temporary loss of breath, but in the desperate hope that the impact of her tubby body against the thin rustic-style woodwork wouldn't be recognised from next door for what it was.

"Did you hear something?" The father, on a choked breath.

"I expect it was Ma MacPherson, eavesdropping." A cold hand clutched at Mrs MacPherson's heart, but let go as the daughter laughed. Not a pleasant sound, but at least it suggested that Judith had been joking. "For goodness' sake, Daddy, try being less jumpy." Mrs MacPherson imagined, more vividly than she found comfortable, the calm face of the girl studying the worried face of the man. Brian Fletcher had been looking increasingly worried of late. "Of course Mrs MacPherson isn't eavesdropping, she isn't the type."

Mrs MacPherson strained her scarlet ears into what she hoped was just a pause, but Judith said, "I'm going in," and after a despairing "Judith!" from her father there was silence.

Mrs MacPherson tried to tell herself that nothing untoward had happened, but after what she had seen yesterday she couldn't manage it. Yesterday, down in this same leafy foot of her garden and tying up some trellised roses, she had caught a movement from the bedroom window that matched hers in the identical Victorian villa next door, and when she had turned to face it she had seen Judith and Brian with their arms round one another, kissing passionately. Under her horrified gaze Brian had at least drawn away, but only to pull Judith out of sight.

Then, too, Mrs MacPherson had stayed frozen to the spot, heart-pumpingly thankful that the climbing rose she was working on was as red as her blouse and that her old brown gardening hat was squashed down on her silver-white hair. No one had come back to the window, but she had kept a motionless vigil through a steady count to a hundred before sinking ever so slowly to the grass and crawling across to the side path behind the low hedge that paralleled it all the way up to her back door.

She followed the same procedure now, gaining the house at a bent-kneed lope and as soon as she was inside pouring herself a tot of brandy and trying not to think of Brian Fletcher's wholesome good looks and kind, courteous manner. And anyway it was Judith she ought to be thinking of. The victim rather than . . .

She didn't want to find a word to describe the new Brian, to define her shock and disillusionment. And it was hard to think of Judith as a victim; Mrs MacPherson had been aware of a toughness, a sort of knowingness, about the girl ever since father and daughter had moved in next door two, or was it three, years ago. Then Judith had looked sullen and mutinous, staring through Mrs MacPherson when asked how she was settling in and how she liked school, answering in a mutter unless her father was with her, and then he had answered for her, with that anxious look that was never far away from his nice face.

Not a nice face! Mrs MacPherson corrected herself, pouring another finger.

About a year ago Judith had changed. She hadn't had any more time for Mrs MacPherson, but she'd stopped looking discontented. Now when Mrs MacPherson encountered her she tended to have a smile on her face and a faraway look in her eye until she noticed she was being observed and went all blank and watchful. *In love*! Mrs MacPherson had thought. *She's got a crush on one of the boys at school. That's nice, it'll make her human . . .*

But not nice. Not nice at all. In fact, if she were to believe her eyes and ears, what she had seen and heard was evidence of incest.

Mrs MacPherson gave a little moan as she wondered what to do and rued the uncharacteristic curiosity that had taken her creeping down her own garden like a thief to try and steal the truth from the couple next door. And spectacularly succeed.

Not curiosity, Mrs MacPherson amended aloud. Just a desperate hope of reassuring herself, by seeing father and daughter together again in what they thought was private, that her eyes or her imagination had played tricks on her the day before and their relationship was as it should be. But what she had done had been to confirm her new fear of why Judith had changed. Of why these days she was looking so – fulfilled, and yet no young men were calling in the evenings to take her out.

Mrs MacPherson conceded the word "fulfilled" reluctantly and with distaste. It described a state of which she had no personal experience and which she found hard to imagine: her brief and infrequent conjunctions with her late husband had left her with nothing beyond the event but her beloved son John. And she simply couldn't tell him about this, even though she was going to stay with him the very next day and the opportunity would so conveniently present itself.

Yet she ought to tell someone.

Mrs MacPherson decided to abandon the brandy bottle

in favour of a couple of aspirins; her head was splitting. Probably because of the words banging about in it. *Duty. Responsibility.*

Incest. No, not incest, surely not – Brian had told her that he and his wife had adopted Judith when Isabel hadn't been able to have a child of her own.

But that didn't alter the fact that the kind, thoughtful neighbour who always told her when he was going to Sainsbury's, with whom she left her key when she went away, appeared to be abusing the young girl who throughout her short lifetime had known him as her father.

She couldn't go to the police, Mrs MacPherson discovered as she made tea, for the same reason that she couldn't tell John. Brian Fletcher had always been so kind to her, and things still just might not be what they seemed.

But she had to do something.

Mrs MacPherson carried the tea tray to her sitting-room window and sat down facing the garden, thankful that fence and boundary bushes made it impossible from her ground floor to see into the Fletchers'. And that Pug, her large and autocratic ginger cat, was making his stately way up the lawn to join her.

Cat! Mrs MacPherson heard the dull thud of his flap on a wave of relief.

"Pug," she said, as he leaped at her lap. "You're a good boy."

Because he had reminded her of what her friend Marjorie Beadle had done about the enticement of her Tiddles by an unscrupulous neighbour. Mrs MacPherson had been scornful at first, *a sledgehammer to crack a nut,* she had thought, although she hadn't said so to Marjorie. She had merely suggested it might be an overreaction, going to a private detective because a cat was sharing its favours. But Marjorie had already gone – "I knew

5

you'd try to put me off, Mary MacPherson" – and had been taken seriously: an inquiry was under way, set up by the owner of the detective agency himself.

His name was part of a tongue-twister she had learned as a child, so it had stuck in her mind. Thank goodness, she wouldn't have wanted to ask Marjorie for it and then have to parry Marjorie's relentless curiosity.

Pug had fallen deeply asleep, but Mrs MacPherson couldn't wait his nap out. She managed to transfer him from her lap to her chair without waking him, and went in search of her *Yellow Pages*.

Yes, there it was, one of two names under the heading of Detective Agencies. Peter Piper Private Investigator. Amazing the things that went on in one's home town of which one was totally unaware.

Mrs MacPherson paused with her hand out to the telephone. It was going to be expensive.

But the late George MacPherson had worked long and hard and had left her very comfortably off. John worked hard too and had no need of her financial help. What else of importance was there in her life that needed money? And this was important. Mrs MacPherson punched out the number.

Marjorie had had to wait for the boss, but the woman who answered the telephone put Mrs MacPherson straight through.

"A very delicate matter," she said. "I need advice. I don't know if you can do anything, Mr Piper, but I need to talk to someone. I assure you that it is not a trivial matter." Such as a wayward tomcat. Which anyway wouldn't have strayed if it had been entirely happy with its owner . . .

"I'm sure it isn't, Mrs MacPherson." The voice was concerned, soothing.

"Thank you. May I make an appointment?" If she didn't make it now, and didn't see anything else wrong next door

6

when she came home, she might weaken. "I'm going away in the morning for a fortnight so I'm afraid it has to be a little while ahead."

The reassuring voice suggested an early afternoon in just over two weeks' time. "D'you know where we are?"

"Thank you, yes." And thanks to Marjorie, she also knew the intricacies of the lift, the layout of the office, and that Peter Piper was "boyish looking".

"Good. I'll look forward to meeting you, Mrs MacPherson."

Mrs MacPherson went back into the sitting-room. Pug was still asleep and the pot still hot enough for another cup of tea. She felt very slightly better.

Chapter Two

"You're being a teeny, weeny bit too athletic, Phyllida darling." Wayne was managing to smile, but Phyllida saw the exasperation in his eyes. "Try to remember you're playing a woman in her sixties."

Because he considered her too old to play the young lead. That role, since Wayne Cryer had taken over as producer for the Independent Theatre Company, had gone to his new and talented young protégée Miranda Delamaine.

Phyllida Moon was a modest woman but she knew her strengths, and that at thirty-eight she could still convince as a woman ten or more years younger. Wayne's predecessor Ken Hadfield had known it too, but Ken had had a heart attack so severe he would never come back to them. Phyllida also knew she could play a woman in her sixties just as credibly, and was content to do so. But Wayne liked to dictate the way his players saw their roles, and found Phyllida the least inclined of them to listen. A lesser egotist wouldn't have been so thrown by this, might even have sought her views as one of the more experienced members of his company, but Phyllida knew that Wayne resented her. He had had to congratulate her on her playing of the small role of a self-effacing secretary in the Company's current production, his first for them, but never having previously seen her acting, and refusing to look beyond her unremarkable real self to the chameleon range of talents so successfully exploited by Ken, he had cast her at face value – wan-haired, sallow-skinned and introvert.

Her fellow players' attempts to tell him there was more to her acting abilities than met the eye had at least secured her the part of sixty-year-old Miss Milton in the production now being rehearsed, although when he had discovered that her last role for the departed Ken had been Elvira in *Blithe Spirit* Wayne's eyes had widened in surprise and he had bitten his lip so as not to laugh.

"Women in their sixties can still move like girls." Since Ken's telephone call none of it mattered, and it was easy for Phyllida to speak mildly. She saw her husband, Gerald, stroll on stage and stop beside Wayne. "And there's nothing in the script to indicate that Miss Milton is arthritic. However, if you really want me to –"

"All right, all right, Phyllida. Just so long as you remember she isn't the young lead. I know how difficult it is to adapt to age change." Wayne had to be referring to her own age, the exasperation in his eyes had turned to spite.

"I'm not aware of finding it difficult, Wayne."

"All right, Phyl," Gerald said in his turn. "No one's getting at you."

"They're not?" Before she had heard from Ken, Phyllida had been finding the combination of Wayne and Gerald, producer and stage manager, increasingly disconcerting. Gerald hadn't got on too well with Ken but he and Wayne had gone into instant cahoots, an alliance from which she was excluded. To the extent, she suspected, of Gerald not having joined the rest of the cast in urging her case for a decent role.

"We'll break there," Wayne called. "Twenty minutes."

Carol, Wayne's wife and the company's wardrobe

9

mistress, came on stage from off prompt. "A word, Phyl?" she suggested.

"Of course. Let's go outside, I want to breathe."

"No coffee?"

"I'd rather get some air."

"Suits me."

The two women descended the steps at the side of the stage, climbed the gentle slope between the empty seats of the small auditorium, and came out into the pink and silver art deco foyer. The Empress Theatre had started life as a cinema in the 1930s and been named, Phyllida had decided, from the list of what were then considered to be appropriate movie-house names – a researcher *manquée*, she had failed to discover in the municipal library any record of past imperial patronage. Seaminster (the name had preceded a cathedral that had never been built) was a proudly Victorian town which saw its small 1930s legacy as an aberration, so that the local civic society had had a struggle to save the Empress from the bulldozers and had celebrated their victory with a restoration which was triumphantly over the top.

"A-a-a-h!" Phyllida hugged her jersey round her against the autumn wind mocking the sunshine and the blue brilliance of the sky, but the air in her lungs and on her cheeks was blowing away her irritation. Across the wide promenade seagulls were motionless on the bright blue knobs punctuating the horizontal rails that barred the short stony slope to the shore, and the details of Great Hill, rising at the east end of the bay behind the pier and the Grand Hotel, were sharply visible – dark green sprawls of woodland, gradated greys of rock, the line of the funicular railway and its attendant red roofs. Only a few figures dotted the broad walk beside the sea, most of them with dogs. Residents rather than visitors; the season was nearly over.

10

"We'd better walk," Carol said. "Too cold to stand and stare."

The Empress was west of town, latched on to the last section of immaculately maintained Victorian stucco. Beyond it towards Little Hill were three pairs of Edwardian semidetached villas to which the Victorian Society had lately extended its protection, and then the sheep-dotted fields of a farm, its low buildings white against the slope of another craggy outcrop.

Phyllida approved the fact of a working farm inside town boundaries, but this morning was glad to turn her back on it and walk against the shelter of the tall narrow hotels into which the adjoining terrace was divided.

"I like Seaminster," she said.

"Yes, it's fine, but most of us are raring to get back to London. Not you, Phyl?"

"I don't know. You?"

"I think so. But . . ."

"What is it, Carol?"

"It's Wayne, of course." Carol's profile was hidden by windblown strands of fair hair, but when she turned to look at Phyllida her habitually cheerful face was glum. "I'm afraid he's interested in Miranda as female as well as actress."

"Oh, no!" Phyllida stood still. "Carol, surely not? Don't tell me you've got proof?"

"Come on, it's cold. Yes, I think I have got proof, although I wasn't looking for it."

"I can't believe it."

"Listen, then. You know, everyone knows, that Wayne escorts Miranda round the corner back to the hotel for her beauty sleep after a measured half hour of sophistication at the Horseshoe."

"I know." Following a tip from their hotel's head barman, Phyllida's husband and Carol's had sussed out

11

the Horseshoe Club together the night the Company had arrived in Seaminster, and headed the hard core of those who remained there relaxing into the small hours for most nights since. "As you say, everyone knows."

"And everyone knows he sometimes takes longer to come back than it takes to walk the few steps each way."

"I suppose so, now I think about it, but I've heard him say he's going to make a phone call while he's at the hotel, or call in at the theatre for something, or . . . or . . ."

"Quite. I've heard him, too, and I've assumed that's what he's actually been doing. I've been a fool, Phyl."

Phyllida squeezed Carol's arm. "It really is hard to believe. But tell me."

"I wasn't checking up on him, it never crossed my mind. But last night after he'd left with Miranda I went back to the theatre; I'd remembered I'd promised to look something out for Gladys for the morning. You know that cupboard just along from the wardrobe, with my overflow?" Carol's voice was wavering, and she had stopped trying to clear the curtain of hair from her face.

"Yes?"

"Well, I'd shut myself into the wardrobe while I was rummaging because of the theatre all dark and silent being kind of spooky, and when I'd found what I was looking for I opened my door again. I had a fearful shock because it was ghosts I was geared up for rather than people, and a real live man was walking along the corridor away from me. I was nearly passing out with fright, thanking Christ I hadn't opened the door a few seconds earlier, and then . . ."

"Come on." Phyllida offered another squeeze.

"Then . . . then Miranda leaned out of the cupboard doorway blowing a kiss and calling goodnight darling." Carol sniffed. "The man stopped and half turned for a second and I thought . . . I think it was Wayne."

12

"You only think?"

"I had to pull back into the wardrobe, didn't I?" Carol said impatiently. "But it was Wayne's height, Wayne's sort of hair. And Wayne and Miranda had left the Horseshoe half an hour earlier. It had to be."

"But you couldn't really see his face?"

"There was only that little ceiling light, and he turned away again so quickly. But Phyl, don't try and tell me you wouldn't have thought it was Wayne, too."

"But you're not *sure*, Carol." Phyllida didn't get on with Wayne, but in fairness she found it hard to see him in the role in which Carol was casting him. "It could have been one of the stage staff, it could have been anyone; I've been thinking it's a bit strange someone like Miranda apparently not having a boyfriend."

"If only!" Carol pushed her hair back, turning to Phyllida with a brief spurt of hope in her eyes. "But I can't go again to make sure, it *would* be spying this time and I just couldn't bear it. But I can't bear the suspense, either."

"Wayne's aware of Miranda," Phyllida said slowly. "But that's a professional necessity. And she does have star quality."

"Are you really so unbitchy, Phyl?"

"She's young and she's talented."

"And Gerald isn't interested. I'm sorry, I didn't mean –"

"Yes you did, but it doesn't matter." As she wiped the wind tears from her cheeks Phyllida could have told Carol that she and Gerald had drawn apart without any help, that they hadn't needed a Miranda Delamaine as a wedge. The odds were, of course, that Carol already knew this from Wayne, but anyway it was easier, with the season so nearly over, not to actually spell the situation out.

"Phyl. Yesterday, Wayne brought me a bunch of red roses."

"And you think it's guilt. All right. I've got an idea."

Phyllida took Carol's arm and sped them across the road and into the seaward-facing seat of one of Seaminster's elegant Victorian shelters, its ironwork as blue as the knobs breaking the line of the rails in front of them. The relief from the north wind was like central heating.

"Listen, Carol. How about if I go and sleuth for you? You know I'm not a great one for hanging on late at the Horseshoe, it'll seem quite normal if I leave soon after Wayne takes Miranda off."

"Oh, Phyl!" Hope gleamed again in Carol's anxious face. "Would you really?"

"I've just said. The sooner the better, the state you're in, so how about tomorrow night? Gerald's going to his mother's, so I'll be a completely free agent."

"The usual thing, he's staying the night in Bournemouth?"

"That's it." It probably was; Gerald was unlikely to cheat on her where it would need the connivance of his formidable mother. "There's a slim chance he may come home to bed but it's unlikely, he always dilutes a session of mother love with a lot of alcohol."

"You don't get on with your mother-in-law, Phyl?"

"I wouldn't say that; I'd be with Gerald I suppose if I didn't have to be on stage. If he does come back, he'll probably go straight to the Horseshoe to make up the drink he hasn't had enough of to stop him driving. In which case he'll assume I've gone back to the hotel. And if he goes to the hotel he'll assume I'm still at the Horseshoe." Phyllida got to her feet. "We'd better start back, no point in inviting Wayne to criticise my timekeeping as well as my acting."

"He's really getting to you?" Carol suggested.

"Only annoying me," Phyllida told her truthfully. Without Ken's telephone call it might have been more than annoyance. "I'm just as happy playing Miss Milton and other eccentrics as I am playing young leads, so long as

14

the part's a good one. I'm not trying to resist getting older, Carol, I'm just resentful at having my scope curtailed by something other than my own and Ken's wise counsel."

"Wayne can be a pain," Carol pronounced. "But lamentably I love him."

"He and Gerald both have a lamentably blokish attitude to women. That may be why you and I are feeling a bit excluded."

"You could be right." Carol stopped in mid-stride. "Phyl, I'd be grateful if you didn't tell Gerald what you're doing for me."

"Don't worry, I won't." Once she would have wanted to, once it would have been the natural thing to make her husband a part of her enterprise. Now, she and Carol saw it the same way. It was a bleak realisation, but the reflex lift of her shoulders showed Phyllida she had at least reached a stage where she could shrug it off. "Come on, or we'll be late."

"I love you, friend."

Wayne was on stage and glaring towards the door to the foyer as Phyllida and Carol came breathlessly through it, but his twenty minutes were only just up and he turned to his leading lady without comment.

"Your noses look cold," Miranda announced as Phyllida and Carol climbed back on stage.

Carol failed to respond, but Phyllida touched her nose with a smile. "They are. The air's glorious, though, it was worth it. You ought to try it sometime, Miranda. Have you ever walked the length of the bay?"

Miranda stared incredulously, and still smiling Phyllida shrugged and turned away, giving the wardrobe mistress a discreet wink.

"Your Miss Milton costumes are ready, Phyl," Carol said. "I'd like a fitting when you next break."

"You didn't have time enough just now to sort that

out?" Wayne looked round his assembled company. "I want to start from the beginning of Miss Milton's search of the room. With Phyl making a teeny weeny bit more business of getting up from her knees."

Wayne and Miranda left the Horseshoe Club the next night at just after half past eleven. Phyllida gave them a ten minute start before leaving too, on a murmured excuse that she was tired and an exchange of looks with Carol.

The evening was moonless and chilly, and it was a temptation to end her walk round the first corner, in the elegant warmth of the Chelwood Hotel where most of the Company were staying. They had played to good houses during their summer travels and had decided to go up-market on their last engagement of the season. The hotel's name in dull gold – no concession to neon – was spread across the last five tiers of symmetrical bay window in the wide street that led to the promenade, and Phyllida's brisk pace lagged as she passed the large letters, in the hope of seeing Wayne descend the flight of steps up to the hotel doors and release her to go to bed.

But street and steps were deserted and Phyllida quickened her pace again as she turned the second corner on to the promenade and the cold wind took her breath.

For security reasons there was only one set of keys to the stage door at the end of the gravelled slit that ran down the nearside of the theatre, and it was held by William the doorman who had long since gone home. The lock on the main door was heavy, and not so easy to turn when one was trying to operate it silently. Not that she needed to be silent, Phyllida reminded herself as she went in; she had the book in her bag that she was ostensibly coming to collect and even if Wayne and Miranda were alerted their presence together in the empty theatre would be indictment enough.

16

But still she crept across the foyer, its pink and silver brilliance barely suggested by the streaks of streetlight slanting across it, and tiptoed down the narrow aisle that broke the faint scallop pattern of the auditorium's empty seats. She slipped on the second of the three steep steps up on to the stage, and the sound seemed to climb into the flies. But it died away into a renewed silence that pressed on her like velvet as it settled back.

The cupboard door from which Miranda Delamaine had leaned had to be passed in order to reach Carol's sanctum, which was the obvious lookout and the place where they had agreed that Phyllida would have left her book. Now the cupboard door was closed and there was no sound from behind it, but the mound of rugs, cloaks and shawls covering the floor made it a ready love-nest and would probably muffle even the human voice raised in excitement . . .

Involuntarily shuddering, Phyllida unlocked Carol's door and went gratefully behind it, glad to discover that it opened inwards and on the side of the cupboard door, so that anyone emerging from the cupboard and looking behind them before moving away was unlikely to spot that the hinge of the wardrobe door was at an angle.

There was no need to take her book out of her bag; if detected she had just put it there and was about to leave. It would have helped to read it, though, and the silence was so palpable it would scarcely have distracted her from her vigil, but the tiny light in the corridor ceiling was far too dim. Phyllida leaned against the doorjamb, counting seconds and advancing her head cautiously out into the corridor each time they became a minute. She thought she had performed the ritual eighteen times, and her back was aching, when she heard the opening of the other door.

And Miranda's voice, actressy and carrying.

17

"It's all right, darling, really it is, if I meet anyone I'll just say I couldn't sleep and came back for my book, I don't know why you're getting so jumpy. Go back to the Horseshoe like a good boy, and I'll toddle home."

An indecipherable male rumble, and Phyllida withdrew in the instant the male figure appeared, edging slowly out again as she heard the diminishing footsteps.

Tall. Dark. Slightly swaggering. Yes, it could be Wayne . . .

"One more kiss, darling."

Phyllida bobbed back as the figure turned, then very gradually out again until she was able to see both the man and the woman in profile in the cupboard doorway, their open mouths in contact.

Not Wayne. Not Carol's husband. *Her* husband, Phyllida Moon's.

Chapter Three

Phyllida had time to bath and get into bed before Gerald came in. And to lie for a while thinking about what she had seen and heard and eventually managing to smile to herself at the irony that was a cliché of stage farce, and to realise with relief that apart from the shock it was only her pride which was hurting.

She snapped her light switch on the second she heard Gerald's key in the door, to read his expression before he had time to adjust it.

Its self-satisfaction started an hysterical laugh somewhere far down inside her. "Gerald!" She sat up. "Goodness, you gave me a shock. I wasn't expecting you till the morning."

"I didn't feel so good after dinner, that damned Nancy made even more of a meal of it than she usually manages. So I decided to come back." And keep his appointment. "Anyway, Mother was a bit under the weather too, she wanted an early night."

"I'm so sorry," Phyllida said politely. "I do hope you'll both feel better tomorrow. You should have called in at the Horseshoe, Gerald, for a digestive."

"I did. What have you been doing?" Questions like that, these days, were never spontaneous. She had seen him disciplining himself to ask it.

"I didn't stay long at the Horseshoe, I was tired. The show went all right, and it wasn't a bad rehearsal."

"Great. God, I'm tired."

Gerald was already undressed, and spent a very few minutes in the bathroom before flopping into his bed. At least she hadn't had to wonder if he might join her in hers.

She was at the theatre early next morning, knowing Carol would be in the wardrobe and on tenterhooks. Carol met her in the doorway and urged her inside her stuffy domain.

"Tell me the worst, Phyl, I'm up to it."

"You really are the most awful pessimist, Carol. I saw the man and it wasn't Wayne."

"Perhaps she's got several –"

"Wayne's height. Hair. Way of walking. As you said. But not Wayne. I swear to you, Carol. Don't *cry*, for heaven's sake."

"I'm not." Carol wiped her shining eyes. "Oh, Phyl, that's wonderful. But who was it?"

"I've no idea. It doesn't matter, though, does it?"

"No! Oh, Phyl, I can never thank you." But Carol's face had clouded again. "You really do promise not to say anything to Gerald?"

"I really do." But Gerald had brought the time forward when there was a need to say other things. Phyllida thought about them during rehearsal.

"A teeny weeny bit more conviction if you can manage it, Phyllida love." Wayne was always at his most polite to the people who most annoyed him. And this morning his annoyance was justified. "Miss Milton is a very positive person."

"I know, Wayne. I'm sorry."

"You know the part backwards. It's just . . ." Wayne looked genuinely puzzled, but Phyllida suspected him of having a higher opinion of her usual performance than he admitted to himself. And this was the first time,

20

she was sure, that she had given him real cause for concern.

"Yes. I didn't sleep. I'll be all right."

The first night was on Monday; thank goodness rehearsals would be over by the end of the week. The play would run for the last fortnight of the season, and then after a short break the Company would be back at its own London theatre to prepare for the winter. Which meant that in two and a half weeks she could be free.

During the mid-morning break Phyllida pulled herself together, and Wayne told her grudgingly that she was fine. After rehearsal she joined the general move to the Chelwood's coffee bar for sandwiches, ate quickly, and slipped away on a murmured excuse. She didn't feel like company and didn't get back into her jacket until she was on the outside steps of the hotel.

Walking felt good, and reminded her how much more dramatic weather changes are on the coast than inland. Today the sun was behind featureless cloud and the land the pale grey of the sea, the details of Great Hill had disappeared and the horizon was the mere stroke of a pencil. Yet it was warmer, the wind had died, and the soft moist air was a light caress on her cheek. The tempo had changed just as histrionically: the sprightly pace of brilliant, windblown yesterday had given way to a monotone pause.

As she had told Carol, Phyllida liked Seaminster. It was the first place since the Cornish countryside of her childhood, she realised as she crossed the road, that she had been aware of as a surrounding entity. She had gone to RADA from school and worked in the theatre ever since, and although other places she had played over the years had had their attractive and interesting features – a park, say, for a fine Sunday, an art gallery for a wet one – they had been no more, really, than triangles of varying shapes

21

linking theatre, hotel or digs, and the place or places of relaxation where first the company she belonged to, and then Gerald, liked to spend the late evenings. London was London, infinitely varied and exciting, but she had never had a real home there, and Gerald's recent purchase of a house too big for them in Wimbledon showed no signs of becoming one.

And never could, now.

But Seaminster . . .

The few people she passed tended to be elderly. A man and a woman touchingly hand in hand. Two women with bright scarves in conversation so absorbed that when their small tartan-coated dog pulled them to a stop to examine a lamppost their dialogue continued unbroken even when the dog jerked them back into motion.

Yes, the season was nearly over, and Seaminster was returning to its private self. When the Company had arrived three months ago there had been coaches parked in the embrasures of the promenade, spilling gaggles of defined groups on to the rails – schoolchildren, old men, confident bright-haired women, bewildered knots of the mentally frail. Ice cream vans had been parked then at regular intervals, their electronic voices tinkling through the grind of steady, slow-moving traffic. On bright days the carriages of the funicular railway on the west slope of Great Hill had looked like kinetic ball bearings, and families had set up house in the open doorways of the beach huts below the railings and trailed dots into the sea.

Now there was only one van, the traffic was intermittent, the beach huts were locked up, and on the sands there was just a man and a dog. The human contrast was as extreme as the climatic.

By the time she turned west the damp in the air had moistened to a drizzle and Phyllida pulled up her hood as she passed the farm. She climbed the rugged but

22

gentle slope of Little Hill to its first Seaminster-facing crag, looking over a low-rise town which was still clearly defined by an arc of countryside sweeping in, parallel with the smaller white arc of the seafront terraces. Knowing as she stood there that she was experiencing one of those rare moments when no alternative remains to radical change, and wondering how it would feel to wake up behind a bedroom window in one of the houses or flats for sale below her.

Back in her bedroom at the Chelwood Phyllida found that despite the hood her hair was damp. And growing out of its perm, she noticed as she sat down before the mirror. In sudden intense irritation she grabbed her brush and beat it against her head with fierce, harsh strokes. Then realised as she stuck her tongue out at her image how much better her face looked without its usual wispy surround. She would have it cut instead of permed, a new style for a new life. And perhaps she could find a halfway house between her own inattention to make-up and the stage's excess of it. She began to try . . .

"Oh." Gerald was in the doorway. "I just saw Carol and she said she thought you'd gone out." Slowly he closed the door behind him. Phyllida could see through the glass that it was reluctantly. "I only want that book . . ."

"I did go out. I walked about in the rain."

"Hardly necessary. But you always . . . Phyl?"

He had turned to the mirror, and remained staring into it.

"Yes, Gerald?"

"You look – different." In the glass, now, he was close behind her, his eyes alight. "Phyl . . ."

For a bizarre moment she pitied him, that in his middle age he had started to live for appearances. "My hair's wet, that's all." She straggled it back into the old dreary frame, then dipped a tissue in cold cream and started rubbing at the new make-up.

Gerald flung away. "Wayne asked me to tell you he'd like a word with you."

"That sounds official." She swung round on the dressing stool. "Where and when?"

"He said he would be in his room at the theatre from teatime on." His eyes weren't meeting hers and she was grateful for their warning: Gerald knew what Wayne was planning to say to her, and that she wouldn't like it.

So did she, and she must get in first. "D'you know what it's about, Gerald?"

He had the book he had come for in his hand and was making for the door. "Just because he assumed I might see you before he did doesn't have to mean he told me what he wants to talk to you about."

"You protest too much," she murmured to his disappearing back. If he hadn't been so anxious to get away she might have told him, done the wifely thing. But he had gone, and she couldn't put off telling Wayne. Anyway, she no longer owed Gerald anything beyond a *fait accompli*.

Back on the steps of the Chelwood Phyllida learned that the weather *entr'acte* was over. The wind was up again and pulled at her hair. The more bedraggled it got, the better for the dowdy character she was currently playing, so she threw back her head and enjoyed the buffeting.

"Afternoon, Miss Moon!"

William's pleasure was genuine. He liked her. Most people seemed to, Phyllida reflected reluctantly – her recent enforced introspection was not to her taste – if they thought about it, which she was contentedly sure they seldom did. Not Wayne, though. Not people who always wanted their own way, even when it impinged painfully on others. People who got a disagreeable shock

24

when they discovered that her unassertive manner didn't mean she was prepared to be pushed around.

"Wayne? Gerald said you wanted to see me."

"Ah, yes. Come in, Phyl." Wayne was put out, shaking his fine head of hair as if there were a fly buzzing about in it; he hadn't been expecting her so soon. But her early arrival would disconcert him only if he had something important to say to her.

"I wanted to see you, too, Wayne."

He came slightly to attention. "You did, Phyl? Have a drink, it's turned cold again."

"Thanks. Scotch." It was only half past four and Phyllida was a careful drinker despite her strong head, but in the circumstances it seemed like a good idea.

"Fine." Wayne poured two, put one into Phyllida's hand. "Sit down, Phyl."

He took his first sip standing, then started pacing the small space of his office.

"Wayne, I'm afraid I have to –"

He wasn't listening. "Look, Phyl." He swung round to face her. "It's about next season. When we're back in London. My temporary post as producer's being made permanent now we know there's no chance of Ken Hadfield coming back, and I want to put my own stamp on the company. I'm planning a few changes and it's going to mean . . ."

"A few changes."

"A number of them." Wayne was suddenly stern before the possibility that he was being made fun of. "New members. And sad goodbyes to a few of the old. Ralph's moving to the RSC – some people! – and Gladys is retiring. I've managed to sign up Simon Moffat, and there's a good chance of Vera Hall."

Vera Hall was in her late thirties. Phyllida had to get his attention. She raised her soft voice. "Before you go

25

any further, Wayne." She had managed it, he was tapping his foot and looking at his watch, his mouth twitching in exasperation. "What I've come to tell you may be helpful. It's that I'm leaving the Company."

"You're *what*?"

"Leaving the Company. I'm sorry if it's a shock," she added mischievously.

"It's a great shock, Phyl," Wayne said sternly. And truthfully. In the wake of his shock Phyllida glimpsed disappointment as well as relief; he'd been looking forward to telling her she had to go.

"You see," she said. "I've been offered a part in the new ITV series Guy Mercer's making based on Paul Cunningham's crime novels." She hadn't had her secret long, but parting with it felt like the loss of a loyal friend. There were compensations, though. "You'll have heard about it, there's been a lot of publicity." Reluctantly Wayne nodded, then started easing his head about on his neck as if something was hurting. "Not a leading role, but rather a nice one that will last through however many episodes they make. I don't know if you've read any of Paul Cunningham's books, but his Detective Inspector Jago Page has a private eye sister whom he can never resist consulting on his cases although he annoys himself by doing so and always goes about it in an undercover sort of a way. I play the sister, so I'm always around yet not exhaustingly prominent."

"Prominent enough. How did you . . ." The fly was back in Wayne's thatch.

"It was Ken. He knows Guy Mercer and asked him if he'd see me. He did and – well, I was lucky."

"You were." Wayne finally shook the fly out and tried to pull himself together. "And pretty secretive, too. I have to congratulate you, Phyl, it's going to be quite a prestige production. Not scheduled till late next summer, though; what will you do in the meantime?"

"I've always wanted to write a history of women and the stage." And now she wanted to work in a detective agency. "Rehearsals start in April, anyway, not so far away."

"No . . . Gerald will be pleased for you. He keeps a secret well, too." Wayne's voice wasn't quite clear of hurt.

To let Gerald learn about her new job and her resignation from other people would be to call in all his debts, but Phyllida couldn't quite manage it. "He doesn't know yet," she said reluctantly. "I only just know myself, and I've kept it a secret from absolutely everyone in case it didn't come off. But now the contracts are signed. I'll tell Gerald tonight, Wayne, so please, no word to anyone until tomorrow."

"Of course not, Phyl." And of course Wayne would be glad to postpone the necessity of appearing pleased by Phyllida Moon's good fortune, at having it known that she had chosen to leave his Company rather than be dismissed from it. "I'm very flattered you should tell me before you tell your husband." The possibility of inflicting at least a small wound had brought a light back into his eyes.

"If you hadn't asked me to come and see you I'd have told Gerald first. But as you're making plans for next season I realised it was only fair to let you know right away." As she stared into his eyes with a polite smile Phyllida saw the light leave them.

"You're a good actress, Phyl," Wayne said. "You'll leave with an excellent reference." He had given up, it showed in every suddenly relaxed line of his body, and Phyllida fleetingly admired him for accepting his defeat without a sulk. "If you need one, now."

"Of course I need one, Wayne. I don't see TV as a

27

new way of life, it's just an exciting and I hope lucrative interlude, not an alternative to the stage." With the exception of the Independent Theatre Company. It was astonishing to realise how recently she had considered staying with it into the spring.

"Of course not." Wayne flopped into his office chair and drew it towards her. "Gerald will like having you at home for a while."

It could be that he was coming in on another tack. Phyllida got to her feet. "We'll see. Thanks for taking it so well, Wayne." Forbearing to tell her he had been about to sack her could, of course, be motivated by politics rather than compassion in the light of what he would see as her enhanced status, but she would give him the benefit of the doubt.

"Can't stand in the way of an offer like that," he said, as he escorted her to the door with a hand on her shoulder.

Politics. But at least he was being honest enough not to tell her he would miss her.

Gerald took the first part of her announcement with more prolonged surprise. And not a little indignation.

"You? A part in the Guy Mercer adaptation of Cunningham?"

"That's right, Gerald."

"And it didn't occur to you to tell your husband you were putting in for it? To say nothing of going for an audition."

"I didn't put in for it, it was Ken's idea. I laughed at him but he insisted I'd be right for the part of Page's sister."

"Page's sister! That's one of the plum parts!"

"I know, I've been awfully lucky. When I went up to see Ken a few Sundays ago – I asked you to come with me,

28

if you remember, Gerald, but you didn't feel like it – when I got there I found Guy Mercer was the other lunch guest. Ken had shown him that bit of film he took of *Blithe Spirit*, and a few other bits, and he asked me for an audition. I didn't tell you, because I was so sure I wouldn't get the part." And then she would have handed him another little weapon. "But we signed last Sunday."

"When you were supposed to be visiting your father. Yes, I see."

"That's where we signed, Gerald, at my father's. Ken brought Guy over, it's not far. I don't think you've ever quite realised what a good friend Ken is to me." Even though he had seen her anguished departures to London following Ken's heart attack.

"He's a good friend to everyone." No jealousy, Ken was gay. "You'll have to get on with telling Wayne, he's planning next season." Gerald turned back to the mirror where before she spoke he had been examining his hairline, not quite quickly enough to hide the sudden wariness in his eyes.

"I just did. As you say, he was making his plans and was going to tell me about them."

"What was his reaction?" Gerald asked, without turning round. But Phyllida could see in the glass that his eyes were intent on her reflection.

"Surprise. But he took it well, offered a good reference."

"Great." The back of Gerald's pyjamas relaxed as he eased his clamped buttocks. The danger had passed of having to admit to her that he had known Wayne was about to dismiss her, and had kept the knowledge to himself. Which meant that he could still be self-righteous about her own secrecy. "All the same, Phyl, I think you might have let on."

"Sorry, Gerald," she said lightly, as she got into bed.

29

He gave her a sidelong glance as he turned from the mirror. "Actually, it will be nice for a change to come home to a supper if not slippers."

And, Phyllida carried on for him, to come home sometimes after supper, at the end of a day maritally untrammelled. Her ever-lurking sense of mischief made her feign surprise.

"Come home to supper? . . . Sorry, Gerald, that's not the break I have in mind. I want to use the next six months getting experience of work in a detective agency."

"Fine." But he'd had to swallow on it. "You may not even have to go into central London to find one."

"I'm staying on in Seaminster."

"You're – what?"

Having settled her immediate future to his own convenience, Gerald was on his way into the bathroom. He spun round in the doorway, too astonished to be indignant.

"I'm staying on in Seaminster. I like it here, it's the first place I've been really aware of since I lived in Cornwall. And it's the same size as Parkton, the country town they're turning into the fictional Annerby as the setting for *A Policeman's Lot*, so it's the right place to find a detective agency."

"Who'll take you on just like that, of course. Don't let this – piece of luck – go to your head, Phyl."

"I'll use my head to make the most of it. I'll rent a flat or a small house and just see how it goes. If it feels right I may even stay here when the series goes into production."

"So you want a separation? That's what you're saying?"

"I'm saying that I want to stay on in Seaminster. I'm sorry, but at the moment that's all I can say. It may inconvenience you, Gerald, but it will hardly upset you. I'm not blind."

"I am, it seems."

30

"I don't think so, sometimes it's just easier not to notice things. I'll go back with you so that I can collect my car." She thought of the handsome, impersonal house in Wimbledon. "I'll have accommodation here lined up by then."

"You've got it all worked out, haven't you?"

"Not really. It can take ages to decide what to order from a dinner menu, but if you think, important decisions are often made in a flash."

In as short a time as it takes to watch your partner betray you.

Chapter Four

The end of season party, held backstage following the last of the last nights, was the usual febrile affair, the level of hysteria heightened by the fact that so many changes were to take place before the Company came together again in London. Phyllida heard more than one tongue speak of "the old order" (one even perpetrated "the old order changeth"), and of course that was how it tended to feel, the narrow world and the mutual dependency stretching back as far as could be remembered.

Like Phyllida's dying marriage, which she was increasingly grateful to Gerald for having put so cleanly out of its misery. Although the fact that he didn't know he had done so, and wasn't going to be told, meant that her own notice to quit had to be on a different timescale.

"Gerald will be glad to have you at home for a while." Carol exchanged an empty wine glass for a full one. The marriage had been terminally ill for so long not even Phyllida's closest friend in the Company appeared to be aware that it had died. But Carol had spoken doubtfully, and might not have made the comment at all if she hadn't drunk more than usual – no one in the Company could imagine that the Waterworths were a loving couple. "But I'm going to miss you, Phyl." Carol's fine bosom heaved dramatically, and her eyes were suddenly bright.

Phyllida was touched. And Gerald would still be stage manager when the Company reconvened, so that

Carol would be sending anxious messages to Wimbledon.

"Look, Carol, I know you can keep a thing to yourself if asked to." She did know, it was something she always knew about people, whether or not she liked them. And Phyllida liked Carol. "I'm staying on in Seaminster. Gerald and I are out of kilter at the moment, it's going to suit us both. Call it a trial separation, if you like." She had thought Carol would prefer to call it something, and saw understanding join the surprise in her worried face. "And don't look so tragic. We're both all right."

"Phyl . . ."

"And Seaminster's the same size as the town they're using for the TV series. I'm going to try and get work in a detective agency here to help me with my part." If she didn't tell Carol, Wayne would, via Gerald.

"You're so *thorough*, Phyl. You'll miss the stage, though."

"I'm bound to. But I'll go back to it if I can when the TV contract's through."

"If you can! You'll always get an engagement, Phyl. Especially now."

Perhaps the TV series *would* make a difference, if only to ease dealings with future Waynes. It had already made a difference in the Company, where since Carol had spread the news Phyllida had been carried shoulder high. It wasn't a position she found comfortable, but to have made Wayne uneasy was a compensation.

"Thanks. I'm going back with Gerald tomorrow to collect my car, and one or two personal things." Phyllida was surprised by the thought of her old teddy bear, banished by Gerald to a cupboard when they moved to Wimbledon and bought new bedspreads. "I've rented a little house."

"Phyl . . ."

33

"I was lucky; the woman who owns it has gone to Eastbourne to look after an aunt who's ill without showing any signs of dying. Perhaps you'll come and see me if you feel like a run down to the coast. I'll press my new address into your hand in the morning."

"Phyl . . . Hello, darling."

Wayne was beside them. Phyllida had been transformed from a thorn in his side to a flowering plant whose prickles could be avoided, so he put an arm round her waist as well.

There was nothing new to be expected from Gerald, beyond a last-minute attempt to fathom the change in her.

It came when they were in bed, Phyllida just falling asleep.

"Why Seaminster?"

"What's that, Gerald?"

"Why Seaminster, Phyl? Truly?" He was bewildered enough to have sat up; when she reluctantly opened her eyes she could see him in silhouette against the thin moonlit curtains. "You won't know anyone here once the Company's gone, you'll be lonely."

"I've got to know a few people outside the Company, Gerald. Anyway, I'm pretty self-sufficient and I plan to be busy. And I've told you why I've decided to stay on here. I want to work in a detective agency in a place the size of Parkton. I also like Seaminster; it's a real place and I was brought up on the coast. It's just what I need. At the moment. I haven't taken a decision to stay here for ever."

"Of course not!" Gerald hissed indignantly. Still going through the motions. Or maybe deciding that because she wanted to go she was worth keeping; he had always been perverse. Which she was being now too, of course: Gerald hadn't changed, hadn't done anything he hadn't been doing for years. Miranda was just another girl in a line of brief affairs he had run in tandem with his married life, and there was no more reason to leave him over her than over any of the other women who caught his brief fancy.

But Miranda was the one Phyllida had seen him make up to, and it had been the catalyst to jerk her out of her inertia. She was grateful to the girl.

"But Phyl . . . Why not just . . ." She had turned her back to him, but she heard the restless movement of his legs. "Why not wait and see how you feel after your TV debut? I'm expecting to be pretty busy one way and another, helping to get the new season sorted out, but there'll be the chance of the odd day out. We can talk . . ."

And his wife rather than his housekeeper could cook his dinner.

"Thanks, Gerald, but there isn't anything to talk about. I've decided what I'm going to do for the immediate future, and you know very well it will suit you, too."

"But Phyl . . ."

"Goodnight, Gerald."

Incredibly, he was the suppliant. But Phyllida had no sense of triumph, she had already moved on.

The morning was all fluster and tearful adieus, and it was easy to pass Carol her new Seaminster address. Her rebuff of Gerald's bridge-building attempt had put him into a sulk that made the journey less fraught than she had anticipated, and they travelled back to Wimbledon in a silence broken only by the radio.

Gerald took his suitcase straight to the spare room, and they had supper on trays in front of the television. After an uneasy night and a silent breakfast Phyllida made immediate preparations for departure, which appeared to surprise Gerald so greatly it became clear he hadn't been expecting her to go. She drove away with a picture of him bemused on the front doorstep, teddy and a few boxes on the back seat of her car, a chair and a small table in the boot. She had been pleased to discover how little she appeared to need.

Once or twice on her journey she sang along with the radio, and when she reached Seaminster she went straight to the estate agent for her key, then drove west along the promenade. Past the Empress, where a man on a ladder was obliterating the Company's last notices with the announcement of an old-time variety show. Past the farm. On a sharp angle up the road that skirted it, where she had so often walked. Short of the eighth house on the left she slowed down, and drove into its carport. When she got out of the car she walked back to the garage gate, closed it, and leaned on it to look across fields and the bay to Great Hill. A long and open view. There were no houses opposite, just another craggy grey wall marking the farm's western boundary.

Phyllida drew a deep breath of contentment. It was the view which had made her decide to rent Number Eight Upland Road. She had given the house the most cursory of inspections, and as she turned to face it she could have been seeing it for the first time. She hadn't even remembered that it was light red brick, although she had retained an image of the art deco front door next to the bay window, its upper glass oval set with stained segments representing a sunburst over a bluebird. Her sensations as she stepped into the bright little hall were unfamiliar: she had married Gerald from digs and had never had a home of her own. Inside, as she now remembered, the walls everywhere were mercifully white, the pictures mostly watercolours, the furniture and fittings uncrowded and making no strong statements.

Phyllida easily placed her chair and table in the sitting-room, then went on a tour which included the views from the windows.

The sitting-room opened via a dining-room and an old-fashioned French door on to a small walled garden, half patio and half lawn and rimmed with low shrubs. She could see only trees and a couple of grey pitched roofs beyond the rosy brick wall, but the back bedroom revealed a loose but complex pattern of houses, bungalows, and flourishing suburban gardens. The view from the front bedroom was the view from the gate writ wider and including an extra curve of the promenade. And the angle of the road meant she would have sun front and back, as well.

Unable to remember when she had last felt so happy, Phyllida put teddy on the bed in the front bedroom, unpacked, and went downstairs to make herself coffee. Mugs and cups were bone china, pretty, and as immaculately clean as everything else. She carried a mug to the sitting-room window – each upper pane was set with a stained-glass rose – and pulled her chair close to it. By the time she had drained the mug she knew that, for the moment, she had done precisely the right thing.

The knowledge wanted to spill out of her, be shared, and the person to share it with was Ken. She had kept him up to date with the wherefores if not the whys of the past few weeks, and he had her new phone number. He would probably ring her that night, but she couldn't wait. Since his heart attack he had worked from home; he was easy these days to get hold of.

"Sounds like a nice place," Ken said, when she paused in her eulogy of Number Eight Upland Road. "Am I to gather Gerald isn't there with you?"

"He isn't here."

"That doesn't really surprise me, lovey. What are you going to do in Seaminster?"

"Find a job with a private eye, if humanly possible. Seaminster's the same size as Parkton, so it should be helpful." Ken's oblique comment on her marriage didn't really surprise Phyllida; they had never spoken of it, but he was observant. "And the money wouldn't come amiss, although thanks to you I'm all right."

"Good for you, Phyl." She heard the approving chuckle. "You've played ghosts and murderers well enough without experience, but where there's a chance of getting it . . . What about your book?"

"I'm hoping to get started on it."

"Good. But with all this you'll still miss the stage."

"I suppose so. But I couldn't have stayed on."

Phyllida decided to tell Ken about giving notice just in time not to get given it herself, then was scared he might have another heart attack.

"*Et tu*, Gerald!" he gasped, when he was able.

"He didn't support me, no, but perhaps he thought Wayne was right. It doesn't matter, Ken."

"But he didn't know then about the TV. He thought you'd be out of work?"

"I suppose so. But he just mightn't have known what Wayne was up to." The sun through the glass oval in the front door was sending a sharp sprawled bird image down the white wall in front of her. On dull days it would be faint or invisible but already it was a friend she would look out for. "Anyway, Ken, you've got to believe me that it doesn't matter."

"I do, lovey, I do. We'll keep in touch, of course, but try to come up and see me sometime."

When she had rung off Phyllida outlined the bird image with a finger, then opened the drawer in the telephone table underneath it. *Yellow Pages* was there with the local directory and she carried it to the sitting-room window and sat down with it on her lap. Seaminster might be the same

38

size as the fictional country town of *A Policeman's Lot*, but that didn't guarantee it a private eye, she might have to look farther afield.

But there was the heading *Detective Agencies*, and under it two names were listed. The Ancaster Detective Agency and Peter Piper Private Investigator.

Peter Piper picked a peck of pickled pepper . . .

The tongue-twister had headed her entertainment repertoire in her extreme youth. And Peter Piper, according to the street map she now had open as well, was nearer to Upland Road than the other agency, and in a more attractive part of town. She would start there. After she had had the remains of her last perm cut out of her hair.

Phyllida made another mug of coffee, ate the sandwich she had bought while buying petrol, and set off on foot down the slope of road to the promenade, where the mild brilliance of the day had provoked a resurgence of tourist activity. She passed two ice cream vans, and there were people in most of the shelters and on most of the open seats, blinking into the sunshine that sparkled on the pastel blue motion of the water. She too could sit down, enjoy the sun and the air and the passing dogs, take a week or too off to potter about her first house and garden; she had earned herself a holiday.

But she didn't want thinking time and she was an actress, discovering as she strolled and admired that even in paradise she would prefer to have work to do.

The woman who had looked after her hair during the season didn't seem particularly pleased to see her, until Phyllida told her what she wanted. Then she said how fortunate it was that she was free to take her right away. When she had cut Phyllida's hair she blow-dried it smoothly round her face.

"It suits you," she said into the mirror. "Please don't have another perm."

"I won't." Phyllida was able to say it with confidence; Kate in *A Policeman's Lot* wouldn't dream of it.

"Your skin . . ."

"Don't worry, more often than not I wear a lot of make-up."

"But one doesn't need to . . ."

"I know. I'm an actress, Peggy."

"And you never told me!" Peggy accused.

"I'm sorry. I don't like talking about myself." That at least was still the case.

Phyllida told Peggy as little as she could manage, and promised to visit her more often. She went into the chemist two doors down, bought some make-up, then set off for Seaminster's central and only square. Four four-storey Victorian terraces looking on to a statue of the local lord highly pedestalled in the centre of a small formal garden. Early Victorian aping the Georgian mode, in immaculate cream stucco. And with some aesthetic success, Phyllida had already decided on her afternoon walks about the town. The terraces had the airy, Italianate look which hadn't survived very far into the century of conspicuous prosperity. The ground and lower floors of Dawlish Square – named for a founding Seaminster father – were offices apart from its south side, which was entirely occupied by the Golden Lion Hotel; basements were flats or restaurants; top floors were flats.

Phyllida went into the ladies room in the Golden Lion and applied some new make-up. Then crossed the square to number thirty-six, the north-east corner building opposite the hotel, discovering from a wall notice like a small honours board that Peter Piper occupied part of its second floor. There was an old-fashioned lift with a gilded diamond-mesh cage, but she took the shallow

40

turning stairs. On Mr Piper's entrance door the gilding was also pristine. When she turned the knob and pushed the door open as invited, Phyllida found a young woman sitting behind a desk in a room with a view across the square from its sash window.

"Hello! Can we help you?" The young woman was friendly. Pretty, too, with big blue eyes in a heart-shaped freckled face that looked small inside a large frame of curly dark hair.

"Perhaps. Would it be possible to see Mr Piper? I'm afraid I don't have an appointment."

"He has a client in twenty minutes, but I'll see. Can you give me your name?"

"Waterworth. That is – Miss Phyllida Moon." Not a good start, Phyllida told herself, but the young woman was nodding in understanding and could be thinking that Miss Moon or whoever it was had to have problems to be where she was. "Fine. Thank you. Miss Phyllida Moon?" Finger out towards an intercom switch but looking invitingly at Phyllida, giving her time to make a further choice.

"That's right."

"Fine. Doctor? I've a Miss Phyllida Moon out here who would like to see you. Do you have a few moments?" The smile widened. "Good, I'll send her in. Dr Piper will see you," the girl said as she flicked the switch. "Straight on through that door."

"Thanks." Phyllida knocked at the door opposite the entrance and a man's voice called to her to come in. Peter Piper was facing his door from behind a good-looking mahogany desk, side on to a window and a view which Phyllida now saw stretched as far as the pale blue sea. His honey-coloured hair matched his carpet and his two small armchairs, and his eyes were brown in a thin, tanned face. A green tie was knotted low on a white shirt, his jacket was over the back of his chair and Phyllida liked his cheerful smile.

"What can I do for you, Miss Moon?"

She hadn't wanted him to recognise her face, but her name had been a possibility. He obviously didn't patronise his local theatre. "I'm not a client, I'm afraid."

"Ah, well." The smile had grown rueful, but it was still there. "You're here though, so there must be something I can do for you."

Either he would go along with her or he wouldn't, no point in beating about the bush. "Would you consider giving me a job?" The brown eyes widened. "Humble and temporary, no big deal. I've been with the theatre company at the Empress all summer and I'm staying on in Seaminster until I start filming a TV series in the spring. I play a private eye, so it occurred to me that a bit of dogsbodying for the real thing might put an edge on my performance." Phyllida paused as she ran out of euphoria and remembered that a few weeks ago she had been shy. "Hack work," she finished meekly.

The eyes opposite were now apologetic, their cheer slightly veiled. "Sorry I didn't see you. I like the theatre but lately I just seem to have been rather busy. And I'm afraid I've got a full complement of staff." The smile came back. "I'm sure you'll be very good, anyway."

"Thanks. And thanks for seeing me."

"Thank you for coming. The best of luck."

"All right, Miss Moon?" the girl asked as Dr Piper, having seen her to his door, closed it behind her.

"Fine."

"See you again, perhaps?"

"Perhaps."

The Ancaster Agency was in a side street and its owner was older and shabbier than Peter Piper. But he didn't go

42

to the theatre, either, and he too declined her services, and less charmingly.

On her way home Phyllida bought an ice cream cornet from a van on the promenade and ate it on a seat facing the sea while she thought about what to do next.

Chapter Five

From the narrow alley where for the second time he was parked, Peter Piper could just see Miss Parkinson's front door and garden path. He was less wary than he had been the first time, having learned that when she put milk bottles out and took them in her suspicious glance swept no further than the stretch of roadway outside her house. He was also less hopeful: even though the road had so far appeared to be free of anyone or anything to cause her alarm, Miss Parkinson continued to walk with a pronounced limp and to lean heavily against the doorpost as she bent down to deposit or retrieve the plastic cage containing the bottles, re-entering her hall with a painful-looking lurch.

"It doesn't look as if she's putting it on," Peter murmured to his passenger as Miss Parkinson's front door closed behind her.

"We shall soon know." Miss Amelia Bailey, his part-time assistant in the field, pulled her old felt hat more securely down on her neat grey hair. "I'm going in."

"Right you are, Miss Bailey. Good luck."

"Perhaps a little more powder." Miss Bailey had glanced reluctantly at her reflection in the sunshield, and now took a compact from the enormous handbag on her lap, frowning into the mirror as she emphasised the pallor of her thin face. When she had replaced the compact she extracted a handful of leaflets. "You're quite ready, Dr Piper?"

"I am, Miss Bailey. On your way."

Miss Bailey got neatly out of the car and crouched the short way to the mouth of the alley without any loss of the dignity which was the hallmark of her appearance. Then straightened up, crossed the road, and went through Miss Parkinson's gate and up the path to her front door. When Miss Parkinson cautiously opened it Miss Bailey immediately entered the narrow space so that Miss Parkinson was unable to close it again. She then held out the leaflets and Miss Parkinson shook her head and put out a hand to repel them.

This was when Miss Bailey sagged against the doorpost. Peter saw the householder disappear at a run, but although he was out of the car with his camcorder at the ready she was too quickly gone for him to be able to make use of it. When Miss Bailey had drunk from the glass of water with which Miss Parkinson reappeared she was gestured inside, but shook her head and started waveringly for the gate.

This was the crux of the matter, and Peter whispered a whoop of triumph as Miss Parkinson remained standing at her open front door, anxiously watching Miss Bailey's progress down her garden path. Miss Bailey reached the gate before falling so that she was able to go down gently, hand over hand on its iron rails.

The camcorder followed Miss Parkinson's precipitate dash to retrieve her, and the return to the house with Miss Parkinson taking all Miss Bailey's weight. Also Miss Parkinson's solicitous seeing of Miss Bailey into a taxi half an hour later.

He followed the taxi to the railway station where it dropped its passenger, parked in the station car park, and got out of the car to open the door for Miss Bailey as she approached.

"Well done, Miss B!"

"Thank you, Dr Piper, I didn't much like it." Miss Bailey

got into the car and fastened her seat belt before replying. "A compassionate young woman."

"And a perpetrator of fraud on her insurance company. But I know what you mean, of course. This business can make you laugh and cry at the same time."

But Miss Bailey had no difficulty in seeing that for the moment her employer was wearing the mask of comedy alone.

"Just so," she said, as she settled her coat around her. "And just now you are laughing at the successful conclusion of a difficult commission. Perhaps, then, Dr Piper, this is the moment for me to tell you my news. Whilst you are buoyant. Not, of course, that I should assume . . ."

Realising that what she had to say to him was important, Peter turned to face her and saw a pink flush suffuse her pallor as she paused.

"Assume, Miss Bailey?"

"That to lose my services would disconcert you. It would be presumptuous of me to assume that."

"It would be the truth." He was aware of a dismay which three years earlier he could not have envisaged experiencing. Miss Bailey had come with the business he had bought on a surge of doubt-defying enthusiasm, and had been one of the main areas of the doubt. But she had quickly justified the seller's embarrassed recommendation. "You must know that."

The flush came and went again. "Thank you, Dr Piper. I had hoped, of course . . ." Visibly Miss Bailey pulled herself together. "Last week was the occasion of my eightieth birthday. I am still fit in mind and body as I trust is evident" – Peter murmured assent – "and it is while I am still able to that I feel I should arrange my life to take me as agreeably as possible into old age."

Which she didn't see herself as having reached, the old

46

stoic, Peter thought admiringly. "And that means . . ." he prompted.

"I have a step-sister who is fifteen years my junior. She lives in Yorkshire and has invited me to make my home with her there."

"And you've decided to."

"After long and hard thought. We get on well. She lost her mother when she was very young and I think I have been in that role to her."

"She isn't married?"

"Her husband is dead. It will be all right, Peter."

She was fifty years his senior, but he was her boss and she had never presumed to use his first name. Her use of it now told him for certain that he had lost her services, and he covered the gloved hands in her lap with one of his.

"If you say so, I'm sure it will. But you'll be very much missed. I'll never be able to replace you."

"Elderly ladies are not essential to the running of a detective agency, and you have employed me on a part-time basis. I have been useful merely now and again. You will find someone much more generally helpful."

"I doubt it. When are you leaving Seaminster?"

"Next week. I apologise for not having told you earlier. But it has been difficult." Miss Bailey paused again. "I've enjoyed working with you very much, Peter, I shall miss it. I'm very glad we have ended with a success."

"So am I. Come back and say goodbye?"

"Tomorrow. I'm a little tired now. Will you take me home?"

Heavy rain began to fall as they drew up outside her small neat bungalow, and Peter rushed her up to the shelter of her porch.

He arrived somewhat depressed at the office, where Jenny was vigorously typing.

"Good morning, Doctor!" Her flying fingers paused

over the word processor keys and she glanced up smiling. "Mrs Porteous is here," she said unnecessarily, indicating the large lady swamping a couple of the chairs by the window.

"Just been settling up." The large lady struggled to her feet. "Thought I'd do it in person so that I could thank you to your face, Dr Piper, for your report."

"That's very kind of you, Mrs Porteous." And very fortunate, as he frequently reminded himself, that Jenny should find machines and people equally manageable. Impressed in the first instance by her appearance and manner he'd taken her on for reception cum telephone while still looking for a typist cum day-to-day keeper of the books, and discovered within a week that he already had both.

"I'm going straight round now to confront that Mrs Godwin. If I'm lucky I might catch her in the act, actually feeding my Tiddles or encouraging him into her house. The impertinence of it!"

"I know it's extremely upsetting for you," Peter said, "but I think you should keep in mind that my member of staff found no evidence of coercion on Mrs Godwin's part. She made no attempt to pick up your Tiddles unless and until he had actually made his independent way to her back door."

"Then she must have offered him prawns once when he was passing. There's no other way my Tiddles –"

"That may well be, but we do just have to remember that Tiddles went of his own free will into Mrs Godwin's garden." He had been up very early and had to stifle a yawn. But two Tiddles in as many months were at least one too many. "Of course you're going to contact her to try and sort something out, but I do think it would be as well to bear that in mind. Don't do anything you may regret with the information we've been able to give you."

"All right, then," Mrs Porteous said grudgingly, as Jenny opened the door. "And thanks anyway."

"It didn't go so well again?" Jenny asked, studying his face as Mrs Porteous's heavy tread diminished towards the lift.

"On the contrary. This time we got her." Peter stroked the camcorder. "Thanks to Miss Bailey. For the last time. She's retiring, Jenny. Has retired. That was Bailey's last case. She's off to Yorkshire to live with her sister."

He went into his office. Jenny followed as far as the doorway. "I thought she'd go on for ever!"

"I hoped she would. Yet if she hadn't been *in situ* when I bought the business nobody could have persuaded me that an old lady could be so useful. She'll be in tomorrow to say goodbye. Get some ideas together about a leaving present and we'll talk at lunchtime."

"Right. Will you think of replacing her?" Jenny asked with interest.

"How could I? But her departure may just hasten the day when I take on another full-time field worker. No need to mention that to Steve at the moment, though." Because his edgy ego would take it as a criticism of his performance rather than a reflection of his contribution to the firm's growing prosperity, and would need preparing. "It's still some way off."

"Of course not." Jenny, too, understood Steve. "Mrs Sunbury's due in half an hour, Doctor," she reminded him before closing his door.

Doctor! thought Peter self-derisively as he flung himself into his chair. A few days ago he'd taken a girl to the cinema on a first-time date, and when someone collapsed in the foyer and she pushed him forward, he'd had to say that his doctorate was in crime fiction. She wouldn't be going out with him again because, she told him, he had made a fool of her. No amount of protesting that the title "doctor" was more accurately his than a GP's could make her change her mind, in her eyes he had misrepresented himself. He hadn't intended styling himself "doctor" when he bought the agency, but Jenny had seized on it when he engaged her and insisted that it added gravitas (his word, coined from her series of entreaties) to the enterprise. Anyway, *Peter Piper Private Investigator* begged the question, and all he had really given in to was her determination to announce clients over the intercom to Dr Piper, and to call him "doctor" herself. He had been amused to learn from Steve that she was a closet addict of *Dr Who*, but had forborne to tell her that he knew. Steve's chosen sobriquet of "governor" came from his addiction to television series about the Met, rooted in rerunnings of *The Sweeney*.

Peter had never been able to take himself or his concerns entirely seriously, and had anticipated some difficulty in his first venture outside academe in distancing himself from a staff only a few years his junior sufficiently to exercise some authority over them. Being addressed as Mr Piper had seemed at the time to be the first step to establishing it, but he had been unable to see himself insisting on the title should a young, democratically minded member of staff decide that first names should apply in both directions. In the event, "Doctor" and "Governor" had come to his rescue. And if they hadn't, he had quickly realised, Miss Bailey would undoubtedly have had something to say . . .

Sighing over his loss, Peter sat down at his desk and dictated his report on Miss Parkinson for the insurance company who had engaged him to investigate the alleged serious damage to her walking abilities caused by a car belonging to one of its clients. People like Miss Parkinson and Mrs Porteous had to be the staple of a detective agency in a place like Seaminster, and were making him and his small staff a good enough living for the prospect of employing another full-time member to have recently appeared on the horizon. But he couldn't help yearning for something unusual. (Although the only out-of-the-ordinary commission he *did* have he could do without and was stalling on.) Steve did his best, bumping up the excitement content of his assignments whenever he burst back into the office, but they neither of them could sustain it much beyond the first few minutes. The trouble was, Peter supposed, that his lifelong desire to be a private eye had its roots in the works of Raymond Chandler, where the uneventful moments were mere preludes to the action-packed.

Perhaps Mrs Sunbury would present the right sort of departure from his bread and butter. Jenny had said she was husky-voiced and possibly transatlantic. "Husky-voiced with an undertone of urgency," had been Jenny's actual words.

Peter glanced at his watch. He still had ten minutes in which to fantasise about Mrs Sunbury, and experience had taught him that if he wanted to indulge in a daydream it had to be done before the client appeared . . .

The advent of Steve cut the exercise short before it had really begun. The rain had turned his brown hair black and flattened it against his head, and his mackintosh glistened.

"Take it off!" Peter ordered quickly, as his assistant turned towards a pale armchair.

"Phew! What a chase!" Steve gasped, complying.

"Mr Molyneux?" Peter asked incredulously. In his mind's eye he saw the stout and stately Charles Molyneux progressing slowly along the street.

"The weather's emptied everywhere and I had to keep back. I nearly lost him, but he couldn't resist the odd shop window." In the act of throwing his mackintosh to the floor Steve caught Peter's eye, and hung it askew on the old-fashioned coat tree that stood by the door. "And he turned into Laburnum Street and knocked at the door of Number Nineteen. That's four Tuesday mornings in a row at ten-fifteen, but there's more. I –"

Peter's intercom interrupted.

"Mrs Sunbury's here, Dr Piper."

"You'll have to keep the rest for later," Peter told Steve. "Go and dry off. Take your mackintosh with you. If you'd like to ask Mrs Sunbury to come in, Jenny."

Steve made his way to the door with an expression of suffering patiently borne, but when he had opened it he turned back to Peter and poked his thumb ceilingwards.

"Thank you, Steve," Peter said.

Steve stepped out of sight as Mrs Sunbury appeared, and the door shut slowly behind him.

"Peter Piper? I'm Anita Sunbury."

"Please sit down, Mrs Sunbury."

Appreciative now of Steve's charade Peter positioned a chair, and with a graceful gesture Anita Sunbury drew it even closer to his desk as she sat down. A tall, elegant blonde with an attractively ravaged face.

"Thank you, Dr Piper."

"How can I help you, Mrs Sunbury?" For once, he was really interested to find out.

"Ah." It was something of a feat to sink back into the depths of a small shallow armchair, but Mrs Sunbury managed it. "I'm looking for confirmation of a sad set of circumstances." Her voice *was* husky. In the Bacall style, and she was American, too. "I don't want it confirmed, but a time has come when I must face facts. Will you have a drink with me at six o'clock this evening in the Connaught Hotel? There is someone I would like you to see as a preliminary to your undertaking an investigation. Without obligation, of course, until you have seen what I have to show you, and I have explained matters. I would

52

be very grateful if you feel you can come." For the first time she smiled.

"That will suit me very well. Shall we meet in the foyer?"

"At a table in the lounge preferably, Dr Piper, it will be less conspicuous. And perhaps in a quiet corner, if you arrive first?"

"Of course. Six o'clock, then? Unless you'd like to tell me something now about –"

"I'd prefer to save it."

When she had left he rang through for tea, which was brought in by Steve.

"Give, Governor?"

"I can't, even if I would. I'm meeting Mrs Sunbury this evening at the Connaught to be shown someone or something and be let into the secret of what she requires."

"Not bad. Shall I hover?"

"No."

"Okay. American, isn't she?"

"It sounded like it."

"Could be the big break."

Peter noted indulgently the surge of hope into the pale, sharp-featured face of his assistant, undernourished-looking despite Steve's hearty appetite. He had taken over no more of the previous agency than its goodwill, its premises, and Miss Bailey, and after failing to be impressed by any of the applicants who had answered his advertisement for a bright young person to assist in the field, had recruited the twenty-two-year-old clerk across the counter of his local building society. Bored out of his mind with his predictable routine, Steve had been ever ready to strike up a conversation with the society's clients. Peter had been impressed by the streetwise young Londoner – Steve got on well enough with his parents to have moved with them to the coast when the Gas Board moved his father – who had the nerve to ask for the job he had told him he was trying to fill. When he learned that Steve also had five GCSEs and an A in English he had invited him for an interview and ended up offering him a three-month trial. This had revealed that Steve's enthusiasm was matched most of the time by good judgement and could be harnessed to practical and useful ends. And that he was prepared to work round the clock. Before it was up, the trial period became a permanent appointment.

Despite the persistently mundane quality of the everyday, Steve still saw his new calling as a progress towards a goal of scarcely imaginable glamour. A *big break*. Peter still found himself hoping for one, too, although unlike Steve he tried to dismiss his vision as a foolish fantasy.

"As you're here you'd better tell me the climax of your report on Mr Molyneux and Nineteen Laburnum Street."

"It could just be that, Governor, although of course I couldn't see what happened in the bedroom. But before they left the sitting-room he'd unfastened her blouse."

Chapter Six

Peter was ten minutes early, and Mrs Sunbury ten minutes late. She came upon him from behind, up the short flight of stairs near the corner he had chosen. He recalled that they led to cloakrooms.

"Dr Piper," she murmured as she sank gracefully down with her back to the wall. He thought she was wearing the same elegant silk suit he had glimpsed earlier under her jacket, and her hair was as carefully careless.

He regretted the absence of a member of Seaminster's comparative glitterati, or even one of its two out-and-about reporters, to see him escorting her. But the lounge had yet to become busy, and at the few occupied tables there were only visitors and the odd upper-end-of-the-market rep.

"What would you like to drink, Mrs Sunbury?"

"A very dry martini," she told him softly.

"Sir?" She was the sort of woman who would always have a waiter hovering. Peter ordered two very dry martinis. When the waiter had gone she asked him about the agency, how long he had had it, how many staff he employed. She spoke in so relaxed and incurious a way he was unable to feel she was out of line and answered her easily enough.

"Do you enjoy your work, Dr Piper?"

"Oh, yes. Although Seaminster is so law-abiding I don't often get the chance to feel like Philip Marlowe." It was a lie: what he didn't get the chance to do was to act like him.

When the drinks came he had money ready and put it on the tray as he gestured to Mrs Sunbury to close her handbag. More seemly for her to pay via his or Steve's expense account.

"To our collaboration," she murmured as she lifted her glass.

"To our collaboration," Peter echoed hopefully. "Now, do you feel able to tell me –"

"Any moment now a man will appear, Dr Piper, whom I shall ask you to observe. While you observe him I shall leave you in order to make a telephone call. Then I shall come back. The man may sit down close to this table, it's in the lap of the gods, but that won't matter, he doesn't know me – as I am now. When I get back I shall explain."

"Good."

"You are being admirably patient." She flashed him a smile, but as she looked away from him towards the lobby her face changed, becoming sombre and watchful. "He's here."

Only one man had appeared at the entrance to the lounge. A small man in a shabby mackintosh whose round shoulders and lagging walk apologised for his presence in Seaminster's smartest hotel. He carried a very unsmart bag and had a few sandy hairs trained across his skull.

"The chap looking so anxiously around? He hardly seems –"

"Dangerous men are all the more dangerous when they look negligible, when you scarcely notice them." Mrs Sunbury drained her glass. "Now, Dr Piper, if you will watch this man closely. I shan't be long away. Perhaps you will order me another martini."

"Of course."

"Sir?" The waiter was back.

As Peter finished his first drink his subject sat dubiously down close to where he had come in, making himself look as small in his chair as he was able. Fortunately its position allowed Peter to see the seated body in profile, study the uneasy movements and admire a master of disguise.

After about five minutes a young woman arrived, advertising a similar state of self-abasement. The man shot to his feet, and standing warily together, exchanging short bursts of talk and looking anxiously around them, they were for all the world like two people keeping an out-of-character assignation about which both of them were beginning to have second thoughts.

It was a relief to Peter when the man eventually persuaded the woman to sit down; however absurdly, he would have felt to blame if they had decided to leave. He didn't have a brief for her and he continued to concentrate on the man, but he would know her again, too, however cleverly she tried to disguise –

"Dr Piper!"

Peter swung round, his satisfaction turning to annoyance as he took in the woman at the head of the stairs. Quietly quality, but in the wrong place at the wrong time, whoever she was . . .

She was the woman who had come to his office asking for a temporary job. Her request had seemed so dilettante he hadn't thought of her again, not even when Miss Bailey had given him her notice.

As she sat down in Mrs Sunbury's seat his annoyance turned to a frustrated anger he could only just control. "I'm sorry," he said. "I'm expecting someone."

"I know, you're expecting me. Phyllida Moon alias Anita Sunbury. I shouldn't have done it, but after I'd been to see you it occurred to me that if you took me on for six months I'd be able to offer you something different, and I wanted to show you what it was. Call it an animated reference, and try to forgive me."

Behind her smile Phyllida was wary. No one knew better

than she the delicacy of the male ego, the resentments engendered by lack of subservience, let alone downright assault, and the stroke she had just pulled had to be a harsh test of anyone, man or woman. But in the next second she had relaxed, remembering she was no longer in the business of trying to please men who took themselves too seriously. She had had fun, and if Peter Piper couldn't take a joke against himself she didn't really want to work for him.

His face was expressive despite his attempts to look inscrutable. Phyllida saw the dawn of the truth, its dismissal, its return. "I made most of it up," she said gently. "But bits of dialogue from some dreadful play I once did kept coming into my mind, so I used them." She would help him a little. "You were puzzled, weren't you? You didn't know me, yet you felt you'd met me somewhere before, I didn't quite take you in."

"Oh, but you did." He didn't need helping. His face now rueful, Peter snorted with what Phyllida was happy to see was laughter. "I *did* have a feeling I'd seen you somewhere before, but I put it down to a photograph in some glossy magazine."

There was no need for him to go as far as to tell her that. Her immediate instincts that he was a nice young man had probably been right. "That's what I was relying on. Dr Piper, I really am sorry."

"*I'm* sorry if you haven't brought me an exciting case after all. That man . . ."

The unhappy couple were now getting to their feet, clasping hands and moving towards Reception. Two people keeping an out-of-character assignation about which they had succeeded in reassuring one another. "The first man to come into the lounge after I'd told you . . . Oh, dear."

"It's funny, actually." Perhaps that was why he couldn't keep up being angry. And perhaps he was flattered that she had gone to such lengths to show him what she could do. And if she could do Anita Sunbury she could do other women. Frail old ladies. Policewomen. Tarts.

"You mean you'd be prepared to sleuth in character?"

"Yes."

"Can you manage old ladies?" The case he was already assigning to her didn't specifically require one, but there had been regular work for Miss Bailey.

"They're mentioned in my latest reference, I was in my sixties for my last show at the Empress. And I can be a lot older than that. And younger than I am." With footlights separating her from the people she was deceiving. What she was offering now would be much more difficult. But Anita Sunbury had worked, and Phyllida already knew from the theatre that she could effect an inner as well as an outer transformation. "What I can't do is tell you I've got experience of working in a detective agency."

"But that's why you want to work in one, isn't it?" It was coming back to him. "For a TV series, you said?"

"It would help."

"Your series character is an actress?"

"No, but if sleuthing in character would persuade you to take me on for a few months . . . Anyway, I'm always happiest when I'm on stage." Phyllida realised the truth of what she was saying as she spoke, and wondered if that was why she was finding herself so anxious not to be a full-time writer even for a safely defined period. And so long as she was playing other people she might be able to put off asking herself who she was in her own right, a question that was threatening to become insistent.

"How many months?"

"Six?"

"All right." Her appearance and manner were pianissimo compared to her performance, but he liked them, she seemed reasonable and reliable. And if she turned out to be too good to be true no real harm could come out of so short a commitment. "Shall we say one month's trial?"

"Thank you." It was a good moment. "I'll bring in my latest reference in the morning. I'm afraid I can't lay my hands immediately on any others." But Wayne in the end had been generous, and one might suffice.

"I'll settle for the latest."

They smiled at one another, until a cloud covered his face. "The work can be horribly erratic. Nothing happening all day, and then to crack something one just has to be around all night. Could you cope with that?"

"I could try; I've no one but myself to consider."

Peter's face cleared. "Good! If there's nothing requiring your presence in the office you can always ring in in the morning rather than come in after a long day's night. Anyway, I expect you'll prefer to make your transformations at home. Have you got a base in Seaminster?"

"I've rented a house."

"Fine. And you've no other commitment during the next six months?"

"Only a long-term intention to get started on a book about the history of women in the theatre. If I do it'll be after work, not instead of it."

"I'm sure. My doctorate's in Crime Fiction, by the way. It's being published next year by Edinburgh University Press." He could feel the blush of his modesty. "Just in case you ever feel ill in the office."

"Congratulations!" They smiled again, each relieved to sense that the other was content to leave it there, for the time being at least.

"I've been getting ideas while we've been talking," Peter said. "What you'll be doing is so different from anything I've ever thought of for the firm . . . As you're going to be a chameleon it might be an idea not to have you openly on the staff. You'll be Phyllida Moon on the books, of course, but there's no need to put just one face to the name. Does that make sense?"

"Oh, yes!" It made the best sense Phyllida could currently imagine. It enhanced the strange but agreeable feeling of being temporarily stranded in a benevolent suspension of real life which would take her safely through the metamorphosis begun with her first glimpse of Gerald at play.

The prospect of being back the following Monday on a species of stage turned the rest of Phyllida's week into pure enjoyment, bringing a relish even to the buying of provisions and house plants and contacting the milkman, the newsagent and the jobbing gardener whose names and numbers the owner of the house had left beside the downstairs telephone, and to pottering about her own house and garden and going to the library to order books and sit taking notes in the reference section.

When she rang her father to tell him why she was still in Seaminster he involved her in a struggle to prevent him setting out at once to see her, which she won through her certainty that the no man's land she was inhabiting was without accommodation for her past, even its beloved aspects.

"I really am all right, darling. I've even got a job in a detective agency to help me with the series."

Her father did not find this information reassuring. But he had married again within three years of her mother's death, and was still working out what Phyllida saw as an unjustified sense of guilt. "That doesn't make me feel happy about you. If only you had a son or a daughter."

If only she had. If only she hadn't let Gerald persuade her, year by year, that it wouldn't suit their lifestyle. "Please don't worry, Daddy. It was time I faced facts."

Over their third dry martini her new employer, whom

Phyllida already suspected of retaining a boyish outlook on life, had suggested she appear on Monday in disguise. "Just to give the staff an immediate idea of your talents."

"They met Anita Sunbury."

"All the more impressive when they meet someone else. And don't tell me how you're going to appear, let's see if I recognise you. Which I suppose means don't come in on the dot of half-past nine."

Phyllida decided an elderly persona would be the most likely to withstand the close scrutiny of three suspicious people. And Peter Piper was feeling the loss of his Miss Bailey. No longer having access to the make-up and props owned by the Independent Theatre Company, she spent part of her free time in London adding to her own small store.

At a quarter to ten on Monday morning it was clear from Jenny's wary greeting that Dr Piper had prepared his staff for a challenge. But after a covert inspection which made Phyllida want to laugh, Jenny accepted Miss Pym as a potential client and rang through to ask Peter if he would see her. Steve was alert in the outer office, but relaxed after one wary glance. When Miss Pym went into Peter's room he came round his desk to hold the chair for her as she sat down.

That was when the laugh escaped her.

"Stay as you are!" Peter urged. He put his head round the door and asked Jenny and Steve to come in.

"This is our new temporary member of staff, Miss Phyllida Moon," he told them. "All right, Miss Moon?"

Phyllida took off her wig-cum-hat and rose to her slender height, removing her padded coat as she did so.

"Meet my permanent staff," Peter said. "Jenny Timmis and Steve Riley."

"Hello," Jenny said, blinking.

"But – Mrs Sunbury?" Steve's surprise was tempered by apprehension.

"I'm afraid so," Phyllida said.

Apprehension gave way to a visible disappointment. "But she was so . . . Gosh, I'm sorry . . ." Red came and went in Steve's pale face.

"That's all right," Phyllida reassured him. "When you compliment Anita Sunbury you compliment *me*. I'll clean my face and get rid of this cotton wool, and then you can meet my real self." If they could do that, they were cleverer than she was.

"I'll show you where to go," Jenny said. There were two doors between Peter's office and her desk, and one beyond it to which she led the way. Phyllida was aware of her flowery perfume, strongest as they passed the desk, and the demure provocation of her back view, short skirt above slender ankles and rounded calves just tight enough to shape rounded hips under a nipped-in waist and spotless white blouse. Jenny opened the door on to an old-fashioned bathroom containing a large unpanelled bath on claw feet, an enormous wash-basin, and a lavatory with a wooden seat like a throne, its pedestal patterned with blue flowers.

"The building started life as a house. I don't know how this set-up escaped intact, but the doctor won't have it touched." Jenny's voice was neutral, but Phyllida guessed that if she had her way she would call in contractors there and then. "All right?" She left Phyllida with a towel and a bemused smile and sped back to Peter's office.

"All right?" he asked in his turn.

"Clever!" Jenny said.

"Women!" said Steve. Where Jenny was exhilarated he was put out, Peter could see, taking the deception personally as a parable of approaching hazards in his own life.

Neither, to Peter's relief, seemed to be resenting Miss Moon's full-time, if finite, appointment to his staff.

"Don't be illogical," he told Steve. "It's her trade. Go and meet her when she leaves the king of bathrooms and show her the rest of the place. Then I'd like her back in here."

Phyllida emerged with Miss Pym in a bag to find Steve in the first of the doorways past Jenny's desk. His critical appraisal ended in a nod, which she hoped meant Miss Moon found more favour with him than Miss Pym, if less than Mrs Sunbury. "Our office," he said, standing aside for her to precede him into a room that ran the length of the outer office as far as the bathroom wall. In the centre was a large table haphazardly surrounded by upright chairs and strewn with newspapers and reference books. More books filled a set of shelves, and three filing cabinets stood together topped with green plants. There were several cupboards and a set of lockers, and the sash window looked across narrow walled gardens to obtrusively drainpiped Victorian backs.

"There's two free lockers," Steve said. "You'll probably need them both." Phyllida hoped the distrustful air with which he handed her the keys was his normal manner, sharpened perhaps by a sense of being one down to her. "Okay?" He led the way out and opened the adjoining door. "Rest room."

In here there were magazines and playing cards on the table, the two chairs were upholstered and there was a comfortably squidgy-looking sofa covered in multi-coloured crushed velvet. The room ran behind Peter's and was a mirror image of the general office with a kitchen in place of the bathroom. Its fitments were modern and included a small fridge and a microwave oven. Phyllida wondered if Jenny had done battle.

"Nice," she said.

64

"It's all right. We'll need another chair."

"There's the sofa."

"That's for stretching out," Steve corrected. "And everyone has to have a chair."

"I can bring one." Phyllida didn't want to expose the chair she had chosen to bring to Seaminster to the harsh life of a general office, but a concession to the deceived male might be no bad thing.

"It's all right," Steve said. "I've only just put Miss Bailey's out in the glory hole on the public landing. I'll bring it back and dust it down for you."

"Thanks."

"That's all right. The Governor says you're doing a TV series." Despite his nonchalant air, Steve's eyes pleaded compensation for her trickery.

"That's right." Phyllida was glad to be able to give him some. "Police series, but I'm a private eye. A straightforward one. I mean, not working in character. I'm the policeman hero's sister, so I shall get to be in every episode, which is nice. Rehearsals don't start until April, so I hope I'll be of some use here as well as learning how a detective agency works. At the moment I don't know anything at all about it. You'll help me, Steve?"

"Sure." Steve had been leaning against the sink, but now drew himself up to his full height. This left him half a head shorter than Phyllida, who was glad to be wearing flat shoes. "The Governor'd like to see you, by the way. He's waiting with a tricky one I'll be glad to miss out on. Coffee or tea whenever anyone wants it." Steve waved a hand round the kitchen and Phyllida went back into Jenny's territory. Jenny nodded towards Peter's door, without interrupting her typing but smiling down at her machine.

"Do you really have something for me already?" Phyllida asked Peter as she sat down.

"Steve, I suppose. But I hope so. We've been rather tiptoeing round it."

"Tell me." Leaning into the close confines of the little armchair, Phyllida was amused by the way it had shrunk from the soft deep luxury it had afforded Anita Sunbury.

"Right. It began with a telephone call from an elderly widow asking if she could see me on a delicate matter, and I invited her to come in. She told me I'd been recommended to her by a friend whose cat ownership problems I'd sorted out so I wasn't too concerned at first, although she struck me as a woman of character who was likely to know her own mind. Which I wanted to be wrong about when she said she'd twice witnessed her widower neighbour behaving as he shouldn't with his teenage daughter."

"Oh, no."

"At least the girl's adopted, so it isn't incest. But she's been his daughter since babyhood."

"What did this elderly widow witness?"

He told her. "Brian Fletcher's forty-something and his daughter's seventeen," he went on. "Mrs M told me that where the girl used to be sulky and monosyllabic, she's now sulky, monosyllabic and looking like she's lapped up the cream."

"Your words?" Phyllida asked.

Peter grinned. "The substance is Mrs M's. She was all the more shocked and upset because until then she'd liked and approved of Brian Fletcher as a nice kind man" – he put the description in quotes – "and a model father. She told me what she could about him, and we've started to follow it up: he has his own small business by Great Hill, Brian Fletcher Ironwork, and sells a lot to tourists and locals who like iron gates and individually designed Dunroamings."

"Any other children adopted?"

"No. And he's been a widower for three or four years."

"She didn't think of going to the police? Or at least the social services?"

"She did, but decided she ought to make sure there really was something wrong first. I gather he's a very good neighbour." Peter hesitated. "Steve's a bit squeamish on this one. So far as personal relationships are concerned, bits on the side between consenting heterosexual adults are his field. I've been hoping you don't have the same taboos."

"I don't think so."

The expressive face lit up. "Good! I've a tame sergeant in the local CID, I could ask him if Brian Fletcher has any dicey form, but that would be halfway to negating Mrs MacPherson's scrupulous behaviour and I don't fancy it anyway. But I do fancy finding out the truth of this particular situation. I gather Mrs M's not short of money, but I won't load the bill. Any thoughts?"

"I'm wondering if Mrs MacPherson is hoping you'll get someone into the house. That has to be the easiest place to find the truth."

"I know," Peter said gloomily. "If there is something going on they've got the privacy of nights under the same roof, they don't have to take risks away from home. I'm prepared to break and enter as a last resort but I'd rather try legal methods first, and with you to help I can. Bobbing about behind them in the street isn't going to tell us anything, but getting to know them . . ."

"Yes." Phyllida felt the prospect of work like a shot of adrenalin. "Do we know anything about the girl's interests?"

"Only what Mrs M said, so far. It's in here, with everything else we've got." He swivelled the thin file in front of him and pushed it across the desk to her. "Now, I've had more thoughts about your work here since I saw you; it's a whole new concept." Peter leaned forward, his eyes sparkling. He might be private sector to Steve's state comprehensive, but Phyllida decided they were both still schoolboys. "I had a word with John Bright last week, the manager of the Golden Lion across the square. The Connaught's the most expensive hotel in Seaminster, but the Golden Lion's the most exclusive. We did a successful job for him recently, and although he paid for it he seems to think he still owes me. It struck me that if you're going to be able to make contact with a subject, rather than just dodging about in his or her rear, you've got to have somewhere you can disappear to without trace if you're followed or if someone insists on seeing you home. And somewhere you can give as your address if asked. So John's booked a room for you at his hotel under our name, where you can take refuge and put your characters on and off and be seen to emerge from and sleep in if it seems wiser or more convenient any time than going home. He's also made discreet arrangements for you to tell Reception the names under which letters and telephone calls may arrive for you, seeing that Phyllida Moon isn't going to exist *vis-à-vis* Peter Piper."

"What did you do for him, Doctor?"

"A few members of his staff got together to rob guests," Peter said dismissively. "John wanted to find out who before going to the police. D'you have a car, Miss Moon?"

"Yes?"

"You'll have to be careful about that, you won't be able to change it each time you change your identity."

He had been thinking more precisely than she had. But the shock was minimal. "I'm a good walker, and I already know how efficient the buses are."

68

"The taxis, too. Don't be afraid of taxis, Miss Moon."

"Thanks, I won't." They grinned at one another. "But this morning . . . Dickens found his plots by walking. I've tended to find my stage characters that way. When I've read this file I'd like to walk home. By the time I get there I should have an idea of where I'm going to start and what I want from my props cupboard."

Steve was still hanging round and Jenny suggested he make Miss Moon a coffee. Having ascertained there were no earmarked chairs in the office, Phyllida sat down at the table with the file.

Brian Fletcher had been a widower for four years. Before coming to Seaminster he had been an accountant in the City, and had registered Brian Fletcher Ironwork three years earlier at the time he moved, telling Mrs MacPherson when they first met that it was an opt-out of the City rat race. In London Judith had gone to the Lycée and was now at Claire College, the well-regarded coeducational boarding and day school just outside Seaminster. She had had outstanding results from the GCSEs she had taken the summer before last and was in the sixth form and her second year of A level studies.

"She didn't seem particularly pleased." The file was quoting Mrs MacPherson. "But then, she was expecting to do well, she's a clever girl and knows it. Oxford or Cambridge seems inevitable."

Phyllida finished her coffee thoughtfully, left the office to the obvious disappointment of her younger colleagues, and set off towards the promenade.

By the time she reached it she had decided to enter the lives of the Fletchers as a woman based on a character she had played early in the Independent Theatre Company's last season. A well-meaning, stupid woman without subtlety or sophistication. This seemed a good idea for two reasons: people might well be less guarded in the company

69

of someone unlikely to pick up their nuances and subtexts; and it would be easier for her, as a novice face to face deceiver, to start with a character so far removed from her own. Always when acting Phyllida aimed to become the person she was playing, and the inner transformation to the woman she already knew was called Jennifer Bond would demand a range of reactions as alien to her as Jennifer's appearance, crowding out her own . . . Which they must no longer be allowed to do, Phyllida realised as she bought an ice cream. On the stage her characters were for their own sake and the sake of the play; now they were merely the means to an end, and the information they earned for her had to be taken in and assessed by her own intelligence.

She sat down on the first seat she came to, all at once weak from her sudden awareness of what she had taken on. But gradually, against the gentle movement of the water in front of her, the image of Jennifer Bond took three-dimensional shape, and when she got to her feet, eager now to get home and get started, Phyllida knew that from there on she must trust to her instincts.

Chapter Seven

"Excuse me. Excuse *me*. This *is* a retail establishment, I believe?"

"Of course, madam. I'm sorry, I hadn't realised my assistant was outside."

Brian Fletcher hadn't realised anything of his immediate surroundings for long enough to provoke this large indignant woman into expressing her dissatisfaction at the lack of service he was providing. The last time he had been aware of her she had been rummaging about in the basketfuls of small objects to each side of the open shop doorway, so careful to avoid his eye he had put her down as an "only looking". Or a thief, which should have had him on alert rather than going off into yet another uneasy reverie. If he didn't pull himself together the marvellous little business he had created would be on its way downhill; goodness only knew how long he had been dreaming.

"These two pieces, madam? Would you like them wrapped separately?"

He got on easily with women, particularly older ones, and by the time he had put the two pretty little parcels into her hand she was disarmed and telling him she would recommend his establishment to the friends she had made at her hotel.

"I'm glad you've found what you wanted," he responded on the usual reflex. "Perhaps you'd be interested in having a look next door and seeing my stock being made. I think I can say that this is the only retail iron foundry in Seaminster."

He knew he could, of course, but the modest turn of phrase always came pat and went down well. He had wanted to make objects in iron ever since a childhood visit to an old-fashioned forge, and moving from his accountant's office in the City to turn that wish at last into a livelihood had been pure pleasure. The business side was all right, too, it was the selling side he had been afraid of, his first working encounter with a public to whom the seller must ideally defer however unreasonable its behaviour. But he couldn't make a living unless he sold what he created, so he had had to get on with it. To his amused surprise, he had discovered something of a salesman's talent and that his patience was on a longer fuse than he had feared. The problem now was lack of concentration; unless he was in his foundry, where his attention was total, he was becoming more and more liable to fits of abstraction as his anxiety became more and more acute . . .

"Excuse me."

"I'm sorry, madam?" There he was again, although this time he had come round more quickly.

"I'd like you to make me a wrought-iron gate."

"Well, fine." He raised his arms and dropped them in a gesture of pleased surrender. He and the woman the far side of the counter smiled at one another. She was attractive in an obvious sort of a way, but he was too preoccupied for his approval to be more than academic, the sort of approval he would give to a showy portrait of a young woman in an art gallery, he couldn't feel it personally. "Do you have a design in mind, or would you like to see some of mine? Or we could work one out together."

"I've got some vague thoughts, but let me see yours. And I'd like to see how you work the iron."

In the end she chose one of his designs as a basis for some ideas of her own which he found so good he asked her if he could incorporate them in his sample book. Her delighted acceptance could be partly a hope that he would feel an obligation to her, Brian thought wearily; she had stood closer to him than was necessary in the forge.

"When shall I come again?" she asked.

"I'll let you know."

"Fine." She hesitated. "You'll have to fit the hinges to my gatepost, won't you?"

"Yes. We'll bring them up with the gate and fit them then."

"I'm not sure my gatepost is worthy. Do you do gateposts?"

"In iron."

"Mine's wood at the moment, but I'm sure iron would be better, it's into a stone wall. You'll need to come and measure, won't you?"

"Yes." He'd send Geoff, unless he felt different in a day or two from the way he felt now, which he couldn't imagine. "When would be convenient?"

"As soon as possible, if you can manage it. I mean, the gatepost's crucial, isn't it? I'll give you my address."

He took it down, made an appointment, walked her to the door and, despite her smile, stayed there while she crossed the forecourt, an elegant figure with a confident, slightly provocative, walk. In almost comical contrast to the woman who was bustling through the open gates, grinning cheerfully as they passed into the first woman's now sombre face, undeterred by its expression. A woman probably the same age as the one who was leaving – late thirties – but in every other way so totally unlike her they could have been different species. This one had untidy brown curls and a shiny, high-coloured skin that would have looked better through make-up. Her cardigan went up at the back over an unspruce cotton dress and she leaned forward slightly from the waist as she walked, as if anxious to win a photo finish. When she stopped halfway across the forecourt and boomed at him, her arms spread wide, she confirmed Brian's fears that she was the type of woman his wife would have described as bright, keen and jolly. A type he had always found particularly repellent.

"I say! Super little place you have here!"

"Thank you."

Jennifer Bond found the man who looked like a proprietor rather attractive, which made her giggle. She liked neat, slender men, and this one had abundant dark hair as well and what she thought of as delicate features. His rueful manner was lost on her, but she approved the brown eyes that proclaimed kindness and reliability.

"Mr Fletcher, I presume?" He bowed, which made her giggle again. "Nice . . ." Gracelessly she swung an arm to indicate the long, low building and the three boundary walls in the same soft pink brick which made a courtyard of the space where they stood. Wrought-iron artefacts from gates through lamp standards to fire screens abounded artistically in all directions, stacked and standing against the walls. "I wondered . . . Do you take commissions?"

"They're my lifeblood. Please come in."

He had an easy smile, which she liked too, although in repose his face looked strained. Sad, even. A romantic hero? "Could I have a Tree Tops? House name?"

"You could. I might even have one in stock, it's fairly . . ." He was still so far away he had almost said "common", although the woman in front of him, breathing heavily like a well-intentioned shaggy dog, probably wouldn't have been put out.

Phyllida was glad when he stopped rummaging and

74

shook his head, they would have to meet again. "No good?" Jennifer demanded.

"I'm sorry. I'll make it for you, but I'm afraid it's going to take twenty-four hours, we're rather busy."

"But it's good to be busy, isn't it? And twenty-four hours is fine; I'm staying in Seaminster while I make up my mind whether to come and live here."

The sort of woman, Brian thought dejectedly, out of whom personal details seem to ooze even when she isn't bent on imparting them. But he felt the anxiety in his face dissolve automatically into a smile.

"You should, it's a good place. Why hesitate?"

"It's my daughter's schooling. If she could get into Claire College . . . She's bright, but it seems to have a bit of a fearsome reputation."

"My daughter's there." There should be parental pride in his face, he could feel it, but he could also feel the return of the anxiety inseparable, now, from thoughts of Judith. "She's bright too, and it does have a high academic standard, but nothing venture . . . How old is your daughter?" Was he trying to punish himself, for heaven's sake?

"Felicity's twelve. She's not at school at the moment because we've lived abroad. I decided to come back to England when my husband died." The constant smile made a token disappearance. "I've arranged for Felicity to have a tutor at least till Christmas while I'm considering schools. I've come to Seaminster because we used to holiday here when I was little and I know Claire's reputation. It's super they've started to take girls, I'd never have believed it . . . How old's *your* daughter?"

"Seventeen." He felt himself wincing, hoped it didn't show.

"What does she want to do?"

"Law. She hasn't decided yet whether she wants to be

a solicitor or a barrister. Whichever she chooses she'll get there."

"You must be awfully proud of her!"

"I am." He was. He had that.

"I worry about Felicity growing up in today's world, you know. I mean . . . I expect I'm silly, but you hear such things . . . Do you and your wife worry about your daughter?"

He'd gone either red or white, he didn't know which. "My wife's dead. But I worry, of course. Although –"

"Gosh, I'm sorry." Tragic hero.

"What for? You couldn't know. Fortunately Judith's a very strong personality, she'll be all right." He had to go on believing it.

"Does she *talk* to you, though? Felicity's only twelve but she's fearfully cagey. I always imagined being such good friends, sharing our secrets and so on, but I don't even feel I know what she thinks about things."

He turned away to open a filing drawer and spoke with his back to her. "I shouldn't worry. It's the same with us. Now, if you'd like to look . . ."

"Yes, of course. Goodness, I'm talking too much, I'm so sorry, do you have just one design or can you –"

"There are a few alternatives." He put a sample sheet on the counter. "As you can see. Plain. Old English. Italic . . ."

"It's like calligraphy, isn't it? I once took a day course in calligraphy. I wasn't very good." Another giggle. If he was with her for long he'd start counting them. "It's for my father. I think he'd like black, and plain."

"Fine. Black and plain it shall be."

"Shall I pay now?" The cash was heavy, she'd be glad to unload some of it.

"Pay when you collect. Late tomorrow afternoon?"

"Super." Reluctantly Mrs Bond swung her bag back

over her shoulder and started to turn away. "See you tomorrow, then."

"I'm just wondering . . ." He had to be trying to punish himself, he was horrified by what he was about to say, and the eagerness with which she turned back to him. "There's a parent/staff meeting tomorrow night at Claire. Would you like to come along as my guest? It seems such a happy coincidence I feel I must ask you –"

"I say, what a piece of luck! I was going back to the hotel this very moment to try and make an appointment to see the head. Look, though, it's a bit of an imposition . . ."

"Not at all, although it would be easier if I knew your name. I'm Brian Fletcher, as you may have gathered."

"Goodness, yes!" If there had been a cartoon balloon above her head it would have been full of exclamation marks. "I'm Jennifer Bond. Felicity isn't with me, I'm afraid." His heart sank even further. But he wouldn't be alone with her; Judith had ungraciously agreed to accompany him.

"So where are you staying, Mrs Bond? I can pick you up."

"I'm staying at the Golden Lion. It really is awfully good of you."

"I live the other side of Seaminster so I have to go through, it won't be any trouble. The meeting's at eight, so if I pick you up at a quarter to? I shan't be able to park, so –"

"I'll be on the step," she eagerly assured him.

"A red Sierra. You were lucky to get in at the Golden Lion, by the way. At any of Seaminster's hotels, come to that, they're always full of Claire boarders' parents this week of the year."

"I got a cancellation, I just thought it was Seaminster's charms."

Another giggle. He'd make sure their second meeting

77

was their last. "I'll bring your Tree Tops, save you coming back for it."

"You really are kind, Mr Fletcher." He really did seem to be. "Till tomorrow night, then."

There was an ice cream van opposite his gates. Feeling disgust for them both, Brian Fletcher watched her buy a cornet and stretch her mouth over the top of it as she bustled out of sight.

"Ralph! Ralph dear, Daddy and I are ready to go!"

"All right, I'm coming you silly cow." He muttered the words, far too low for her to hear, as he pushed the chair back irritably from his desk. He was eighteen, for God's sake, why did she still have to call her husband "Daddy" when she spoke to him? She'd do it at school tomorrow night, even if at the last minute he told her not to. He was glad they were going away and so wouldn't be able to come. It meant that he didn't have to go either, but he couldn't miss out on an extra opportunity to see Judith. And maybe manage to use the crowd to eavesdrop and find out what she and the Elite did in the afternoons . . . When he'd told his mother that he'd go on his own she'd congratulated him on his conscientiousness.

"Off, then, are you?" he said on the landing. His father was disappearing round the curve of the stairs, accompanied by the bumping sound of suitcases. Apart from her handbag his mother was carrying just a shiny PVC bag with a Liberty pattern. She was staring at him anxiously, increasing his irritation.

"You're sure you'll be all right, dear? There's plenty in the fridge and freezer –"

"As you've told me. Of course I'll be all right, Mummy." He kept forgetting that now he was a prefect he'd decided to call her "mother". But probably this wasn't the best time to remember, just when she was going on holiday.

She'd be upset, and he didn't want his free fortnight to be tinged with guilt.

"Well, I hope so, dear. You've got our number safely?"

"*Yes*. I'll ring you if there's any need. There won't be. Just have a nice holiday."

"Are you coming, Daphne?"

Ralph put his hands on his mother's shoulders, propelled her gently towards the stairs, and followed her down.

"The rush hour should have cleared," his father said in the hall. "As much as it ever does." They were driving to Heathrow, where they'd leave the car and spend the night in an hotel before an early flight to Rome.

"Don't work too hard," his father said on the doorstep. It wasn't a joke, Ralph wanted to read chemistry at Oxbridge and spent most of his spare time studying. His mother thought this was exactly right, but his father sometimes wished his only child had a lighter touch and would show some evidence of a sense of humour.

"I won't," Ralph answered automatically. He was trying to imagine having Judith with him in a parentless house.

"Goodbye then, darling." His mother's arms were round his neck. Automatically he returned their squeeze, kissed her cheek, shook hands with his father.

When they had gone he felt depression rather than the elation he had so much looked forward to. He stood in front of the hall mirror and removed his glasses. Not so bad, blurred, apart from his lifeless hair, if he took himself feature by feature; it was just that it didn't add up to the way he would like to look, the way boys looked who were popular. Perhaps his expression was partly to blame, but when he tried to smile at himself and then look nonchalant it was equally ridiculous and anyway it didn't reflect how he generally felt, there were far too many people doing irritating things.

But at least with his glasses on he looked serious and intelligent.

When he had put them back he went to the telephone and dialled Judith's number. He'd never dialled it before but he knew it by heart. As he was giving up hope the dialling tone cut out and he heard her voice.

"Yes?"

"Judith . . . It's Ralph."

"Ralph?

"Unsworth," he completed humbly.

"So?"

"Judith . . . I've passed my test, you know, can I give you a lift to college tomorrow night? Your house is on my way to Claire." Which was the reason for his sudden burst of courage, and would have made his invitation sound casual and unimportant if he hadn't been the fool he was, letting her and everyone else see how he felt about her. But at least she couldn't deny the practicality of his suggestion and she hadn't taken her driving test yet. Driving her to college, letting her experience him in charge of a car, could earn her respect even if she didn't let him drive her home. And if she did let him he could suggest a coffee at his place . . . He tried to forget her reaction when he had shadowed her into the house kitchen a couple of days ago after lunch and asked her what she was doing. He'd asked her without thinking because she'd looked so sort of – well, furtive when she first saw him, standing in the recess that led down to the cellar as if she was hiding from someone. She'd told him to mind his own business, and for a moment he'd thought he had seen real dislike in her face. It just might not have been for him, of course, but he couldn't forget it, he was crazy to have rung her. Now he'd done it, though, he had to go on. "My parents are away, I've got the car."

"If I go to college tomorrow night I'll go with my father. I'm sorry, Ralph. Goodnight."

He heard the click, the trailing whine of his disconnection. He went and sat on the bottom stair, his head in his hands.

In view of her choice of hotel and her hopes of an interview with the Headmaster of Claire College, Jennifer Bond had packed her floral two-piece. She put it on for the parent/staff evening, congratulating herself on its suitability. It had been another day of Indian summer, and after a drink and sandwiches at the bar she came out of the Golden Lion a little early to await Brian Fletcher, standing under the pillared porch and admiring the north facade of Dawlish Square. Most of the windows were dark, but light shone from two side by side on the second floor. As she looked across at them the outline of a man appeared at the brighter one.

"Here we are!" Brian Fletcher was springing from his car, to usher Mrs Bond into the front passenger seat. "My daughter Judith's in the back. Judith, this is Mrs Bond."

"Hello, Judith."

Phyllida didn't catch a response, but when she turned round and saw the sullen face of the girl sprawled in the corner she decided there hadn't been one.

"I'm afraid I've taken your seat, Judith," Jennifer gushed, unsnubbed. "You should have let me sit in the back. I'm so grateful to be in the car at all . . ."

At last there was a small pained smile. "It's OK."

Street lights swooped across Judith Fletcher's face, but the intermittent shadows were so black and frequent that Mrs Bond's regular, polite backward glances gave no real picture of it. It wasn't until they were standing together beside the car, surveying one another by the debilitating sodium glow of the safety lights shining from the Palladian facade of Claire College, that Phyllida really saw the closed, neat-featured face, the smooth dark hair and the small slender figure. Under the chandeliers of the entrance hall she discovered that Judith Fletcher really was pale, with a strongly defined mouth just touched with pink and grey-green eyes which were her most noticeable feature in their skilfully darkened surround.

"Let's go through." Brian Fletcher's hand descended towards his daughter's shoulder, jerked away. "I expect you'd like to find your friends, Judith."

"Eventually." Judith's eyes slid from her father to Mrs Bond in an expressionless face.

"All right. Wander off when you want."

"Thanks, Daddy."

"Through here." Phyllida was aware of Brian Fletcher's hand just touching her arm as they moved in a small crowd towards a double doorway. "Ah, the Molesworths! A plus for a mixed school, wouldn't you say, Mrs Bond, having a married couple as joint Heads . . ."

Mr Molesworth was small, sparse-haired and skinny, making Brian imagine his large, elaborately coiffed wife draining his reserves. The contrast of their side-by-side position in the doorway made him want to laugh, and he killed the impulse with a glance at Mrs Bond. Her expression of eager approval of all before her hadn't varied, but she had already made it clear that she had no sense of humour.

He introduced her. "Mrs Bond is hoping to live in Seaminster and would very much like her daughter to come to Claire."

"I know Claire's reputation, but Felicity's pretty bright . . ." Jennifer went through her breathy paces, turning the wide doorway into a bottleneck and securing from the Molesworths – in self-defence, Brian thought –

82

the promise of a conducted tour of the school in tomorrow's daylight.

Mr Molesworth's rich baritone and his wife's soft treble made him want to laugh again, but the impulse died as he spotted the severe-faced youth staring hungrily towards them. Towards Judith. He'd done the same thing the other day when he and Judith had come out of the ironworks on to the promenade. He must have been hanging about and he'd come towards them and Judith had had to introduce him. Ralph Unsworth. Judith had imitated his priggish, unattractive way of speaking the moment they were out of earshot. She didn't have any time for him, thank God, all he had attracted was her scorn. But he was obviously keen on her and he was male and young, he might wear her down . . .

He was coming towards them again, and now he was isolating Judith with a hand on her arm, leaning so close to her the wisp of hair that stuck out from his forehead was brushing her ear.

Judith, her face coldly angry, was shaking herself free, but Brian Fletcher had already been hit by a wave of anguish so strong he had to stand still a moment until it ebbed.

"You all right, Mr Fletcher?"

If the terrible Mrs Bond hadn't been bouncing so eagerly forward he'd have been nearer to Judith, able to interpose himself between her and the boy. "It's nothing, just a twinge in the knee."

The boy was in retreat, but Brian's suffering had generated a determination to use tonight's unique opportunity and speak to him. Suggest, as if kindly, that he was wasting his time. Play King Canute and try to stem a tide to which, even in the guise of Ralph Unsworth, his dearly beloved daughter might all too easily surrender herself.

Chapter Eight

Ralph had arrived too early as usual, but for once lacked the energy to go to his form room and take advantage of the spare twenty minutes. He was mooching round the entrance hall when the anxious face of the Assistant Bursar, Miss Turner, peered out from the Bursar's office. It lit up as she saw him.

"Ralph Unsworth!"

"Can I help you, Miss Turner?" Faces didn't usually light up when people saw him, but he had a reputation for reliability and he never made excuses. She must want him to undertake some duty during the evening.

"A letter for you. It came through the slot." Miss Turner waved a hand at the gleaming brass rectangle in the centre of the mahogany door. "It's marked 'urgent' so I hoped you'd be here."

She handed him a small white envelope, smiled formally, and withdrew. If he'd been Tim Rowland or one of Tim's cronies, Ralph thought bitterly, she'd have shown at least a flicker of curiosity.

No one else was showing any, either, but he went behind a pillar to open the envelope. The flimsy sheet of paper inside was typewritten, but the ink was faint and it took him a few seconds to take in its message. Then he stood with it in his hand and read it again and again. *Ralph. Meet me please in the storeroom round the corner from the visitors' cloakrooms at nine o'clock tonight, or as near to nine as you can make it. Don't tell anyone, or speak to me about it. Close the door if you get there first. Explanations when I see you. I shall be alone. Judith Fletcher.*

Judith Fletcher. The name was typed, but Judith had already developed one of those tiresomely illegible signatures, so this was understandable. *Judith.* The incredible truth kept hitting him as if for the first time. Judith wanting to see *him. I shall be alone.*

If she hadn't said "alone" he'd have half expected the rest of the Elite to be in attendance, she was hardly ever to be seen without them, those three tall and frighteningly attractive girls who went round with her almost as if they were her bodyguard. And disappeared with her in the afternoons . . .

But tonight she would be alone. When he thought about the storeroom he had to lean against the pillar. He'd been sent there once by his form master to collect some stationery. It had shelves everywhere to the ceiling but its central area was small and there was no window. A perfect private rendezvous for two, and Judith had asked him to meet her there. Even if she just wanted him to do something for her it would be a start, it would put her in his debt. He'd suffered all his school life for being well-behaved and always doing what the staff wanted – not that that seemed to have made him popular with them, either – but when it came to needing help, someone to rely on, that was the time even Judith could start looking at him in a different light . . .

Unless . . . He didn't know for a fact that Judith didn't fancy him, he'd never seen her smile favourably on anyone, not even Tim Rowland. She had a reputation for never doing the expected thing so couldn't there just be a chance?

Ralph glanced at his watch. There was at least the chance to dream. For a whole long hour. He went into the party room and took up a position behind the Heads, from where he could watch the arrivals. Judith appeared promptly with her father, and a woman who reminded him for a moment of his mother.

If he went and said hello he could show her how well he could match her cool. But when he was beside her he found himself putting his hand on her arm. Leaning close to her to look reassuringly into her eyes . . .

She was twitching free, turning away after staring through him. But there was no need to be upset, now. Judith was so perverse it could mean that when they were alone she would do just the opposite. And he knew her well enough to be certain that whatever her private thoughts they would not be reflected in her public face . . .

"Ralph? You're OK?"

To his annoyance he had been spotted by Tim Rowland, the Head Boy, whose face he always thought of when he looked at his own. Popular. Good-looking. Decent, too, although Ralph couldn't help hating him.

"Of course, yes." He was glad the note was safely in his pocket. "Why shouldn't I be?"

Tim shrugged, still amiable. "I thought you looked a bit put out. Sorry if I was wrong. No parents tonight?"

"They're on holiday."

"Conscientious you for turning up."

Another sixth former would have said it sarcastically, or made a comment about his not having anything else to do. He should make an effort to be less aggressive to Tim. "I don't expect I'll stay the course. See you."

He could do with a coffee, and pushed his way through the crowd. Judith was standing near the large table where coffee was being served, still with her father and the woman who on a closer look wasn't really like his mother, who had a fashion sense.

"Hello again." It was easy this time to sound indifferent

because in the moment of speaking he was distracted by the sudden anger in Judith's father's face. He wondered what had caused it. "Good evening, Mr Fletcher. Ralph Unsworth, Claire prefect. We met –"

"I remember."

And remembering that he was going to have a talk with the boy was enabling Brian Fletcher to subdue his apprehension, even though Unsworth's face as he looked at Judith was so sickening it was actually a relief to turn to Jennifer Bond. "This is Mrs Bond. She's hoping to send her daughter to Claire."

"She'll have to be bright." Ralph Unsworth's tone of voice matched his prevailing expression. Brian had suspected him of being a prig, now he was certain. "The school has a very high academic standard."

"She *is* bright," Jennifer pleaded.

"I'm sure she is," Brian assured her. He was glad to see a familiar figure on its way towards them. "Ah, here's Mr Williams." He and Alan Williams, Claire's Art Master, had discovered at an earlier of these get-togethers an interest in each other's craft. Alan came over to the shop now and again with some pictures under his arm, but Judith had been so unenthusiastic about her father's idea of asking him to dinner he hadn't done so. His disappointment at her reaction had been tinged with relief; she had once told him, albeit scornfully, that a lot of the girls at Claire fancied themselves in love with the Art Master.

Ralph deemed it politic to leave them before Mr Williams's charisma rendered him invisible.

"I'm sorry, that was unnecessary," Brian said to Jennifer, as he sent daggers into the rigid retreating back.

"Not to worry. But Felicity really *is* a clever girl!"

Judith shrugged. "Ralph Unsworth's a total pain. Hello, Mr Williams."

"Judith. Brian. And?"

Brian introduced Mrs Bond, who rapidly explained her presence.

"Mrs Bond!" Mr Williams sparkled, as she ran out of steam. "I teach art, and I look forward to meeting Felicity." His handshake was firm, his green eyes radiant and, for a heady moment, exclusively hers.

"Mr Williams is the school heart-throb," contributed Judith.

Mr Williams gave an amused laugh, it was a description he was clearly used to. Phyllida could see why: the radiance was accompanied by striking good looks, an easy manner, and the sort of smile that seems to belong solely and for ever to the person at whom it is currently directed. It made Jennifer blink, in delighted embarrassment.

"Felicity loves art. Do you paint, Judith?"

Judith shrugged again, and Mr Williams said, "Judith has talent. Selfishly I could wish she were less academic, I'd like her to study art seriously."

"That's good to hear." But parental pride was no more than a flash across Brian's tension. "I like some of her paintings, as you know," he said to Alan. "But I'm no expert."

"Non-experts are entitled to likes and dislikes. Art snobs are too disdainful of people knowing what they like without being able to explain it in art establishment terms." Someone was tapping the Art Master on the shoulder. "Now, I've arrived at the place where I'd like to linger, but I'm reminded that my duty tonight is to circulate. I'll call in sometime soon, Brian."

"Make it at lunchtime if you can. My sandwiches are as good as my coffee."

"I'll try. And I hope to see you again, Mrs Bond." The sort of man who would always remember names after one hearing. "Here's Miss Hind now to take her turn with you. Excuse me." With a final graceful smile that managed to be intimate with three people simultaneously, Mr Williams moved swiftly away.

"I say, what a charmer!"

Brian wondered what sort of a man Mr Bond had been. Conscientiously he introduced his guest to a circulating succession of Claire staff. Miss Hind (history), near to retirement but blinking as happily as Mrs Bond from the impact of the Art Master's passing smile. Dr Court (physics and chemistry), with a lot of teeth under a ginger moustache and a reputation for getting young scientists into Oxbridge. Mademoiselle Dupuy, flirting with Brian and expressing her *grande déception* that she didn't see more of him. (Judith had to explain to Mrs Bond that *déception* in French meant *disappointment*.) Mr Bell (English), a morose cynic.

"Are you tired?" Brian asked Mrs Bond as Mr Bell went on his world-weary way. Perhaps it was because, unlike his guest, he had been able to respond to the combined and impressive intelligence of the Claire staff that he was so tired himself.

"Not a bit!" Mrs Bond laughed, as he had already learned she so often did when nothing amusing had been said.

"Good, we'll hang on a bit."

"I wouldn't mind . . . Judith, could you show me the ladies' cloakroom?"

"Sure." Judith looked at her watch. "I want to go to my form room, I'll take you on the way."

"I say, thanks awfully."

Judith indicated that Mrs Bond should walk ahead of her. Halfway across the room Phyllida turned and saw Judith nod gravely to a tall and strikingly attractive blonde, who immediately excused herself to the group she was with and followed Judith.

"Hi!" In the hall another tall striking girl with a cloud of black hair and an excited expression.

"Fiona."

Judith didn't introduce either of the girls to Mrs Bond, but then they hadn't exactly joined them, it was as if they just happened to be going the same way.

"We're in School House," Judith told Jennifer in the wide, handsome corridor. "This part's usually out of bounds to students. That's what Claire pupils are known as; I suppose it's meant to make us think university."

The corridor was interrupted by a seating place with small tables, easy chairs and sofas, where a girl was perched on an arm and flipping through a magazine. Another exchange of nods, and the girl got to her feet. She was as tall and good-looking as the other two Judith had collected, and had long, wavy red hair. She glanced at Mrs Bond, who smiled at her, and then, without returning the smile, at Judith again, before starting to walk alongside the dark girl.

"I say!" Jennifer exclaimed cheerfully. "It's like the pied piper!"

There was no response, but the girls exchanged glances. They were approaching a door in the left wall from which two middle-aged men were emerging. The disagreeable prefect who had been so severe about Felicity's chances at Claire was approaching the men's room from the other direction, looking at his watch and not seeing the women right away. When he did he stood still. Phyllida wasn't aware of the girls quickening their pace, but they were all at once ahead of her, surrounding him. Moving as he moved, keeping him enclosed, their hands out, strange and upsetting expressions on their faces . . .

Phyllida was glad there was a portrait on the wall beside her which Jennifer could turn away to look at, the living picture seemed somehow so private.

When she turned back the young man was disappearing

90

into the men's room and Brian Fletcher was standing watching him.

"Oh, hello," Jennifer said. "We're just . . ."

"Here we are, Mrs Bond." Judith was at her side again, and her friends were by the women's room door.

"See you back at the party," Brian said quickly, without catching Mrs Bond's eye. He didn't want to risk being delayed, missing the opportunity which was presenting itself without his having made any effort. His apprehension resurging, he followed Ralph Unsworth into the men's room.

Judith walked Jennifer on to the women's. "We're going to our form room," she said at the door. "Find your own way back?"

"Yes, of course. Thank you, Judith."

Two younger girls had had their way into the cloakroom blocked by Judith's friends, and got in only when they moved aside for Mrs Bond.

"That Elite!" one of them said crossly as they joined the small queue for cubicles. "Judith Fletcher and her gang! You'd think they owned the place."

"Who decided they were the *crème de la crème*?" the other asked.

"It was sarcastic, didn't you know? Oh, but you're new. It was because of the way they go about as if they're superior to everyone else. The name stuck and they love it, they think it's just the word to describe them."

"They *are* rather something though, aren't they, Rosemary? I mean, they're awfully good-looking and all of them are clever and well, sort of sophisticated, sure of themselves as if they know something . . ."

"Fiona Jeffcoate?"

"Well, perhaps not quite Fiona, although she's the most human, I should say."

"So the others'll probably kick her out."

The conversation ended as a cubicle became free. Phyllida washed her hands hurriedly, hoping she might emerge at the same moment as Brian and be able to walk back with him, but when she came out into the corridor it was deserted. She was unable to find him in the party room, or Judith or her friends. So she went for another cup of coffee, and got into conversation with the mother of a twelve-year-old student whose conversation was of interest only to Jennifer.

When he came out of the men's room Ralph went round the corner to the storeroom for the second time. The first time had been just to look at the sign on the door and anticipate. He was still too early for his tryst (a word he had only just thought of, and liked), but he wanted to be there first. He felt very slightly uncomfortable at the way he'd put Judith's father off, telling him he couldn't talk just then because of having an appointment. If he hadn't been so excited about his meeting with Judith he'd have wondered what her father could possibly want to talk to him about, and why he had looked so strange, almost as if he was angry again. At least he'd told Mr Fletcher he'd be happy for them to get together later.

He paused casually outside the storeroom door and looked up and down the corridor. It was deserted, and he turned the handle and walked quickly inside, finding the switch for the naked overhead light bulb before fastening himself in.

As he had remembered, the shelves went to the ceiling and were stacked. He had noted stationery, loo paper, drawing pins, twine and carbolic soap when the door slowly opened and the light went out.

"Don't speak," a voice whispered. He heard the door close again and then, from behind, hands came down on to his shoulders. He leaned his head towards one of them, and suddenly it was withdrawn and both of them were passing softly down his face.

"Judith!" he sighed, before something the hands must be holding began to restrict his throat and he started choking.

When he had ceased to breathe the hands eased him carefully to the floor, switched on the light, and freed the envelope he was still clutching. When they had opened it and spread out the sheet of paper inside, there was a grunt of satisfaction.

Chapter Nine

On the drive back to the Golden Lion Brian Fletcher was as unresponsive as his daughter, but Mrs Bond was undeterred and kept up a steady flow of enthusiastic comment on the evening and its personalities.

"I was very impressed by the staff, Mr Fletcher. I was very impressed by the staff, Judith." She had turned round to repeat herself. "And the atmosphere of the school, too," she said to Brian. "I liked it enormously." Again she turned round. "You've got some very attractive friends, Judith, but I think that prefect – Ralph, isn't it? – has a rather unfortunate manner." Brian Fletcher jerked in his seat beside her. "Anyway, you and your friends put him in his place all right." The sharp movement this time came from the back of the car. "But that was a very small fly in the ointment. I'm having a conducted tour in the morning. Oh, but you know that, of course, how silly of me, in fact I should be thanking you for it, Mr Fletcher. If you hadn't invited me this evening . . . I really am grateful."

"Not at all," Brian Fletcher murmured. When he stopped outside the hotel he reminded her about the wrought-iron house name.

"Goodness!" she said. "I'd forgotten." Despite the special care she had been taking of her handbag.

"That's just as well, because I'm afraid it isn't ready." He'd been so busy all day he'd forgotten about it too, to his annoyance. It meant he would have to see Jennifer

Bond again. "Would you be able to call for it say tomorrow afternoon? Or I can drop it in at the hotel."

"How kind, but I'll be very happy to call for it. I'm always glad of a walk in Seaminster."

"Fine, then." He got out of the car and went round to the passenger door.

"Goodnight, Judith." Jennifer smiled towards the back seat as she inelegantly alighted. She stood on the steps until they had driven away, then went into the hotel, bustled across the lobby, and climbed the stairs to the first floor. At the end of a wide corridor there was a door into a narrow one with a carpet that felt thinner under her shoes.

"In here," the girl from Reception had said that morning, opening a bedroom door. "Mr Bright's personal orders." Curiosity had been no more than a flash of prurience across the indifferent face. "Here's the key. Mr Bright said you wouldn't have much luggage."

"That's right." The girl had drifted out without properly shutting the door, and standing with her back against it after completing the operation Phyllida had approved her first private office: a small single bedroom with a bathroom *en suite*. As suitable as her house for a transformation so that, after a day in the agency learning about its business and its routines, she had decided to bring Jennifer to the Golden Lion in an overnight bag.

She had shed the floral two-piece and was in the bathroom cleaning her face when the telephone rang, making her start so violently she had to smile the next second at her large startled eyes.

She raced back to the bedroom.

"Yes?"

"Miss Moon! Peter Piper here. Forgive me, I know it's late, but I saw you from my window. First when you were leaving, although I only knew you because of Mrs MacPherson giving me Fletcher's registration number. Then just now. Would you feel like coming across for a nightcap before going to bed, or are you too tired?"

"I think I'd be glad to talk about my impressions while they're still vivid. Give me ten minutes?"

"As long as you like."

He was waiting for her in his outer doorway.

"Do you live in your office?" she asked as he followed her in.

"No, but since my girlfriend left I seem to be staying here later and later. Anyway, I'm an owl and I had a report to write. Scotch? Soda?" He opened what she had thought was a small filing cabinet, and poured both as she nodded. "Is Mrs Bond really as awful as she looks?"

"Yes. Silly, ignorant, and stricken with verbal diarrhoea. Little or no awareness or insight. We don't have to stick with her but I thought she might be a good start, that people might be more relaxed – indiscreet, even – in front of someone who didn't count. She could have made Brian Fletcher think twice about his invitation, of course, but I hadn't imagined a stroke of luck like that." During her day and a half in the office her employer and his staff had insisted it was a stroke of genius, and although she had tried to turn their tributes aside with her honest opinion that it was a happy coincidence which deserved their congratulations, she had enjoyed the unfamiliar sensation of working with a director and company who considered her brilliant. "Cheers."

"Cheers. And would you say Mrs Bond *was* a good start?"

"I think so. She was completely beneath Judith's contempt, and didn't inspire Brian Fletcher to make any real effort to hide the fact that he's a bundle of nerves and desperately jealous of anyone who makes sheep's eyes at his daughter."

"Someone did?"

"There was a prig of a sixth former with a tight little mouth who was very prissy with Mrs Bond about her daughter being up to Claire standards. When he looked at Judith his mouth went all trembly and full the way men's mouths tend to when they feel like that." She dismissed an unwelcome memory of Gerald.

"Do they? I've never thought . . ." He was almost sidetracked. "What was Judith's reaction?"

"Apparent indifference. When he'd gone she said he was a pain. But Brian Fletcher's reaction was the spectacular one. He didn't say anything, but for a moment he looked really sick."

"Which could be telling us what he wants to do, if not that he's done it. And if another kind of woman can get to know him . . . Anything else?"

Phyllida hesitated. "I don't know. Judith agreed to take Mrs Bond to the visitors' cloakrooms, and on the way she collected three of her friends."

"Collected?"

"It was as if – as if it had been arranged in advance. I know that sounds ridiculous, but the first girl was absorbed with a group, yet as we passed it she and Judith both nodded very gravely and deliberately and the girl excused herself and came after us. The second encounter seemed to be more casual, the girl was standing by herself in the hall, but Judith just said 'Fiona' and she came along too. The third one was reading a magazine in a sort of little lounge we went through, and she and Judith exchanged nods like with the first one and she got up and joined us. Judith didn't introduce any of them to Mrs Bond, and I got the feeling it was only partly because she didn't consider Mrs Bond worthy of an introduction, it was also because

97

the girls hadn't joined her in the normal way. Yes, it does sound ridiculous. And it's nothing to do with Judith and her father."

"Never mind, I've learned in this business that everything is grist to the mill. What happened then?"

"The youth who's keen on Judith came from the other direction on his way to the men's room and suddenly" – Phyllida shook her head and took a drink – "the girls were all round him, sort of hemming him in; they had their hands out as if they'd stop him if he tried to escape, almost as if they were baiting him. It wasn't all that nice, it made me think of a group of witches. Mrs Bond turned away to look at a convenient picture on the wall by where she was standing, but I don't think I missed anything. Then Brian Fletcher came up and suddenly the circle had broken, Judith was beside me and her friends a little way ahead, and Brian and the boy – Ralph Unsworth – went into the men's room and Judith and her pals left me at the women's. That was when I had my last bit of luck."

"The Lord helps those who help themselves."

"Two younger girls wanted to go in, but they had to wait until Judith and co. got out of the way, which they did for Mrs Bond. One of them was annoyed, and I learned that Judith and her friends are known as the Elite and tend to ride roughshod. So all that ritual of getting together could just have been schoolgirl mystique. I'm sorry, it doesn't really amount to anything, does it? Nothing you can tell your client."

"Not yet." His smile was resolutely encouraging.

"But Jennifer *did* secure an invitation to be shown round the school tomorrow morning, which at the least will be an opportunity to invite a few comments on Judith Fletcher. I'll ring first thing to pin it down. From the hotel, I thought I'd stay there tonight, even though Mrs Bond is unlikely to receive an early morning call from Brian

Fletcher." Phyllida tried to be amused by the absurd pang of homesickness.

"But if there's the least possibility of it you'll need to stay there. I hadn't thought of that, but what you're doing is new for me as well and I expect there are several things I haven't thought of. There's no problem?"

"None."

"Good. John Bright's coming over here tomorrow evening, by the way. Six, if you can make it. I decided that in the circumstances he was the one person outside this office who ought to meet Phyllida Moon. He doesn't know or want to know anything beyond the fact that there are times when you won't be recognisable, and that the name of the woman in room 247 could change in the course of a day, but he's a star pupil in the school of discretion and if you ever need his help he'll be there."

"Thanks."

"He and I have already agreed that you provide Reception with your changes of identity by telephone rather than face to face. Which you've probably worked out for yourself."

"Well, yes."

He grinned his approval. "One other thing. Steve calls me Governor and Jenny calls me Doctor. What if you call me Peter?"

"If you'll call me Phyllida. So long as Steve and Jenny won't disapprove."

"On the contrary. They both have a strong sense of suitability; they'll consider it entirely appropriate between two professionals who are also contemporaries."

"Near contemporaries." Phyllida wondered if it was his patent enthusiasm which made her feel a larger age gap between them than there probably was. "But I'd rather be Phyllida than Miss Moon."

Or Mrs Waterworth. Who, Phyllida realised as she

strolled back across the neat floodlit gardens, had *de facto* ceased to exist.

"Mrs Bond? I'm Jane Turner, Assistant Bursar, nice to see you. Let's start right away, shall we?"

Miss Turner closed the door of the Bursar's office behind her and swung her bag over her shoulder. She was the sort of young woman Jennifer Bond approved of: tidy, businesslike, wholesomely pretty.

"I think we'll begin with the houses," she pronounced with a smile.

"The houses?"

"Ah! Come and see!"

Miss Turner ushered Mrs Bond through the front door, down the steps and in a straight line across the forecourt to where the curve of lawn began. There she stopped, and turned to face the college.

"The contemporary outbuildings are to the left, as you can see. They're extensive enough to provide Claire's assembly hall as well as our art and crafts room. The houses are to the right."

All that could be seen to the right was a wide screen of variegated bushes. Miss Turner led the way obliquely back across the drive, and round the screen.

"Goodness!" Jennifer exclaimed, as they stopped beyond it. The terrace of tall, red-brick Victorian Gothic villas had three acute-angled gables, three identical front doors between pairs of bay windows, three flights of stone steps up to the front doors, and could hardly have been further in feeling from the mansion on which they encroached.

"I know. Quite a cultural shock, isn't it? But so convenient, Mrs Bond! Claire was sold out of the Sheldon family in the late nineteenth century and the new industrialist owner built the houses to take the overflow of his large staff. Claire is quite a small stately home, you know.

The houses wouldn't have got planning permission today, they're much too close to the mansion, but they do fit in awfully well with a school . . . The industrialist – forgive me, I've forgotten his name – screened them with a heavy shubbery, so perhaps he did feel a little ashamed of himself, but as you can see it's quite attractive now with the different kinds of bushes. Let's go into St Bride's."

Miss Turner led the way up the flight of steps nearest to the school and pushed open the heavy door. The hall beyond it was dark, its gloom relieved by no more than the rich splash of colour from the sun's impact on the glass images of fruit set into the door's upper panels.

"I think the only difference between the houses is the arrangement of the stained-glass fruit." With a little laugh Miss Turner pressed the switch for an overhead light. "As you perhaps discovered last night, Mrs Bond, Claire started taking girls as day students fifteen years ago, and about eight years ago a comparatively small number were admitted as boarders to this house, under Miss Hind. That may sound rather old-fashioned, but St Bride's does have dayboys as well as daygirls as house members, and the three other houses – Bart's under Mr Smith the French Master, St Jude's under Mr Williams who teaches art, and School House under the Heads – have daygirls although they board only boys. There's a very strong house spirit at Claire and the students are encouraged to use their houses whenever they're not in the form room or on the games field." Miss Turner paused and looked at Mrs Bond with slight embarrassment. "It's still rather difficult for girls to get into Claire as boarders, I'm afraid. But I gather you're thinking of coming to live in Seaminster?"

"Oh, yes, and anyway I'd want Felicity to live at home with me. A fatherless child . . ."

"I see." Phyllida saw the scepticism in Miss Turner's face. "Well, that should greatly improve her chances of

101

acceptance. As a day student she could of course find herself in Heads, where I'll take you when we've had a brief look round here." Miss Turner waved a hand towards the stairs. "Day students can use the bathrooms for bathing and showering. The upstairs rooms are on the small side, being one-time servants' quarters. But Claire isn't the sort of school that would have wanted large dormitories."

Miss Turner's feet showed no signs of following her gesturing hand. "Sitting-rooms, studies," Mrs Bond said. "Are they upstairs too?"

"No, indeed!" Miss Turner opened a door to the right of the hall. "This is the common room. The place where every house member tends to flop down when he or she comes in, as you can see." Miss Turner laughed as unnecessarily as Mrs Bond, embarrassed this time by the cheerful untidiness of St Bride's common room, where the shapes of bodies still showed on soft cushions and there were biscuit crumbs on the carpet. "The room will have been cleaned this morning of course, but some of the students come to their houses for the mid-morning break and make their own coffee in the kitchen."

Miss Turner ushered Jennifer out, closed the door, and opened one behind it. This room was smaller and tidier than the common room, but gave the same impression of having been hastily vacated. "This is for the prefects and sixth formers to get away from their juniors and perhaps watch a different TV programme. They can use it if they want during free periods. Games aren't compulsory at Claire, Mrs Bond. They take place each weekday between two and three, but the students who don't want to play work in the library or in their houses, or pursue some special interest or hobby somewhere on the school premises." Miss Turner was quoting from the prospectus Mrs Bond had taken home with her the night before. She led the way out of the study. "The door opposite is Miss Hind's office and sitting-room, she won't be there at the moment of course . . . Now, I'll just show you the kitchen and then we'll go back to school."

The kitchen was large and so pleasantly old-fashioned the fridge and electric stove looked ludicrously out of place. There was a scrubbed central table and a deep embrasure containing a heavy door.

"Cellars," Miss Turner said.

"Are they used?"

"Only for storage. I'm told they're quite extensive but I've never been down into one. I believe –"

There was the sound of a door slamming, a voice yelling. "Miss Turner!" the voice shrieked again. As Miss Turner and Mrs Bond hurried into the hall a young woman reached them at a run and clutched Miss Turner's arm. "One of the cleaners has just found Ralph Unsworth's dead body in the storeroom near the visitors' cloakrooms in School House. Strangled, he's been strangled!" Jennifer Bond cried out, and Miss Turner leaned against the wall. "The police are on their way and Mrs Molesworth would like you back in the office."

"Of course. Yes." Miss Turner had gone intensely pale and spoke in a whisper. "I can't believe it. You've seen, Deborah . . ."

"Mr Molesworth has."

At the foot of the steps Miss Turner remembered Mrs Bond. "I'm sorry," she said dazedly. "Perhaps another time." She and the young woman started back towards the school.

"I was here last night!" Mrs Bond bawled excitedly as she kept pace. "The police will want to see me. I'm only in Seaminster a short time so perhaps I should wait now and give them my statement."

"Your statement . . ." Miss Turner hadn't really heard

her. As the school facade came in sight the two members of staff broke into a run and charged up the steps, Mrs Bond stumbling in their wake. The Heads were in the hall, a reception line again but now in trembling disarray. Jennifer Bond could have disappeared without being noticed, but she hung about on the edge of the distracted group, making ineffectual attempts to gain attention.

When five minutes later the police arrived, she still hadn't managed it.

Chapter Ten

"Mr Fletcher?"

"This is Brian Fletcher."

"This is Jennifer Bond, Mr Fletcher! You remember –"

"Yes, of course." A pause and a sigh. "Your house name will be ready by four o'clock this afternoon, Mrs Bond, as I said last night. All right?" The voice was calm, normal. Unless he'd killed the boy himself, he hadn't heard.

She drew a breath. "I'm not ringing about the house name, Mr Fletcher. I've just got back from Claire College, and I felt sure you'd want to know . . . I was being shown round by the Assistant Bursar and someone came running up to her . . . Hysterical, shouting . . . That boy who was rather rude about Felicity's chances last night – oh, dear, one shouldn't speak ill of the dead, should one? – well, he'd just been found by one of the cleaners in a storeroom near the visitors' cloakrooms. Strangled. Someone had strangled him. Mr Fletcher?" Mrs Bond inquired anxiously, into the silence.

"I'm sorry. You said . . . Ralph Unsworth has been strangled?" The voice, now, was scarcely above a whisper.

"I'm afraid so. Terrible, isn't it? Apparently it happened last night, during the get-together. I suppose the murderer chose a time when he – or she, I suppose it could have been, how absolutely *awful*! – could be lost in the crowd."

"How do you know – it was last night?" The voice was

stronger again, but seemed to be coming from a very sore throat. Odd that Brian Fletcher should be so cut up by the death of someone he'd scarcely seemed to know.

"The police!" Jennifer said impressively. "I thought people who were there last night might have to be interviewed so I stayed around in hopes of getting it over with and I saw the police doctor leave and then the police said it had happened between eight and ten o'clock, so you see . . . The police *did* interview me." She paused to draw breath. "They only wanted to know where I'd been and when and if I'd seen anything which might be helpful, and of course I was able to tell them the poor boy was alive well after eight, as you and Judith will be able to tell them, too . . . I just thought I'd put you in the picture, Mr Fletcher, in case the police came to see you before Judith had a chance to tell you, or it was on the news. Actually, I think Judith could be with you soon because when I left the Heads were talking about closing the school for the day."

"Thank you, Mrs Bond." With a painful effort of the will he pulled himself together. "You've been very kind and thoughtful. Now, if you'll excuse me, I have a customer." He wondered if he would be able to stand without the support of the counter.

The transistor on Peter's desk was silent, and he asked Phyllida in a relaxed way how Mrs Bond had enjoyed her conducted tour.

"It was fine as far as it went. It came to an abrupt end when Ralph Unsworth's body was found in a storeroom round the corner from the visitors' cloakrooms. He'd been strangled."

"Good God! How terrible!" It was a struggle to make his face a reflection of what he was saying and conceal his excitement.

106

"Jennifer was being shown round St Bride's by the Assistant Bursar, and one of the girls from the office came screaming in with the news. They were inclined to forget Mrs Bond, but she followed them back to school and was hanging around unnoticed when the police came into the hall and said the boy had probably died between eight and ten the night before. I knew then that everyone at the parent/staff do would have to be interviewed, and I thought if I could get Jennifer's interview over at a time when she wasn't prepared for it then it wouldn't seem so strange that she wasn't carrying any means of identification. Luckily a CID sergeant took her measure and decided that the best way to get rid of her was to let her make her statement."

"Well done. What did she say?"

"That she'd been introduced to Ralph Unsworth soon after her arrival and had seen him go into the men's room when she was on her way to the women's, probably round about nine o'clock although she hadn't looked at her watch. I had to say that much, because Brian Fletcher and Judith and her friends will have to say it too, and the police would be more interested in Mrs Bond for keeping quiet than for admitting she'd seen the boy at nine o'clock."

"You think Brian Fletcher and Judith and co. will say it?"

They stared at one another.

"Brian Fletcher will, now," Phyllida said at last. "Because the first thing Jennifer did when she got back to the hotel was to ring him with the news and tell him she'd been interviewed and what she'd said."

"You're pure gold, Miss Moon. What was his reaction?"

"He sounded poleaxed. By the murder, so I couldn't tell if he had a second unfavourable reaction when Jennifer mentioned her interview. Or, of course, whether his devastation was for real anyway. But I might get a clue when Jennifer collects her house name this afternoon. At least I'll have saved him from perjuring himself, if he was tempted." Phyllida paused, searching for words that didn't sound pious. "I felt I had to tell the police about seeing Ralph Unsworth at nine for another sort of reason. If Jennifer as well as the Fletchers and Judith's friends had kept quiet, police time could have been wasted on that first hour and maybe the wrong person spotlighted, which could have helped the murderer."

"You did your duty," Peter said, after another uneasy silence. "Did you tell the police about Brian Fletcher following the boy into the men's room?"

"Yes. That was an even more difficult decision, but at least I'd had a bit of time to think about it while I was hanging around. I just hope Brian Fletcher will tell them that, too, and anything he can about how Ralph Unsworth seemed. If he doesn't, I could have done him a very bad turn."

"If he's innocent. And if he isn't, what he tells the police won't be of much help to them anyway. Did you tell them about that mime Judith and co. performed around Unsworth?"

"No. And that decision was easy, when I came to it I couldn't. I suppose because I knew that if I did it would turn what could just have been schoolgirl bitchiness into something that would make those girls the number one suspects."

"If they're guilty they might remember what Mrs Bond saw."

"Are you trying to frighten me?" In that safe bright room, he had for a moment succeeded.

"I think Mrs Bond ought to check out of the Golden Lion."

"The police have told her to stay there. Or let them know if she leaves."

"I think we should take the chance that they won't want to see her again. And that if they do and she's disappeared without trace, they won't divert their resources to trying to find her."

"All right. But after she's paid her last visit to the iron-works. It's a unique opportunity to observe Brian Fletcher before he's had a chance to pull himself together. Which he may need to do whether he's innocent or guilty. If he's innocent, he could be wondering about his daughter."

"If he's innocent of murder. If he's guilty of seducing his adoptive daughter and we prove it, we'll have to think very hard now about reporting to Mrs MacPherson, she'd be bound to take the information straight to the police. Abusing his daughter wouldn't turn Brian Fletcher into a murderer, but it would make him look a lot more like one than anyone else, especially with the victim having been keen on Judith. I know you've seen evidence that he was hostile to Ralph Unsworth, but I don't like the idea of handing him obliquely to the police as suspect number one."

"Neither do I. And how many people murder people they aren't too keen on? Anyway, there must have been a hundred people at Claire College last night, and judging by what I saw of Ralph Unsworth he could have got the wrong side of half of them."

"Yes. So if we get a positive result on Fletcher's domestic activity I think we'll stall Mrs M unless and until the police make an arrest. My tame Detective Sergeant will tell me how the land lies. He expects me to take an interest in local crime and I can quiz him without bringing the Fletchers into it. But I want Jennifer Bond to disappear after she's visited Brian Fletcher."

"I promise. And I'm going to take her away from the

Golden Lion in a bag so that she can set out this afternoon from Upland Road." Phyllida Moon was her own disguise, that was why she would have to obliterate herself whenever there was the possibility of face-to-face contact, however peripheral, with someone she was investigating. And if the Elite really were concerned about Jennifer Bond it would be at the hotel they would look for her.

After a morning trying to satisfy the excited curiosity of Jenny and Steve to the extent of being able to learn more from them of agency business, Phyllida sauntered home through the sunshine under the protection of her own identity (whatever that might be), savouring a day that was pale and soft-edged like a faintly coloured Victorian steel engraving. She lingered a few moments at the gate to gaze across the silver-grey bay, but as soon as she was in the house she went to the telephone and rang the Golden Lion.

"I'm calling on behalf of Peter Piper. Any messages for Mrs Jennifer Bond?"

"Mrs Jennifer Bond . . . Ah, yes. Two young ladies came in about half an hour ago and asked for her. I said I didn't know when she would be back. They didn't leave a name but they said they would call again at five o'clock this evening. All right, Madam?"

"Fine. Thank you."

Two young ladies. For a moment, staring at the distorted bluebird slanting down her wall, Phyllida had to remind herself that Judith Fletcher hadn't met her, was unaware of her existence. Then she picked up the telephone again, but abandoned her call when it was half punched out. If she told Peter now there was no doubt whatsoever that he would abort Mrs Bond's final assignment.

"So." Brian Fletcher faced his daughter across his shop counter. "You're to go back to school this afternoon to talk to the police." As always, he found himself in total ignorance of what was going on behind those cool, steady eyes.

"That's right, Daddy. They reckon they'll be up to F by three o'clock."

"The parents who were there last night" – he tried to turn the curious choking sensation in his throat into a cough – "will they want them at the school, too?"

"No, they're going to call on them at home. I should think sometime today. I gave them your two addresses and told them when you were likely to leave the works."

"Thank you. Mrs Bond's coming for her house name at four, as you know. I could manage without a visit from Mrs Bond."

"I'm sure you could."

Something flickered behind her eyes, increasing his unease. "Judith . . . When she rang to tell me about the murder, she also told me she'd given a statement to the police and that she mentioned the three of us seeing Ralph Unsworth by the cloakrooms round about nine o'clock."

"Of course she did, Daddy. If she hadn't done, the police would have found it very strange when they heard it from us."

"Yes, dear." Her eyes were so straight, so unevasive, yet they offered him no clue as to what she thought, what she knew. "Judith . . . will you stay for a sandwich, coffee, with me?"

"I'm sorry, Daddy. I've arranged to meet some friends."

Friends . . . Male? Female? He didn't know who Judith's friends were, she never brought them home. "All right, dear." Relief and apprehension together, a queasy *mélange*. "I'll see you this evening, then."

"Of course, Daddy."

He watched her cross the forecourt. Neat, discreet,

111

knowing where she was going. Which she had always done. That was why there had always been difficulties. But when he had had Isabel with him they had coped together and they had managed . . .

"Sandwiches, Mr Fletcher? Prawn and ham?"

He didn't want either, but he had to eat. And be seen to do so. "As usual, Billy, thanks."

"You all right, Mr Fletcher? You don't look too good, to me."

"I'm fine, Billy. Just shocked by what happened last night at the school. But life must go on, eh?" His forced laugh sounded pretty feeble, and although it got rid of the unwelcome concern in his assistant's face it replaced it with surprise. He'd have to pull himself together, remember that all he had to do to be lost in a crowd of people who had disliked Ralph Unsworth was to behave normally. The way Judith would behave . . .

As the afternoon crawled on and the police failed to come through the gates he found his unease turning to irritation as it focused on the inevitable appearance there of Mrs Bond. Knowing her the little he did, she would probably jinx fate so that she and the police arrived together. He spent most of his waiting time in the forge, where to his solace he found himself still able to muster total concentration. Mrs Bond's voice sounded enthusiastically behind him whem he was nearing the end of a tricky piece, but faded as his other assistant, Geoff, steered her on a muttered instruction towards the shop.

Brian followed when he had finished, glancing anxiously as he crossed the forecourt towards the empty gateway. No police, but in the road a taxi with a driver at the wheel which he profoundly hoped had been engaged by Mrs Bond.

"Been interviewed yet?" she asked him from the shop doorway.

"Not yet. Let me get you your Tree Tops."

"Thanks, I've a taxi waiting outside. I'm leaving Seaminster in an hour or so, Felicity's got chickenpox. Just as well I saw the police this morning, isn't it? Disappointing about the rest of my holiday, but I'll be back."

"I'm sure. I hope your daughter isn't suffering from too bad an attack."

"Not too bad, my mother says, but I ought to be there. Have you seen Judith, Mr Fletcher, how is she?"

"She's all right. Shocked. As we all are."

"I should say so! I mean, we must have seen him just before . . ."

"I suppose we must." His mouth felt as if he'd had a stroke and he wondered about his colour. This was just the first of innumerable small ordeals ahead of him, he'd have to learn how to cope with them.

"Judith isn't here?"

"The students are being interviewed at school. The parents at work or at home." He managed a smile that felt fairly normal.

"Well, I hope they soon find who did it. If they don't it'll be awfully uncomfortable at Claire, won't it? Everyone wondering about everyone else . . . From what Judith said the boy wasn't very popular. It was clever to choose a staff/parent evening, wasn't it? I mean, such a lot of suspects."

The handsome twist of iron he was holding out for her inspection was trembling in his hands.

"Super! Exactly what I wanted!" She paid for it in cash, glad to be relieved of the unaccustomed wadge of notes. "And now it's *au revoir*. I'm still jolly grateful to you for inviting me last night. I'll be in touch when I get back."

He had been braced to receive her address, and it was

the one consolation of a terrible day that she didn't press it into his hand.

Jennifer bustled into the Golden Lion just short of four-thirty, and vanished forever inside the grade two single room assigned to Peter Piper. As soon as she had gone Phyllida rang him.

"Brian Fletcher was in a bad way, and Judith wasn't with him. But there was a message at Reception for Mrs Bond." It was a very white lie. "Two young ladies called to see her this morning and are coming back at five."

"When you and I will be having precociously early drinks in the lobby bar. Separately, I'm afraid. I suggest you ring down now and tell Reception that Mrs Bond has checked out and that her home address has unfortunately been mislaid. I'll be over in five minutes."

Although her back was to the lobby, Phyllida saw Peter from her bar stool in the rococo mirror which ran the length of the long bar and reflected the hotel door as well as Reception. He chose a stool some way off, but close enough for reflected eye contact. It was precisely five o'clock by the gilded clock set into the C scrolls at the top of the mirror when the two girls came into the hotel and went up to the counter, Judith demure in navy skirt and neat white blouse, the tall redhead in sweatshirt and jeans. Phyllida kept her back to the lobby until Judith's glance had raked it, then swung idly round on her stool, glass in hand.

She couldn't hear, but she could see that the talk was a dialogue between Judith and the male clerk, the other girl making no attempt to join in. The clerk's obvious discomfort had to be a reflection of Judith's insistence, but it was he who won.

As Judith turned from the counter Phyllida held up her left arm so that her watch was prominent as she faced the

114

lobby, seeming to scan it for the person she was awaiting but seeing nothing beyond the cold rage in Judith's white face, the fury of her frustration.

Followed at an amble by the redhead, Judith marched out of the hotel. Alone with the pair of them, Mrs Bond could have had more to fear from the boss than from the heavy . . .

Peter paid for his whisky and left. Phyllida lingered a few more moments over hers, then followed him out and across the square.

The three of them were in the outer office.

"Jennifer could have been lucky to die of natural causes," Phyllida said. "You saw Judith's face, Peter?"

"Yes. There's a hoarding outside the newsagents in Moss Street," Peter informed them. 'Murder at Claire College.' Whether or not they committed it, Judith and her friends wouldn't like it if tomorrow it said 'Female students help police with their inquiries.' Mrs Bond could have made that a possibility."

"I know," Phyllida said. "But Ralph Unsworth could have made other enemies."

"One was enough, wasn't it?" Steve demanded.

The telephone rang as Peter was telling him and Jenny it was time they went home. Jenny handed over to him with a thumbs up sign. His part of the exchange was a succession of grateful monosyllables, and when he rang off he was grinning.

"My tame Detective Sergeant. The murder weapon was strong twine, the kind that was stacked on the storeroom shelves. In fact, the murderer hadn't bothered to cut a piece off, he or she'd just let the ball unroll on to the floor and it was still attached to the double twist round the throat."

"He or she," Phyllida repeated. She saw Jenny shiver. "So it could have been a woman."

"If he was taken by surprise, my DS said. He was attacked from behind, so he probably was. Look, John Bright will be here any moment. Try not to worry, Jenny, it's only like watching a creepy movie. It makes you feel frightened, but the fright's in your mind; everything's just the same with you as it always is, just as safe."

"I'll walk you to your bus," Steve offered, and Jenny left on a burst of edgy laughter.

John Bright was a short, plump, twinkly man who suited his name.

"Thank you for your hospitality," Phyllida said as he gripped her hand.

"And for not asking questions," Peter said, opening his fridge. "That's the heroic bit."

"In my job you learn to mind your own business. And I owe Peter," John Bright told Phyllida. "For saving that business from a small league of gentlemen who were robbing my guests. Two on the staff, two coming and going as guests in varying guises. So you see our new arrangement is quite appropriate, Miss Moon. And the only additional price I'm paying is to run the risk of my young receptionists deciding I'm a dirty old man. I'm sorry the room's so basic. It's normally an overflow for when we're exceptionally busy. Which we are from time to time, thanks to Peter, but the room will be yours now so long as the agency wants it. Ah, thanks, Peter. Cheers. Good luck with whatever you're currently up to. What about Seaminster's murder?"

"Terrible."

"Terrible. Claire College has a reputation for academic excellence, but I don't suppose that will do much for it now. Does something like this make you wish you were a policeman, Peter?"

"In some ways. Such as automatic access to all the facts."

116

"Jennifer Bond has left Seaminster," Phyllida told John. "Her daughter has chickenpox." Seaminster wasn't a very large town and he could know Brian Fletcher, but Jennifer Bond was not the kind of woman to be voluntarily remembered. "Another woman will probably arrive tomorrow."

"Whatever suits you," John Bright said.

When Phyllida turned her front door key in the lock the telephone was ringing. She fell on it trembling, dreading a breach of her anonymity even while her reason told her it was impossible.

"Phyl."

"Oh. Gerald." She hid her relief, he would misinterpret it.

"I rang earlier."

"I've just come through the door."

"You've found your detective agency, then."

"Yes." There was so much to say about that, she couldn't make the effort to begin. "Everything all right?"

"Of course not. But I'm kept pretty busy, planning the winter season. It's going well." Phyllida didn't fill the pause. "Things all right with you, then?"

"Fine, thanks."

"The work interesting?"

"Yes."

"Good. Shall I come down?"

"No." Phyllida realised that her mind was only half on what was being said, that she was thinking about her props and wardrobe. "I'm sorry, Gerald," she said sincerely.

"I deserve it."

The concession was unprecedented, but too late to have an effect beyond surprise. "There's no deserving or undeserving in situations like this. I'm glad company planning's going well."

"Thanks." Another pause. "This house is too big, you know. Goodbye, Phyl."

By the time Phyllida was at the top of the stairs the surprise was already fading into the excitement of wondering who she would get to know during the course of the evening.

Chapter Eleven

"Hello again!"

"Hello?"

Brian Fletcher's wariness of the highly charged battery of charm being beamed across his counter was instinctive; he had seen the woman before but he couldn't recall where or in what circumstances.

"Belle Bryson!" Hurt pride had scarcely dimmed the beam.

He remembered, made himself smile. "I'm sorry, I was miles away."

"So I saw, Mr Fletcher. I've just come to tell you what a good job your men have made of my new gatepost."

"I'm glad to hear it. The gate should be ready next week."

"Ah." Her eyes challenged him to bring it in person. "I've some more design ideas, by the way."

"Good." He shouldn't be having to force the word, it was time he had some more design ideas. But not yoked to a predatory female. "Perhaps you'd like to bring them in and show them to me sometime." Asking the girl to wait in the hall while he brought the etchings down, that ought to make things clear. He realised he felt desperately tired. "Unfortunately, at the moment, I'm rather tied up . . ."

Brian turned hopefully towards the room behind the shop where he relaxed and ate during the working day and into which his lunch guest Alan Williams had just wandered. And from where he was now strolling back, having heard his cue.

"Ready, Brian?"

"Just about."

Mrs Bryson's eyes had narrowed at the sight of Alan and his intimate smile, giving Brian a moment of respite as his anxieties dissolved into an amused reading of her sudden hesitation. Was there better prey?

There was certainly someone better equipped to deflect the battery. Binding the wound with his smile even as he inflicted it, Alan said that Mr Fletcher was about to go out to lunch.

Brian nodded as she turned to him for frustrated confirmation. "Sorry. Do bring your designs in sometime."

"Okay." She had shrugged, but he couldn't take her defeat for granted. He could only hope that tomorrow or the day after he would feel strong enough to cope with her.

"Yes, I should say that one's after your body, Brian," Alan observed as they watched Mrs Bryson's provocative crossing of the forecourt.

"Or yours."

"Given the circumstances. You observed that I didn't lie to her? The weather's so good you're bound to be serving the sandwiches and coffee in the garden."

The garden, walled and tiny, was sheltered and the pale October sun felt hot on Brian's forehead.

"I should think it must be a relief to be away from Claire," he ventured, as Alan put his empty plate down on the wrought-iron table between them.

"It is." Alan stretched his legs out towards the small square of grass. "The atmosphere's very tricky. Particularly in house. Some of the youngest are tending to hysteria, and some of the naughtiest are inventing new games. The Molesworths have talked of closing for a while, but we all know it isn't an option. At least half term's coming up." He glanced at his watch and got to his feet with a sigh. "Time I was back, I should never really have left. Does this business seem to have affected Judith? She was in my class yesterday, but she's not easy to read."

Renewed anxiety took Brian to his feet as well, and halfway across the lawn. He had to force himself to turn slowly and saunter the few steps back to Alan. "She hasn't said anything. I gather the boy had a crush on her, but she seemed to find it a bit of a joke. You knew, didn't you? That's why you've just asked me about her. Alan, was it common knowledge?" All at once it seemed vital to find out.

"These emotions usually are," Alan said gently. "Particularly if they're a lost cause. Ralph Unsworth wasn't in my house and didn't take art, but there's an inevitable small spotlight on prefects and everyone knew this one tended to go in with both feet and make a fool of himself. I mean, you've only got to get a student's form master or house master thinking aloud in the staff room . . . And Judith was so obviously out of his reach."

"Was she? Was she, Alan?" Brian tried to speak calmly, but despite his efforts his agitation was still so strong he was afraid of communicating it.

As it was, Alan was looking at him in surprise. "Well, yes. She's fairly self-possessed, isn't she, and that's enough in a school to gain a reputation for sophistication. She and Unsworth were chalk and cheese."

"I see. I didn't know the boy, of course." Following him into the men's room didn't constitute knowing him, even the police couldn't imagine that; anyone who had been around Unsworth in his last moments would have been asked to spell them out second by second . . . He knew it would be foolish but he desperately wanted to say more to Alan's smiling, understanding face, to ask more, and it was a relief to see his senior assistant appear in the open French window. "Yes, Geoff?"

"A woman, come over queer. I've taken her through to the back and given her some water. I think she's all right now she's sitting down."

"Ladies' day," Alan murmured as they followed Geoff indoors. "Or one lady on another tack."

Brian was well disposed in advance towards any woman who was not Mrs Bryson, and the one leaning back in his old armchair was reassuring in her own right. Red-gold hair round an almost pretty face which wasn't trying to promote its owner's charms, and, for the apology, a soft Scottish voice. He'd say late thirties.

Margaret Morrison's outward self had not been difficult for Phyllida to assume: all she had needed was a wig, a transformation of sallow skin into pink-cheeked pallor, and an Edinburgh accent. Inwardly, the qualities her instincts already suggested would appeal to Brian Fletcher – a light touch, a wry humour, self-awareness without self-absorption – were qualities she herself admired and aspired to. So the inner transformation, the essential assumption of the character she was playing, was the most difficult she could remember, and a potential pitfall.

But at least it was Jennifer Bond Brian Fletcher had met, not Phyllida Moon.

"Please," he said. "Just relax. Are you feeling any better?"

"Yes, thanks." He liked her laugh. "I was looking up to your higher shelves and just went dizzy."

"That was all?" Alan asked.

"I hope so. I'm in Seaminster to convalesce and I've probably been a bit ambitious. It's such a nice place, I keep on walking."

"Is there anyone we can contact?" Alan again.

"No. And anyway it wouldn't be necessary. Look, I'm

fine now." The woman got to her feet, than sat down again with an apologetic grin. "Well, almost. If I can just sit for a little bit longer . . ."

"Of course," Brian said. "We'll make you some tea." He went into the kitchen corner, added water to the warm kettle, detached a mug from the wooden tree. "Sugar?"

"Just a very little milk. Thanks."

"Then Brian will see you get safely home." Alan waved a hand across the room. "Brian Fletcher, master forger."

"Thank you for reminding me. I came in for a house name, Mr Fletcher."

"Of course. As soon as you're feeling better. Where are you staying?"

"The Golden Lion."

"Seaminster's nicest hotel," Alan said. "Wasn't your prospective fellow parent staying there, Brian?"

"Don't remind me." Brian shuddered, although, the way he felt these days, a Mrs Bond was less daunting than a Mrs Bryson.

"We'll leave you in peace to recover." Alan strolled towards the shop as Brian approached the armchair with the mug of tea, signalling to him to join him as the woman bent her head to drink. "On her own, at least in Seaminster. Nice. Slightly in distress," he said judicially when they were through the shop and on the forecourt. "And about to place an order which you're likely to have to see her a second time to fulfil. Don't let her disappear, Brian, offer to show her round. All right, I'm taking advantage of what you told me about your reclusive tendencies, but I think you should resist them before they become irreversible."

"What about you?"

"A house master in term time? You're joking. Anyway," he said smugly, "I'm too young for her. Thanks for lunch, Brian, I've enjoyed it."

123

"So have I." As much as he was capable of enjoying anything, these days. He'd have another go with Judith about inviting Alan to dinner. "Come again when you can."

Brian went into the foundry and helped Jim finish off a finicky flourish, then warily back to the snug. The red-haired woman had put the empty mug down on the table beside the armchair and was lying back with closed eyes. He had made the slightest of sounds, but she opened her eyes and smiled at him, sitting forward.

"I'm too soon, I'm sorry."

"No, I really am all right now, I've tried myself out. I'm Margaret Morrison, by the way."

He sat down on a hard chair nearby. "I hope this won't spoil your holiday, Mrs Morrison." She appeared to be wearing a wedding ring.

"It won't, I'll just take it a bit easier."

"You've come by car?"

"By train. I do so much driving at home I thought being without the car for a while would make part of the change and encourage me to walk." She smiled again, still unprovocatively. "It has done." She got to her feet, stayed there. "Could I see the foundry?"

"Of course."

He had a reluctant arm ready, but she didn't need it. When he had talked her through Jim's next flourish they went back into the shop and she ordered "The Wilderness" in black Roman.

"I'm afraid that's something I don't have in." They smiled at one another. "I should be able to manage it by late tomorrow, though. The summer rush is over but I'm still opening all day Saturday. Would you be able to call for it, say, four o'clock?"

"I would. Thank you."

"Good." He thought of what Alan had said, but it had been easier to punish himself with Jennifer Bond

124

than it would be to attempt to divert himself with Margaret Morrison. Anyway, there had been a reason for propositioning Mrs Bond, and Mrs Morrison didn't strike him as a woman prepared to accept an invitation without a reason. Which was probably why he was half attracted to the idea of issuing one. "Let me order you a taxi," was what he said.

"No, thanks, I'm all right. And I'll sit down at some point on the promenade to look at the sea as I always do."

"Quite right."

He walked with her to the gate. She had flat heels and an easy walk, and was as tall as his ear. As he said goodbye he had a memory of an ordinary, everyday life.

The outer grounds of Claire College were open to the public and set with elegantly designed wrought-iron seats which had been the enabling commission for Brian Fletcher's business. The mansion faced downhill to Seaminster, the garden side looked over a terrace and a lawn to tennis courts, playing fields and a cricket pitch, and the fields and woods beyond them. There were a few narrow exits in walls and hedges, but the day students had only one way to come down into town.

At half past four that Friday afternoon an unglamorous elderly lady took a short stroll among the trees and the begonia-dominated autumn flowerbeds, then sat down on a seat near the foot of the drive. Phyllida had easily decided on the safest disguise for a situation where eyes and ears were her only requirements. No one would really notice the shabby woman in the felt hat like a mushroom, her face pale and blank, her handbag held firmly to her lap with both her woolly-gloved hands.

As the first of the students came straggling down the slope Miss Pym smiled vaguely toward them. Four notably attractive girls came into sight quite early in the exodus, walking like grown-up women and not lolling against one another in the sloppy way of so many of the others, but quite clearly a group. The Elite. They wore the uniform of navy kilted skirts and red cardigans over white blouses and red ties, but as they moved along they somehow managed to make the regulation outfits appear to flatter them.

When they strolled between the wide-spaced gateposts Miss Pym got to her feet and ambled behind them.

Across the main road and down the hill between the Victorian villas they kept loosely together, turning right together into the road where the shops began. And the cafés.

They passed two, but they gave off a sense of purpose, and Phyllida was hopeful of their having a public destination.

Miss Pym didn't carry much weight and was nippy on her pins, but she slowed down and leaned for a moment against a postbox as the girls turned into a doorway and disappeared. When she had recovered her breath she walked on, and when she peered in at the doorway and saw that it led to the Marigold Café she followed the girls and sank gratefully into a seat at a table for two beside the larger table where they were settling.

It was ten to five and most tables were empty. A middle-aged waitress who ought to have known better looked unenthusiastically at Miss Pym, then approached the girls with a smile.

"The usual, is it?" she asked Judith.

"That's right, Grace."

"Earl Grey for four, lemon, no milk, four chocolate surprises."

Phyllida found the order rather touching: four young women drinking sophisticated tea, four little girls craving sweetmeats.

126

The inappropriately named waitress made a note, then moved grudgingly over to the elderly lady.

"Yes?"

Miss Pym looked up from the menu in her hand. "Oh, dear, could I have a pot of Darjeeling tea, please? And a toasted teacake?"

"No toasted teacakes."

"Ah. Then a Danish pastry?"

"One Darjeeling tea. One Danish pastry." The waitress moved away, nodding to the girls as she passed their table.

Judith and two of the others sat calm and expressionless but the fourth was agitated, the girl with cloudy dark hair and pink-cheeked complexion whom Judith had called Fiona. Her large, light-blue eyes passed indifferently over Miss Pym, the only person within earshot of her table. "We're safe," she said. "So spill, Judith!"

"When we've got the tea," Judith said severely. There was no doubt about her leadership.

"Don't be stuffy, Judith, we're all on tenterhooks." The blonde, tossing a long thick strand of hair over her shoulder.

"Unless we discipline ourselves in public we'll get careless." Judith spoke more quietly than the other two, Phyllida could only just hear her soft, stern voice. "It's especially important now, with police all over the place, probing into every corner."

"And Ralph having been so soppy over you." Phyllida saw the brief flare of hostility in the blonde girl's face before it closed up under Judith's cold gaze.

"That's enough, Becky. Judith's right. And we don't need to be silly, either." The tallest, the one with the red hair and brilliant green eyes. Phyllida wondered if she was the second in command.

127

"Thank you, Gill." But Judith didn't show her gratitude.

"Ah, tea!" Fiona exclaimed with nervous enthusiasm, as the waitress reappeared. Perhaps she was the unreliable one.

If there was something to be unreliable about.

The tea was served on Willow Pattern china, reminding Phyllida of a set from her childhood and how attractive it looked when massed. She was resigned to a long wait for Miss Pym's small order, but the waitress was soon back to set it dourly before her.

"So?" Fiona persisted, when the waitress had disappeared for the second time.

"So, my dear Fiona." Phyllida saw the contempt in Judith's eyes. "We've got to possess our souls in patience, accept that for the moment we're closed down. Even when the police have finished their main going over of Claire they'll be back for one reason or another. So no arguments." Judith dropped her stern gaze to her plate, where she cut a neat square off her chocolate surprise.

"You're quoting, of course." Becky pulled some hair forward, wound it round her finger.

"Oh, no!" Fiona begged.

"Oh, yes." Judith's gaze circled the table. "And I agree with my text. I hope you all do, too."

Two of them nodded, but Fiona let out a wail.

"It was so wonderful. It seemed so long since the summer term, and then when it was all going to be the same this term it seemed too good to be true –"

"Which at the moment it is," Gill said, her eyes on Judith's scornful face. "That should be obvious even to you, Fiona."

"It's Judith's connection with Ralph," Becky said, taking a bite out of her cake which left her mouth outlined in brown.

"It's self-preservation. And I had no connection with Ralph."

As Judith's gaze again challenged her companions Phyllida saw it abruptly leave them, to focus on the eruption into the Marigold Café of a young woman dressed, made up, and moving in a way that suggested a career at the kerbside. Judith watched her sit down at a table for two the other side of the room. Phyllida thought they exchanged glances, and then Judith's attention was back with her friends.

"No languishing," she said. "No nostalgic visits to an entertainment that's closed down. Understood?"

"I suppose so," Fiona muttered sullenly.

"Good." Judith put the last small piece of her chocolate surprise into her mouth. "This is a business meeting and I declare it closed," she said, when she had chewed and swallowed.

"Right." Gill visibly relaxed, Becky and Fiona followed suit. "What are you doing this weekend, Judith?" Gill asked.

"Working," Judith said.

"A's are ages off." Fiona.

"Some of us are ambitious. But I might play Scrabble with my father."

"Big deal." Becky's scorn quickly withered under Judith's exclusive gaze. "Don't you ever go out at night, Judith?"

"If I want to." Judith's customary face, Phyllida decided, was a steady, unsmiling challenge.

"If that's it, then I'm off." Becky pushed her chair back and stood up, throwing long blonde hanks of hair over her shoulder.

Judith glanced up as Gill and then Fiona got to their feet. "I'll stay here a while, I want to make a note of something Miss Jackson said this afternoon in English

129

before I forget." She felt in the bag on the floor beside her and produced an exercise book, then brought a ballpoint out of her jacket pocket.

"Hark at her!" Fiona tossed her dark head. "Since English she's had the meeting of our lives and she's still thinking about something Miss Jackson said!"

"It'll be an Elite of three, Fiona," Judith said softly, "if you won't be warned."

"Yes," said Gill.

"All right. I'm sorry. I'll try, but it really is harder for me, I'm" – Fiona looked at the three impassive faces – "I'm more ordinary than you three." Phyllida wondered if Fiona had wanted to say "more normal". "I haven't got your superhuman self-control."

"Try," Judith suggested. "Hang on a moment, all of you." The instruction was as softly spoken as everything else she had said, but the three other girls were instantly at attention. "I suggest we go our own ways out of school for a bit. If we dwell on – things – together they'll feel four times as bad and there'll always be a risk." Judith's gaze sought out Fiona. "I'll let you know if and when there's a change. All right?"

"All right," was repeated in unison, Fiona protesting only with her eyes, and the three girls on their feet swung gracefully out of the café.

When they had gone Judith took her time writing a few lines in the exercise book, then put it carefully away. By the time she looked up the young woman she had acknowledged was showing obvious signs of impatience. When Judith nodded to her the impatience became a sulk and she came laggingly across to Judith's table.

"I thought you was never going to be ready!"

"Everything in good time." Judith's voice was even lower than when she had been speaking to her school friends, and Phyllida had to strain to hear her.

130

"So? Why d'you need to speak to me again? You said it was all fixed up."

"It is. The person, the place. As we agreed. But at ten o'clock instead of nine. All right?"

"All right if you're as sure as you were last time that I won't regret it."

Judith smiled, producing a prickling feeling in Phyllida's spine. "Oh yes, Candy, I'm still as sure as I was that you won't regret it."

Chapter Twelve

"I used the name of my father's house," Phyllida told Peter. "'The Wilderness.' I felt fairly confident Brian Fletcher wouldn't have it in stock, and judging by the work on display I don't think it'll be wasted. Margaret's to collect it tomorrow afternoon."

"Well done."

"In the late afternoon an elderly lady went for a stroll in the public part of Claire College grounds, and walked back into town behind four attractive girl students."

"Yes?"

Phyllida watched polite bewilderment turn into surprised understanding.

"Don't make yourself indispensable," he warned her. "Where did you all go?"

She told him what she had overheard in the Marigold Café. "So it looks as though whatever activity they'd carried over from the summer term had begun again, then come to a premature end because of the murder. I couldn't tell from what they said whether they were involved in the murder or were just afraid of the police stumbling on whatever they've been doing – which is enough to show, wouldn't you say, that it was something illegal even if it didn't have anything to do with Ralph Unsworth's death. One thing was very obvious: it's enormously important to all four of them. Fiona was the only one to show any feelings, but the sophisticated way the other three kept themselves on such a tight rein was just as telling of how seriously they're affected by whatever it is. I was grateful to Fiona; if she hadn't rattled them no one would have said anything. Although it was Gill who cut a corner."

"How?"

"She asked Judith what she was doing over the weekend, and Judith said she might play Scrabble with her father."

"Reactions?"

"How unutterably boring."

"That was all? Not the teeniest flicker of knowingness?"

You're being a teeny weeny bit too this and that, Phyllida darling . . . For the first time in days Phyllida thought of Wayne, and the way he would barb his criticisms of her by appearing to understate them. He seemed a very long way away. "Not the teeniest. So we've learned that whatever Judith's activities involving him and the Elite, they don't overlap. But I'm learning about Judith, too. She has tremendous self-control and obviously tells people only as much as she wants them to know. I should say she's the rare sort who can live their lives very comfortably in separate compartments."

"Yes." Peter leaned back and put his fingertips together. "You've done wonders, Phyllida, but since we last talked I've decided there's something else we have to do as well. Because Mrs Bond saw Fletcher follow Ralph Unsworth into the men's room just before he was killed, I think we have to use the direct way to try and find out whether Fletcher's carrying on with his daughter." He offered his quick smile to her reluctant nod. "I called on Mrs MacPherson earlier today and told her it would be helpful if she could let us have her set of keys to the Fletcher house. She just happened to have them in her handbag, as I suspected she might, and was holding them out to me before I'd finished asking for them. It's too late this week, but Steve will watch for father and daughter to leave on Monday morning – he takes her to school before going on to his works – and then he'll go in and have a look around. The Fletcher house has a neighbour on the other side too, but there's generous Victorian space and a lot of greenery. I told Mrs MacPherson she was unlikely to see anyone, but that if she did she wasn't to worry so long as he fitted my description of Steve."

Phyllida would have been interested to hear that description. "And if we get positive evidence? We'll still keep it from Mrs MacPherson and the police?"

Peter shifted in his chair. "A man who's corrupted a daughter who was the object of the murdered boy's affections . . ." He groaned. "It's a paradox, isn't it? It's because the wretched business is so serious that I want to find out all I can, and it's because a positive result would be so damning that I don't want to pass it on – if Fletcher's innocent of the killing he'd have a terrible time establishing it. So whatever we discover, for the time being I'll go on hoping the police will find enough evidence of their own to make an arrest, in whatever direction. And that they'll manage it before Mrs M gets impatient. Anyway, a few days is a long time in a murder inquiry as well as in politics, and we know there have to be a lot of people who disliked Ralph Unsworth. If there are signs of the inquiry being scaled down, we'll pass on what we know. For the moment, we'll have a drink." Peter leaned down to his cupboard. "Stepping up our activity over the possible abuse doesn't commit us to any other course of action. But I think, being in the uniquely knowledgeable position we are, we ought to step it up. I don't like it, but murder is even nastier than abuse of a minor and cuts unlawful entry down to size. Or so I keep trying to persuade myself."

"Mrs MacPherson hasn't seen – anything else?"

134

"No. But what she did see – if she interpreted it correctly – must have been a carelessness the Fletchers are unlikely to repeat. Come in!" he called out, in response to the knock on his door. Steve appeared, followed by a hovering Jenny as Peter nodded. "She told me Judith was her usual cool and indifferent self when she saw her in the road yesterday, and she had a chat with Brian Fletcher over the back fence last night when they were working in their gardens and he didn't seem embarrassed at all, although she thought he seemed a bit" – Peter glanced down at the piece of paper by his hand – "'tense and gloomy'."

"He hadn't met Mrs Morrison then," Steve said. "Shall I go through everything, Governor?"

"Yes. Steve never leaves a trace," Peter assured Phyllida's wary look. "It's a native talent. I suspect the father of being more likely to offer us something. From what Miss Moon's told us he doesn't sound anything like as calculating as his daughter and he might be less careful."

"I don't think I've ever met anyone as calculating as Judith," Phyllida said.

"And only seventeen. Her father could have done that to her as well, couldn't he?" Jenny suggested. "I mean . . . It's bound to have affected her, isn't it, quite apart from the obvious . . ."

"OK, Jenny." Steve took over, with an air of benevolent worldly wisdom, as Jenny floundered. "We know what you mean. And we'll get the bastard."

"Innocent until proved guilty," Peter reminded them. "On both counts. Like Judith and her friends so far as the murder's concerned." He stared at them meaningfully. He wanted to get it across to them, as obliquely as possible, that he was aware the Elite might not be innocent of the killing of Ralph Unsworth, and as they stared silently back he knew he had succeeded. "Now, I've a report to write before I leave for the night. Jenny comes in for a couple of hours on a Saturday morning to man the phone," he told Phyllida as she got to her feet. "If you or anyone else wants to make contact the rest of the weekend it's mobile through me or Steve. So no one will be expecting to see you in the office."

In the morning there was no sunshine to illumine her thin bedroom curtains, and Phyllida slept late. When she awoke rain was driving against her window, and she brought tea and toast and the newspaper up to bed.

The pleasure of cosy idleness on a day when it was more agreeable to be indoors than out was only slightly disturbed by a telephone call from Carol, obliquely intimating that Gerald didn't appear to be enjoying life.

"That's a pity." But Phyllida to her relief couldn't work up any sense of responsibility. "How's Wayne?"

"Busy as usual." Always that sudden yielding note in Carol's voice when she spoke of her husband. But a woman as nice as Carol could stay with a man like Wayne only if she was madly in love with him.

"That's splendid."

"Phyl . . . Are you very lonely?"

"Lonely?" The question had no meaning. "Not in the least."

"I know it's not my business . . . But – you're in touch with Gerald?"

"He's rung."

A pause while Carol suppressed the major portion of her curiosity. "Have you found a detective agency?"

"Yes. I'm enjoying my change of occupation." The job was already too complex for her to start explaining that she had in fact adapted her occupation rather than changed it. "And my house. I'm all right, Carol, but it's nice of you to worry."

"I do worry, Phyl."

"I know." Phyllida could see Carol's anxious face as clearly as if she was looking at it. "But I promise you there's no need."

The conversation petered out on ever vaguer assurances of mutual concern. But Phyllida was fond of Carol. It was just that it seemed easier, at the moment, not to go into detail.

She got up mid-morning and typed notes from her library reading beside a streaming window, pleased to find herself able to switch her attention to historical skulduggery. After coffee and a sandwich she began to suspect her unaccustomed self-satisfaction and rang Ken to make sure she hadn't dreamed of being given the role of Page's sister in *A Policeman's Lot*. And to discover there was one direction in which it was no effort to define her new job, if not the way it was developing. When they rang off Ken was still yelping his delight.

The bluebird had appeared on the wall above the telephone, and Phyllida opened the front door to discover that the rain had stopped and a thin blue rift was widening between the dark blocks of cloud over Great Hill. When Margaret set off along the promenade an hour later the cloud had flattened to a dark band above the horizon and the sun was out.

Brian Fletcher was on his forecourt, talking to Billy. When he saw Mrs Morrison he realised he had been looking forward to her return.

"Your house name's ready." He was enjoying what felt like the rare sensation of smiling because he wanted to. "Come into the shop."

He laid it on the counter in front of her.

"It's lovely! You won't mind cash?"

"Whatever's most convenient. How have you been?"

he asked as he made up one of his attractive parcels.

"Fine. It was that high shelf."

"Good. I was worried –"

"If Mahomet won't come to the mountain . . ."

It wasn't Mrs Morrison's soft voice. Mrs Bryson was in the shop doorway, a folder in her hands.

"Please don't go!" He hissed the plea under his breath on a reflex, before responding in his normal voice to Mrs Bryson's disconcertingly rapid return. "Ah. You've brought your design ideas."

"As I said I would." Mrs Bryson checked short of the counter, looking from Brian to Mrs Morrison and back again. "But I have the feeling the time still isn't ripe."

"I'm sorry. I'm about to go out. May I introduce my friend Mrs Morrison?" He found out what he was going to say as he said it. "Margaret, this is Mrs Bryson."

"Hello." Margaret Morrison was going along with him, he even saw amusement in her violet eyes.

"Hello, Mrs Morrison." Mrs Bryson was amused, too. And probably relishing a stronger challenge.

"Would you feel you could leave them with me? I'd very much like to see them." It was a concession: if she didn't come back for them he would have to make a move towards her. But for the moment he was winning, and anyway he'd like to assess the designs coolly; he knew they could be good.

Mrs Bryson shrugged. "Okay. In case you've lost my phone number it's on page one. See you."

"I'm sorry," Brian said again, no more sincerely than the first time, when he and Mrs Morrison had watched Mrs Bryson's undeflated departure in silence. "I shouldn't have done that."

"Don't worry." The eyes were still amused. "I'm glad if I helped."

138

"For the time being, at any rate. Could I thank you by showing you some of the countryside round Seaminster? Unless you know it," he finished feebly, his pleased surprise at his unexpected enterprise immediately ebbing.

But her smile was still there, still unwary. "I don't know it, Mr Fletcher, I'd like to see it."

"Good. Tomorrow afternoon, perhaps, Sunday? I know just the place for an old-fashioned tea." Just the place to go in agreeable company, but Judith had been bored and restless from the moment they went in, mimicking the refined elderly ladies who served the small tables and sold home-made lemon cheese, with a deadly accuracy which had made him at the same time angry and admiring . . .

"That sounds very nice."

Edinburgh, he thought. "Good. If I call for you at two, say?"

"That will suit me very well. I shall look out for you. And now I shall walk slowly back to the hotel."

Sunday morning was sunny, and Phyllida cleaned the house and tidied the garden before setting out at noon for her room at the Golden Lion, from where Margaret descended for a sandwich and a shandy in the lobby bar. Brian Fletcher arrived a few minutes late, tense and *distrait* and with the excuse of some unexpected business. Phyllida was aware of the tension ebbing as they drove along, and put it down to Margaret's serenity and the fact that she reserved her attention for the view beyond the windows.

They talked of nothing but Seaminster and what they saw until they were sitting over tea and home-made cakes in the café Brian had discovered with his daughter. Then he made himself say, "Judith will be in this evening, and I hope I can persuade you to have supper with us. It won't be the splendid meal you'd get at the Golden Lion, but between us Judith and I don't do too badly." Judith hadn't replied to his suggestion when he made it, but when he had gone into the kitchen before lunch she had been preparing the small chicken they'd had in the fridge and remarked that there was enough on it for three.

"I'd like that, thank you." Phyllida was favourably amused that he had waited a couple of hours before issuing his invitation, giving himself time to decide whether he liked Margaret enough to want to prolong his afternoon with her into an evening. "Has Judith made some good friends at Claire?"

He winced, hoped it didn't show, and was thankful Mrs Morrison was so unappraising. "I think so, although she doesn't bring them home. I wish she would."

He sounded as though he meant it. "I'm sure you do."

"On the other hand," Brian said, examining the piece of cake in his hand, "she doesn't go out much at night and I nearly always know where she is."

"That's a great deal." And perhaps even more than it sounded, suggesting as it did that Judith found a live-in lover more satisfying than dates with boyfriends. But it could, of course, mean something else: that what the Elite had once done at school was so important they didn't feel the need to do other things. "Although you must wish in a way that she did go out more, make her own life."

"Judith has her own life." He thought of the long evening hours she spent alone in her bedroom, his sensations when he at last heard her door open . . . "I didn't mean she's dependent on me, just that she's exceptionally self-sufficient." Was she, still? "You may see what I mean when you meet her. I'm rather proud of her, actually, and I respect her intellect. That may sound like a fond father's talk, but I think she'll go far."

Margaret murmured polite congratulations, and Phyllida decided that Brian Fletcher was less tense when facing the subject of his daughter head on than when it came at him obliquely, at times not of his choosing.

"Do you have children?"

It was a riskily personal question, so it could be that he was relaxing. Or trying to appear relaxed.

"No, to my regret. But I don't suppose there's a minute's real peace once the first one is born."

"No." He took a gasping breath, tried to turn it into a cough. "What do you do, Margaret, do you have a career?"

A man like Wayne Cryer, almost totally self-absorbed, would have been easier. "I'm a librarian." Phyllida had played a librarian last year, in a jolly comedy. "I enjoy it."

"I enjoy my work, too. It's being creative, I suspect, in my case. I used to work in the City, and when my wife died I sold my partnership and came to Seaminster to set up the iron works."

"Had it been a hobby?"

"Only at evening classes. But that was enough to show me I had the will." Brian paused, struggling with his modesty. "And the talent," he managed.

"I think that's wonderful. Judith didn't mind?"

Tension again, because he hadn't been ready. "No. She was only fourteen, but she was grown up for her age. And she's never been attached to places, or . . . or people and things, perhaps." Brian shook his head, in what Phyllida saw as an attempt to dislodge an unwelcome realisation. "She encouraged my enterprise all the way."

"And you're happy about her move to Claire?" She had made such a gentle transition to her catechism it wasn't disturbing him.

"It's a good school with an excellent academic record, and it will get her to Oxford."

"I hope what's just happened won't do it or its pupils any

lasting damage." Margaret didn't know that the pupils were called students. "The dead boy must have been Judith's age. Did she know him well?"

It was the key question, but Edinburgh voices were of all voices unalarming. Margaret asked it casually, reaching for the teapot as she spoke.

As she looked up with it in her hand, she saw a tic at work in his cheek. "I don't think so," he said. "She's never mentioned him." If Jennifer Bond or Belle Bryson had been the other side of the table he would have left it there. "But then, she doesn't mention anyone." The cry for help was muffled and he couldn't expect her to hear it.

On the drive back to the coast they talked of books and plays and domestic architecture, and as she got out of the car at Brian's house Phyllida showed her pleasure at the look of it. Judith came slowly down the stairs as her father was helping Margaret out of her jacket, matching the Victorian elaboration of bannisters and newel post with her composed face and full-skirted modest pose, a short-haired Tenniel *Alice*.

"Hello!" Margaret said cheerfully. "I'm Margaret Morrison. You're Judith, of course."

"Of course." Judith stopped at the foot of the stairs and the two women looked at one another. Matching sang-froid with sang-froid, Phyllida decided to let Judith speak first.

"Come into the sitting-room," Judith said at last. Suddenly half-smiling, giving Phyllida no clue as to whether her appraisal of her father's guest had been alarming or reassuring. Other schoolgirls of seventeen in the position where Judith could be would surely reveal whether they welcomed their father's interest in another woman as a chance of freeing themselves from his sexual attentions, or resented it because they had come to need those attentions

142

as much as he did. But not Judith Fletcher. Appearing gracious could mean no more than that it suited her just then to enter that particular compartment.

And Judith did appear gracious. There was no sign of the contempt she had so clearly felt for Jennifer Bond, or the stern chill of her dealings with her peers. All that was lacking, to Phyllida's attentive eyes and ears, was a sense of commitment to the situation in which she found herself. She matched their whiskies with a sherry, asked them where they'd been during the afternoon and Margaret's views on what they'd seen, let Margaret carry dishes through into the kitchen at the end of dinner and dry them while her father washed up and she put away. But all the time Phyllida felt that Judith's real concerns were elsewhere, that she was using the evening to work something out, come to some decision. A couple of times at table her father had to repeat a question he had asked her, and when she heard him the second time she seemed to have come from a long way off.

Phyllida chastised herself as Margaret stacked plates, for trying to drag significance out of what could be explained in the most ordinary of ways. Judith was tired, she was thinking about her homework, she was trying to work out how to cope with the loss of the activity she had shared with her friends, the secret of which had made her young face in the café look so old and so hard.

She was wondering if she had got away with murder . . .

"It must be uncomfortable," Margaret said over coffee, "at school just now. I hope no one's rushed to any private conclusions and made them public."

"If they had, the odds are they'd be about me." Judith crossed her ankles in the buttoned Victorian armchair, and Phyllida searched her memory for a specific *Alice* illustration. "Ralph was silly about me."

"I'm sorry, Judith . . ." And for Brian, who had been discovered in a lie which his new friend could be expected to find surprising.

But he had, of course, a way out. "Judith!" he exclaimed. "I didn't know!"

But Phyllida had seen his face at the parent/staff evening when Ralph Unsworth had looked so hungrily at his daughter.

"It wasn't important enough to talk about," Judith said dismissively. Playing with her father, perhaps. Dropping him in it, then fishing him out when he swam to the bank. "Nobody's said anything, actually." But who would dare, in Judith's hearing? "And Ralph Unsworth made a nuisance of himself to lots of other people. You're right though about it not being a very nice atmosphere in school at the moment. Would you like to play Trivial Pursuit?"

Judith turned out to be knowledgeable in most directions and it was an equal contest, won at last and by a whisker by Brian. When the game was over Judith immediately tidied it away, said goodnight, and left them, kissing her father lightly on the brow. But short of going with them in the car to the Golden Lion there was no way she could prevent them being finally alone together. Three hours in her company, and Phyllida had been offered no clue to her views on the prospect.

Despite Steve's confident belief in Brian Fletcher's comprehensive abnormality, Phyllida in the car found herself braced for the overreaction of an unhappy man to the easy companionship of a day.

But he got out the moment he had drawn up in front of the Golden Lion.

"I've enjoyed your company," he said on the step.

"I've enjoyed yours."

144

"I'm glad. I'll ring you. Soon. All right?"

"Yes. Thanks for a lovely day."

"My pleasure, Margaret."

Margaret went up to the refuge, and half an hour later Phyllida took a taxi home.

Chapter Thirteen

On Monday the Elite came fragmented down the hill from Claire. Becky and Gill first, keeping pace with one another but with more speed and less grace, not communicating and with set faces. Fiona a few moments later, talking animatedly to the outstandingly handsome Head Boy who was offering her very little response and making her walk more quickly than it obviously suited her to keep pace with him. Nevertheless she persisted until they reached the wide gateposts, where he gestured to her that he was turning back and eventually, pinker cheeked than usual, she tossed her head and went out into the roadway alone.

Judith appeared when the exodus had passed its flood, walking briskly and clearly not seeking company. When he was certain Fiona was out of sight Tim Rowland had wandered back to the gates, and he went up to Judith as she reached them. Frowning, impatiently tapping a neat foot as if marking time, Judith stopped.

"Yes, Tim?"

". . . word with you . . . Fiona . . ."

The androgynous figure in trilby hat and mackintosh leaning against one of the gateposts could only make out snatches, and tried to read gestures and lips.

Judith's body was a denial even before she shook her head. ". . . up to you." The foot tapped more briskly.

". . . Head Boy of Claire College!" The soft stern voice had strengthened on those words.

The boy's arms went out in a mock-anguished gesture and Judith suddenly smiled.

". . . word with her? Oh, all right, Tim."

Judith nodded and went quickly between the gateposts to make it plain that she wanted to walk alone. Tim shrugged, ran his fingers through his fine head of hair, then strolled into the road. The androgynous figure watched him disappear down the hill, letting the gap between himself and Judith gradually widen.

Although she was alone Judith sat down at her usual table in the Marigold Café, at her usual place. She gave a quarter of the usual order to Grace, whose eagerness to ask questions she quelled with a single glance. Then, as Grace withdrew frustrated, she extracted an exercise book from the bag by her feet and drew a ballpoint from a pocket. Miss Jackson had quoted interestingly yet again, and good as Judith's memory was, she wanted to be certain not to forget.

If it is not necessary to change, it is necessary not to change . . . Lord Falkland on the eve of the English Civil War. A small sigh escaped Judith's beautifully shaped lips as she placed a dot at the end of the neatly written words. Change could creep up on one, it could operate without conscious human agency. However painful and regrettable. And then, somehow, however much one hated it, it couldn't be reversed . . . Although she, Judith Fletcher, would never give in to it without a struggle if it concerned something she was happy with as it was –

"What the hell!"

A woman had come flying in to the café, had caught the strap of her shoulder bag on the corner of Judith's table as she went past and stumbled almost into Judith's lap, sending the exercise book to the crumb-scattered floor.

"Jesus, I'm sorry! Of all the clumsy bints . . ." Panting, the woman retrieved the exercise book, handed it back to Judith with a rueful grin.

A grin that reflected Phyllida's relaxed attitude to what had to be her last character in the Fletcher case. Sharon Lane was so dramatically different from both Margaret Morrison and Jennifer Bond that even a Judith Fletcher must be deceived by her. She was dramatically different from Phyllida Moon too, who had had the good fortune to be offered a model at close quarters during Judith's brief meeting with the woman she called Candy. Phyllida might even enjoy herself.

"It's all right," Judith said. "Sit down and get your breath back."

As it took in the woman's appearance Judith's face had changed. It wasn't welcoming, despite what she was saying, but there was a spark of interest in the eyes.

"You're a mate. Phew! Warm, isn't it?"

The woman's heavy make-up was beginning to break up under her eyes and in lines down from her nose, making Judith decide she wasn't quite so young or so glamorous as her impact had suggested. But she was striking enough, with her fizz of blue-black hair and tall slim figure straining at the thin tube of skirt and low tight neckline.

"Very warm." But Judith was wearing her red school cardigan and looked cool. "Have some tea."

"That's why I come in. But I don't see –"

"That's all right." The waitress had reappeared and was looking unfavourably on Judith's companion, the words "Sorry we're about to close" trembling on her lips.

"Another cup, please, Grace." Judith scarcely looked up, she was putting the exercise book back into her bag.

"And another chocolate surprise, I suppose." Judith had succeeded in making Grace swallow, if unwillingly, on her disapproval. Sarcasm was the only advantage she had left.

148

"That's an idea." It was like pushing aside the muzzle of a gun. "They're very good. You'll have one?" The woman nodded, open-mouthed. "Yes, please, Grace. And we'd better have a jug of hot water."

"Very good, miss, I'm sure."

Grace stalked off, and the woman half found her voice.

"Look. I wasn't trying . . . You don't have to . . ."

"Relax. As you said, it's warm. What's your name?"

"Sharon. Sharon Lane. You're at Claire, aren't you?"

"That's right. Where are *you*?"

"Work at the Golden Lion."

"Really?" The grey-green eyes opened wide.

"Not on the Reception counter, as if I had to tell you. Bedrooms. When the customers are out of them, worst luck. Very high class of commercial." Sharon's leer found no response in Judith's impassive face. "Bathrooms when drunks have used them. You name a scummy job, I do it. Well, too." Sharon bridled, as though Judith had called her standards in question. "I like a clean place. I reckon they'll keep me on when my probation's up. If I want to stay. At the moment I've got no choice. Got into a bit of trouble in London."

"I can tell you're from London." Judith leaned across the table. "You're on your own, then?"

"At the moment. A hundred years ago I had a husband. I was unlucky, I was only helping out a friend."

"Of course. Where are you living?"

"In the hotel. Part of the deal."

"But they've got to give you free time." Judith looked Sharon up and down. "You're not a teenager but you still deserve some life." Indifferent to her companion's feelings, she was thinking aloud.

"Thank you." About to bridle, Sharon decided it was a luxury she could do without. "Yeah, I've got free time. Afternoons two till five. And evenings to eleven. *Eleven!*"

"It does seem a bit harsh on a mature lady. You must have been naughtier than you're letting on." Judith's face was watchful and intent, no hint of a smile despite what she was saying.

"Well, I suppose to be called a persistent offender a girl has to be a bit naughty." Sharon laughed, a large generous sound. "Anyway, I was broke by then, and I always liked the sea."

"Um." Judith stared thoughtfully at Sharon. "Your offence was prostitution, of course."

"No of course, if you don't mind!" But Sharon's rebuke was automatic. "That's what they called it, but as I said, I was only helping out –"

"Did you enjoy it?" Judith's gaze now was brilliantly intense.

Sharon shrugged. "When I fancied them. Which wasn't often, I'm choosy. When I didn't, I thought about the money. Which I made honestly!" Protest against another accusation that hadn't been levelled. Judith nodded in approval, she respected spirit.

"Of course. Have you met anyone you fancy in Seaminster?"

"You cheeky monkey!" But Sharon was smiling. "Have I been invited to Buckingham Palace? They're a right limp lot at the hotel, and . . . well, by the time I've finished wiping hairs out of baths I just don't seem to have the energy to look for trouble. That was the idea, I suppose. But if I was to meet the right sort . . ."

"I have connections." There was nothing youthfully boastful in Judith's claim, she was simply stating a fact. "I might be able to introduce you to the right sort."

Sharon leaned away from the table, her face suspicious. "What d'you mean?"

150

"I mean that I know someone. Someone I think would suit you."

Sharon gasped. "And you a school kid! I ought to report you to your teachers."

"I wouldn't do that, if I were you."

"No, well . . ." Something in Judith's stare made Sharon suddenly respectful. "OK, then. I can see you can take care of yourself." She hesitated, leaned forward again. "There wouldn't have to be anyone else involved."

"There wouldn't be. But I can't be certain at the moment that it's on. I'll have to see. If you're interested you'd better tell me your name again and I'll ring you at the Golden Lion."

The arrival of the hot water and chocolate surprise gave Phyllida a moment to form Sharon's reply. "Not the telephone," she said when the waitress had gone. "I'm a bit low down in the pecking order and they don't like it. And everyone in the hostel's so nosy and I want to be squeaky clean. Send me a note at the hotel, or hand it in. Sharon Lane. You can write Staff on the envelope, might save time."

"All right." Judith ate the last piece of her chocolate surprise and wiped her fingertips on her paper serviette.

"You going to tell me any more?"

"No."

"Come on."

"All right. I'll tell you that you won't be disappointed."

"He might."

Judith looked Sharon up and down a second time. "I shouldn't think so."

"That's kind of you. What time would it be?" Sharon spoke cautiously, but there was a light in her eyes.

"Evening. Not late. Say nine o'clock, but I'll let you know."

"Okay." Sharon in her way was as inexpressive of emotion as Judith. "I'd better be going now, I just fancied a bite and a cuppa." She stuffed the last of her chocolate surprise into her mouth, washed it down with a long draught of tea. "I'll see you."

"I don't think so," Judith said, her level gaze suggesting that the Marigold Café would now be out of bounds to Sharon Lane. "If it doesn't work out that'll be the end of it. And if I've anything to send you a note about, it isn't me you'll be seeing."

"It had better not be any girl!" Sharon said sharply.

"It won't be any girl." Phyllida thought she saw distaste as well as impatience flash across Judith's impassive face. "Look, if you don't feel comfortable . . ."

Sharon shrugged. "I feel comfortable enough, thanks." A wistful look came into her face, and she leaned her elbows on the table. "I could do with something good. But I can't . . ." Sharon scratched her head, grinning. "When I'm out in the street I'll think I've dreamed you."

"You haven't. I'll hope to be in touch," Judith said primly. She pushed her plate away so that it nudged Sharon's, and leaned down to take the exercise book out of the bag where she had replaced it. Sharon got to her feet.

"Well, cheers. Thanks for the chocolate and other surprises."

"Goodbye." Judith didn't look up from the reopened exercise book, and after a few hesitant seconds Sharon sauntered to the door. Grace was looking grim by the curtain hiding the kitchen, and Sharon pulled a face at her as she went out.

As soon as she was out of sight of the Marigold Café Phyllida quickened her pace and lowered her eyes, and was accosted by no more than guarded glances. Nevertheless she decided at the last moment not to run the gauntlet

152

of the Golden Lion's discriminating foyer, and turned off Dawlish Square on its other side.

Relief on the bottom stair had brought Sharon back by the top one. Steve and Jenny were both in the outer office, Jenny with jackets on herself and her word processor, and Steve lounging against a doorpost. When Sharon came through the door he jerked upright and stared so long and hard that Jenny nudged him.

"Good afternoon," she said doubtfully, staring as well. "I'm afraid we're just closing. Tomorrow –"

"The door was open!" Sharon stated aggressively.

"That's true." Steve moved swiftly forward to lay a reassuring hand on a bare arm. "So you can tell us your troubles here and now."

"I want to see the boss."

"Sorry!" Phyllida was uneasily surprised, as what looked like sexual jealousy crossed Steve's face. "The boss is tied up at the moment, but if you'd like to tell us what the trouble is we can be getting it down." Steve waved an arm towards Jenny's desk where Jenny, her mouth tight with disapproval, already had a notebook in her hand and was sitting down.

"Only the boss." Phyllida was surprised again, to hear herself keeping it going when she didn't want to.

"The boss is busy, I'm afraid." It was the coolest Phyllida had yet heard Jenny.

"He just might be free by now." Steve knew how to make the best of a bad job. "If you'd like to wait, I'll go and see."

"He asked not to be disturbed, Steve," Jenny said severely.

Phyllida was opening her mouth to resolve the argument when Peter appeared in his doorway. "Anything I can do?"

"This – lady – wants to see you, Governor. I was just telling her there was a chance you'd be free."

"And I was telling her you'd asked not to be disturbed."

Jenny was getting upset, which was more than the charade was worth. And Peter's wary face showed he had been taken in.

"It's all right, Jenny, Steve." Phyllida spoke in her own voice and Steve groaned. She put an arm round Jenny's shoulders. "I'm sorry. I'd intended going to the Golden Lion but hadn't the courage at the last moment. I didn't intend to play a silly game but when I saw you didn't know me I couldn't resist . . ." *Something came over me that mustn't come over me again.*

"Of course you couldn't, and we don't mind that sort of silly game."

But both youngsters looked shaken, as if they had suddenly acquired some unwelcome knowledge of themselves. As she thanked them for being sporting Phyllida felt ashamed.

"What have you been doing?" Peter asked. Since she'd come back to her own voice and facial expression his eyes had kept away from her. "Why are you looking like a tart?"

Phyllida hadn't told them about Sharon because she hadn't told them about the girl she had seen talking to Judith Fletcher in the Marigold Café. She pulled off the wig and wiped her mouth before answering. "It was a gamble that came off. I'll tell you if I'm not too disreputable to come into your office."

"You'd better all come," Peter said, making an ironically expansive gesture. "Steve has things to tell, too, and we haven't heard them yet either because we've been waiting for you."

"Thank you." Phyllida found herself glad her own

154

activities had precluded much dwelling on the fact that some results of Steve's could be available that day.

"Now," Peter said from behind his desk, when they had trooped in and disposed themselves. "Who's to be first?"

"Miss Moon!" the young ones chorused. But Phyllida nodded at Steve, whose eyes were determinedly above the expanse of bare leg there was no way she could get her minimal skirt to conceal. She didn't know whether to feel amused or resigned at the respectable image he and Peter were so clearly showing her belonged to Miss Moon.

"Steve first," Phyllida said firmly. She didn't want time to wonder what he had discovered about Brian Fletcher.

"Okay." Steve swaggered across the room from his peripheral seat and posed negligently against Peter's desk. "The Fletcher side gate was locked and I had to climb over but there was so much greenery I wasn't bothered. The back door key was easy and so was the alarm, thanks to Ma MacPherson. There's only one double bed in the house, which solved another possible problem. In Brian Fletcher's bedroom. Which is not especially macho but hasn't any female knick-knacks. I should say she only visits." Steve swung along more and more easily, managing, Phyllida thought, to see the Fletcher case like one of his usual adultery set-ups. "Upstairs too there's an obvious twin-bedded guest room – empty drawers and just a man's dress suit in the wardrobe. A third room's got an easel and paintings and stacks of do-it-yourselfery, and the fourth's so small it would have put me in mind of a nun's cell if I'd ever seen one, I can't imagine anything going on *there*."

"Judith's room," Jenny said.

"Yep. And not much more personal stuff than a nun would have, either, apart from the condoms. There's some good clothes in the wardrobe and drawers, good shoes. A couple of pictures you can understand and a couple of non-ones – you know, lines and squiggles. Both sorts signed 'Judith Fletcher'. There's a little desk with pigeon-holes, but they only had things like medical card and invitations and bumph from charities. All very tidy. There was just one thing that'll interest you." Steve paused for someone to ask what it was. Phyllida obliged. "An exercise book – just an ordinary lined exercise book – which she's used as a diary. What she'd written seemed ordinary enough too, but I photographed every few pages because . . . well . . ." Steve scratched his head. "She wasn't writing about anything shocking or even unusual – but it was sort of, well, sort of cool. I mean, she'd describe a person, a situation, without any feeling in it, as if she was describing a film she was watching, as if she wasn't there herself, even her own reactions were sort of detached."

"That figures," Phyllida said, as Steve's own descriptive powers ran out. "She *is* detached, that's the word. Thanks, Steve."

"Don't mensh." Steve was briefly pink, with pleasure. "That was how it was," he resumed, "until she and her old man had been a couple of years in Seaminster. Then there's just a rough edge where the pages have been torn out. Last entry left in was just under a year ago."

"Then blank?" Peter asked.

"That's the funny thing." Steve attempted to sit on the edge of Peter's desk and cross his legs, but they were not quite long enough and he resumed his original careless pose. "The few pages left *are* blank, but there's one sentence written very large across the page following the ones that have been torn out. I photographed it, of course, but I can remember it. 'When love is murdered,'" Steve quoted slowly, "'it doesn't know how to die.'" He

156

repeated the words, with relish. "Funny, isn't it? I've got my own darkroom at home," he told Phyllida, "and I'll get the pics developed before I go out tonight, so you can all see I didn't have a brainstorm."

"Something happened," Peter said. "With her father, or with the Elite?"

"It's dreadful!" Jenny said indignantly. "Her life became so terrible she couldn't bear even to read about it!"

"Unless her father tore the pages out," Peter said. Professionalism had taken over and he was now watching Phyllida's face. "I can't see your reactions through all that paint, but from what you said to me this morning I don't think you were aware of any repressed hostility or resentment on either side when you had supper with the Fletchers last night."

"No. Although Judith's no ordinary teenager. She's cleverer and more sophisticated than any girl of her age I've met. But Brian Fletcher seems . . . straightforward."

"Well, he would, wouldn't he?" Steve said. "That kind always do."

"What kind, Steve?" Under Peter's mildly quelling gaze Steve went back in silence to his seat. "What about Fletcher's room?"

"I didn't get farther than my head round the door. There was a noise at the front door so I shot out the back. It turned out to be the local freebie. I'll go back tomorrow."

"Good lad. Phyllida?"

She told them first what she had seen as Miss Pym, then what she had done that afternoon. "It was the wildest of gambles, but I didn't feel it had any real risk attached and so I decided to go ahead and try it before telling you."

"And you learned that Judith Fletcher's a pimp," Peter summarised.

"For her father," Steve added.

"Which would mean it was nothing to do with the Elite," Phyllida said. "But there could be other men in her life besides Brian Fletcher."

"If it is him, he must be a monster!" Jenny stormed. "Making his own daughter . . ."

"No one could make Judith Fletcher do anything against her will," Phyllida said. "That's the one thing I'm sure about her."

"But he could have made her like that," Jenny protested. "And if she loves him . . . The strongest person goes weak from love. There was a film on TV a couple of nights ago –"

"You could be right, Jenny," Peter interrupted her. "The primary aim of people who love is usually to please the loved one."

"You say people who love, you don't say people in love." Phyllida couldn't imagine Judith in either category. Unless, perhaps, obsession . . . "So you think it could be filial feeling on her side?"

"Don't you?" Peter asked.

"I don't know. Whatever it is, she propositioned Sharon on behalf of some man."

"You're sure it's a man?" Steve asked, looking sophisticated.

"Sharon made sure it is. And Judith's reaction to her insistence on a heterosexual contact made me pretty sure she and the Elite aren't interested in their own sex. Judith made it clear, incidentally, that Sharon wouldn't be welcome again in the Marigold Café."

"Which doesn't affect Miss Moon's comings and goings." Jenny looked wistfully at Phyllida. "That must give you a sense of power, Miss Moon."

"I like it," Phyllida said. "Sharon's awaiting a note from Judith at the Golden Lion. I'll go over and tell them when I've changed and washed my face."

158

"What will you do?" Jenny asked. "Above and beyond the call of duty doesn't go *that* far."

"I can see who Sharon's date is without getting into his car."

"We'll decide what to do," Peter said, "if and when Judith delivers. And if it turns out to be Brian Fletcher I'll lose my scruples about going to the police. Now, I think it's time we dispersed, unless anyone has anything else to say?"

"There is something else," Phyllida said. "Fiona came down from school trying to hang on to Tim Rowland, the impossibly handsome head boy I saw at the parent/staff evening. It was a bonus, because I'd first thought of going straight to the Marigold as Sharon in the hope that Judith would be there on her own – I was pretty sure she got the message across to the rest of the Elite when I was listening as Miss Pym that the café was to be out of bounds to them in the immediate future. But then I thought I'd start at the school gates and see what form the Elite appeared in, so when Fiona and Tim came down there was this person lounging against a gatepost. Tim managed to extricate himself from Fiona at the gates, and she went reluctantly off on her own. Tim hung around obviously waiting for someone, and it turned out to be Judith." Phyllida shook her head regretfully at Jenny's shocked catch of breath. "Nothing significant, I'm afraid. Judith didn't seem pleased to see him, but she stopped. I couldn't hear everything they said but I think he was telling her Fiona had become a nuisance, and asking her if she could warn her off. Judith started by telling him it was up to him, but when he made himself look helpless she suddenly smiled and said she'd speak to Fiona. At least that's what it seemed to be about."

"Fiona trying to make up for whatever it is the Elite can't do any more," Jenny suggested.

"It could be. Judith went off on her own and Tim let her get away. I followed him down into town and saw Judith in the Marigold when I passed the door, writing in her exercise book. So Sharon emerged from the street loo and went into the Marigold too, and the rest you know."

"Enterprise rewarded," Peter said, into the impressed silence.

Phyllida broke it. "Can you tell us any more about Judith's paintings, Steve?"

Steve screwed up his face. "It was kind of funny, the way they were so different. The ones you could understand were all sort of calm and clear. Blue sky, green grass like a photograph, only you got the feeling something nasty was going to break through and spoil it all. The other sort with the lines and squiggles didn't seem to mean anything, but they made me feel uncomfortable, too. In a different way from the other lot. Like if you looked too long you might see something you'd rather not."

"I could kill that man with my own hands," Jenny said.

In the outer office she and Steve and Phyllida exchanged amiable goodnights, and Phyllida went to wash her face determined to remain in charge of her cast of characters. Not just in order to be fair to a team which felt as equal and united as any theatre company she could remember being part of. Also because she had seen the danger, so long as she was living in limbo, of one or other of those characters becoming more real than she was herself.

Chapter Fourteen

Despite having blunted Sharon's impact in the cloakroom at Peter Piper, Phyllida sped through the foyer of the Golden Lion on her way upstairs. Fifteen minutes in the small bedroom completed her self-recovery, and when she was back in the foyer she strolled across to buy an evening paper from the hall porter before sitting down at one of the small tables and ordering herself a drink.

Ralph Unsworth's murder was no longer front-page news, but because the paper was local it reassured its readers without their having to open it that the police were pursuing their inquiries and reported that the dead boy's parents had gone away, reviving Phyllida's reaction of mingled disappointment and relief that there were no siblings with whom an appropriate persona would have been duty bound to strike up an acquaintance. On an inside page there was an angry letter from Appalled, Seaminster, that a week had gone by and the murderer of a Claire College student was still at large.

Phyllida took time over her drink, enjoying the rarity of being herself in public and the paper's predominantly cheerful trivia. It was seven o'clock when she decided the break had been long enough, and got up and went over to Reception.

"Any letters or messages for Mrs Margaret Morrison?"

"Ah. I rather think . . . Yes, there was a telephone call half an hour ago." While she was sitting there, but the

161

staff's only brief had been to ring the small bedroom and, if there was no reply, put the message into the pigeon-hole marked "Peter Piper". "No letters."

The girl held out a piece of paper. The message asked Mrs Morrison to ring Brian Fletcher, and gave a number. If she didn't ring he would try again later.

"Thanks." Phyllida went back upstairs.

He answered quickly.

"It was just that I've had a thought. You'll still be here on Wednesday?"

"Yes."

"Good. Well, I hope it's good. Wednesday night's the night of Claire's annual concert. The top musical talents on parade. They don't include Judith but last year they were mostly worth hearing and anyway day students' parents are encouraged to attend. It would be nice to have a companion. Could you bear it, Margaret?"

"I'm sure I could." Phyllida was surprised by the possibility of Brian Fletcher not having a regular female companion, then wondered if he found his relationship with his daughter so satisfying he had no need of one. The third thought, some way behind, was that he might simply want the company of Margaret Morrison. In the way of normal men. "Judith will be with you too, I suppose?"

"Judith will be with her cronies in the rear stalls. Segregation of parents and students is the usual thing on these occasions, I suspect so that the students can be less inhibited in their reactions to the performers. If I call for you at seven? There's a refreshment break half way through. Substantial."

"Thanks for the warning. And for Sunday, I enjoyed it."

"I did too, Margaret."

And the night that followed? Phyllida shivered as she hung up.

162

No note had arrived for Sharon when she left the hotel, but at 8 Upland Road there was a telephone call for Phyllida from Gerald, in emphatic contradiction of Carol's opinion that his life was a ruin. But before ringing off he asked if he could come and see her. Phyllida again said no.

She spent Tuesday learning the work of the agency from the office standpoint, and wondering about Steve's second visit to the Fletchers. He came in as Jenny was making the end-of-day brew, and Peter said he supposed they had better have it together in his office.

"Well?" he asked, after he, Phyllida and Jenny had spent several minutes watching Steve silently drinking tea.

"Only one thing," Steve said, avoiding everyone's eye. "But I should say it's a clincher."

"Yes?"

"I went all over downstairs this time, and through his bedroom. No condoms, and his desk's as boring as hers, except for one thing." Steve paused, an expression on his face Phyllida couldn't read.

"You really are the most maddening person!" Jenny exploded. "For goodness sake tell us!"

"It's a poem," Steve said reluctantly, his face flooding pink. Phyllida realised he was embarrassed. "A love poem. Well, a bit of one."

"To his daughter?" Phyllida heard herself asking.

"Who else? I copied it out." Steve slowly pulled a crumpled piece of paper from a pocket and stood with it in his hand.

"Go on," Peter said.

"'Bright girl of mine, too early woman, what blame do I bear?'" he recited in a low, hurried voice.

"That's a question he hardly needs to ask!" Jenny commented tartly.

"Innocent until proved guilty," Peter reminded them.

163

"But all right, it doesn't sound too good. What next, Steve?"

"Phyllida'll tell you." Steve crossed the room to put the paper into her hand. "Capitals," he said encouragingly. "You can read it."

"If you will, Phyllida," Peter asked.

"'Bright girl of mine, at once child and woman, where did I go wrong?'"

"Don't answer that."

"All right, Steve, let's hear it through," Peter suggested.

"'Bright girl of mine, full-blown before blooming, how great is my guilt? Christmas tree fairy, so firmly fixed, how did you fall down? How did I help you lose your crown?'"

"I'm sorry, Doctor," Jenny said, "but I just can't take any more of those questions."

"There aren't any more." Phyllida folded the paper and held it out to Steve.

"In all fairness," Peter said, not looking at her, "he didn't write it to submit to the Poetry Society. I used to produce stuff myself at one time to ease the pressure."

"I'm glad I'm not going out with that man tomorrow!" Jenny said. "Gosh, sorry, Miss Moon."

"I'm not going out with him either," Phyllida automatically pointed out. "Margaret Morrison's his date. And she's unlikely to find herself alone with him. I expect Judith will go and come back with them even if she sits with her chums when they get there."

"Margaret needn't worry if she *is* alone with him." A wary eye on Peter, Steve had returned to his theory. "That sort isn't interested in anything normal. I could do with a straightforward case, Governor. Get the taste of Mr Pervert Fletcher out of my mouth. Anything come in?" Steve blinked hopefully at Peter.

"Yes, but it will keep till tomorrow. Let's pack up."

Peter called Phyllida into his office as soon as she arrived the next morning.

"The nationals have revived our murder story with a report of the local Super's defensive press conference yesterday afternoon."

"So I've seen."

"I've had words with my tame Detective Sergeant. The Super told it how it is. There's no lead, but the boy seems to have been on the wrong side of quite a lot of people. No wonder the Super's rattled."

"Your DS doesn't have any theories?"

"We tried a few out between us, but I was hamstrung knowing things he doesn't. Like about Brian Fletcher, and the Elite."

"You didn't tell him anything?"

"Without a conference here first? What I say eventually goes, but not before discussion. Which you and I should have now. Sit down, Phyllida. That poem."

"Yes."

"It's not in Brian Fletcher's favour, but it doesn't give us an answer. Does it?"

She had spent most of the night wondering if it did. "I don't know. Which could be to agree with you that it doesn't. But –"

"Look, we agreed we didn't feel the time had come to damage Brian Fletcher. Does the poem change that?"

He saw the relief in her eyes before she spoke. "Not while I've a chance of finding out if we'd be initiating an injustice. Which means not before tonight, and not until it becomes obvious Judith isn't going to fix a date for Sharon. At least – that's how I feel."

"Me too. And the police are still going all out for the murderer. We'll start looking at things differently if they show signs of closing the case unsolved. For the moment, we'll just hope Mrs M doesn't get impatient." He hesitated. "And that it doesn't get too difficult with Brian Fletcher."

"I can take it. And Steve's views on the nature of perverts might just be right. Anyone outside the scope of their perversion could be out of focus."

"Let's hope so, if Brian Fletcher is one. I think you should be off duty until tonight, by the way. Do something different, like writing your book."

"Like driving along the coast, and then walking."

It was only ten o'clock and Phyllida had come into town by car, so there was time to go quite a long way. Before she was out of town she had confirmed her suspicion that putting places before people made her feel less unreal. With land and seascape her only companions, life felt as vivid and substantial as it used to be, as it would surely be again when her coastal limbo had turned into a conventional weekend retreat from the TV studios. She walked for an hour along a stretch of uninhabited shore, then drove inland and bought a piece of cranberry glass in a village antique shop before having a sandwich at the village pub. A dog sat beside her and shared it with her, reminding her how upset she had once been that Gerald didn't care for animals.

The sun shone all day, and when she got home Phyllida's head was filled with serene images of coast and countryside. But finding it so slight a transition to Margaret Morrison restored her sense of unreality and brought a slight unease.

Brian Fletcher's face as he drew up at the Golden Lion looked tired and anxious, but it relaxed into a smile as he saw Margaret.

"I'm on my own, Judith elected to go with her friends. Hasn't it been a lovely day? It's brought me a lot of customers, and I've been glad half my stock's in the open air. What have you been doing?"

"Walking, mostly. Yes, it's been a lovely day." Because of the poem small talk was harder than it had been, and Phyllida found it a help that a comfortable silence had already been established between Margaret and Brian.

Students were stationed at Claire's gateposts to control the parking. Brian and Margaret were waved up the drive, and found one of the few remaining spaces on the forecourt. People were strolling into the largest building of the one-time stable block, now a handsome hall starred in the dusk by a lighted chandelier through each long window. The back rows of chairs were already filled with boys in white shirts with red ties and girls in a variety of no doubt statutorily demure short-sleeved floral dresses. Phyllida looked for the girl she knew. Brian found her first.

"There's Judith, Margaret."

Three members of the Elite sat motionless and with set faces. Fiona fidgeted and peered anxiously around.

"Yes, I see her. With her friends, I suppose."

Phyllida turned her attention to Brian, whose glance was playing lightly over his daughter's companions.

"I suppose so, but I wouldn't know. As I told you, Judith doesn't bring friends home." They were of necessity close together in the narrow aisle space, and she felt him wince.

The Heads were standing together in the aisle near the front, provoking in Phyllida a frightening desire to laugh hysterically at their conjunction and making her thankful there was little time to socialise before the entertainment began, although they had a moment's chat with Alan Williams and Brian introduced Margaret to Judith's History Mistress, and the world-weary schoolmaster archetype who taught her English and whose attention Mrs Morrison had more hope than Mrs Bond of attracting.

The first half of the concert featured a pianist, a violinist, a flautist, two solo singers and a choir, in pieces fairly divided between the familiar old and the difficult new. Phyllida liked music, but had no means of telling how well the Claire students were tackling the new, which sounded as hard to play as it was to listen to. It received the same loyally rapturous applause as the familiar old, whose performance in each item impressed Phyllida and made her look forward increasingly to the second half of the concert, to be devoted to the school orchestra and the school's star pianist in the Schumann Piano Concerto. The first half ended with an abrasively modern liturgical piece from the choir (to be offset, according to the programme, by *Jerusalem* at the end of the second).

"You're right about the high standard," Margaret murmured to Brian when they were part of the crowd meandering into the school dining hall via an elegantly proportioned gallery overlooking the garden terrace through a series of slender glass doors. The long tables held buffet supper dishes interspersed with flowers, and the many identical chairs stood about at ease.

"Yes. They're good, aren't they?" He seemed less relaxed, newly on edge, but it could be that despite Phyllida's efforts Margaret's response to him was less spontaneous than it had been on Sunday.

"Shall we look for Judith?" she suggested.

"I'm looking now."

They didn't see Judith, but Phyllida caught the eye of the world-weary English master and was gratified that this brought him to Margaret's side. When Brian saw that she was enjoying the encounter he excused himself and disappeared. Phyllida had to make an effort to bring an enjoyable discussion of Shakespeare's women to a close in order to express the hope that Claire's murder wouldn't affect the school's reputation. Denis Trevelyan shrugged and said that three sets of parents had so far removed their little darlings and Ralph Unsworth had been a poisonous prig with a talent for stirring it and he personally wouldn't be upset if the police never found out who had cut him off, which he suspected they wouldn't, and did she share his special feeling for *A Winter's Tale*?

Brian's reappearance was timely, coinciding with Mr Trevelyan being enticed away by a parent and the beginnings of the drift back along the gallery.

As she and Brian strolled side by side Phyllida noticed Tim Rowland dart from a side corridor and slip in among a group of his peers. He was grinning and blowing out his cheeks in what looked like relief, and two other boys were slapping him on the back.

A moment later Judith came alongside. "Hello, Mrs Morrison. Are you enjoying yourself?"

Phyllida could see that the red-haired girl the far side of her was keeping pace, although she and Judith were paying each other no attention.

"Very much."

"You missed a good supper," Brian said.

"I didn't, Daddy. I heaped a plate up and ate in School House sixth form room with some friends. I didn't think you'd miss me." Judith was looking at the ground, it was hard to know whether or not she was being sarcastic.

Again Phyllida felt Brian Fletcher wince. "It was a very good supper," she said. "And now I'm looking forward –"

The screams were so powerful they cut like a knife through the buzz of chat. They came again and again, and then other people at the front of the crowd found their voices and the crowd was tight around what, from its back edge, Phyllida could see only as the upper part of one of the glass doors on to the garden terrace, open.

She turned to Judith, but Judith and Gill were no longer

169

beside them, and when she looked at the door again she saw them sliding through the scrum towards what was wrong.

Information was being passed back through the swaying crowd, spreading the shock as if a stone had been thrown into a pool. Bringing it closer to Brian and Margaret, although when the Art Master's head and shoulders appeared against the top of the door it still hadn't reached them.

"Ladies and gentlemen! Please!" Urgency lent power to his normally murmurous voice, producing an instant stillness. "Thank you. I have to tell you that a terrible thing has happened: one of our girl students has fallen to her death from an upper floor on to the terrace behind me. It must have been instantaneous, but until the police come we can't tell . . . I'm sorry, but this has to be the end of our concert. However, if you'll all be good enough to go back to your seats in the hall, I'm afraid we must wait for the police." Alan Williams paused, his face even at a distance looking strange to both Brian and Phyllida without its smile, and passed a hand across his forehead, ruffling the dark hair that had so attractively fallen forward. "Two terrible things for Claire," he said, his voice at last faltering. "But at least this one appears to have been an accident. Please all go quietly back into the hall."

The head and shoulders disappeared, and two young men began urging the crowd forward, making Phyllida think of a flock of sheep being headed off by border collies.

The open door had to be passed, and when Brian and Margaret reached it two other senior boys already stood guard and a cover had been thrown over the small mound intermittently visible behind them.

The audience drifted like sleepwalkers, and only those who had left coats and wraps were bothering to find their

170

former seats. The hall now was dotted throughout with students seeking adult reassurance, and those still at the back were as agitated as a field of wild flowers in a gale. The Heads stood solemnly side by side at the front of the platform, and other members of staff rushed aimlessly about. Alan Williams appeared as Margaret and Brian sat down somewhere near the chairs they had occupied before, and was detained by a hand put out from the edge of the row in front of them.

". . . most likely the second floor balustrade," Phyllida heard him say. "There's a door . . . It's supposed to be out of bounds but I suspect most of the students at one time or another . . ."

Brian Fletcher made a sound Phyllida could only call a moan. "And if you wanted to . . . Judith. Where's Judith? I must go —"

He was struggling to his feet and Margaret put her hand on his arm, nodding across the aisle.

"She's there. See? She's all right, Brian."

She heard his deep sigh. Judith, Becky and Gill were each of them discreetly active, looking round the auditorium and towards the doors, then expressionlessly at one another. Except for their eyes, which as time moved on grew wider and more anguished.

So that when two men in grey suits eventually joined the Molesworths on the platform Phyllida, too, knew what to expect. The grand piano was still centre stage, and the men stood in the curve of it.

"I think you will all have heard," the older man began. Phyllida recognised his face from newspaper pictures of his press conference. "A senior female pupil of this school has fallen to her death from the top floor of this building. I now have the unhappy duty of telling you that that pupil is Fiona Jeffcoate." The shocked murmur would have been the same whatever name had been spoken, but Judith might not have bowed her head to her knees, Gill and Becky have clasped hands.

There was no physical reaction from Brian Fletcher. When Margaret turned to look at him he was looking at Judith, who had raised her head and was staring into space.

"D'you know her?" Margaret asked him in a whisper. "No."

But someone, since the murder of Ralph Unsworth, had been acting as professionally as Phyllida Moon.

Chapter Fifteen

"Above and beyond the call of duty, as Jenny might say." Phyllida smiled at Peter over the rim of her glass. Waving Brian Fletcher away, she had seen the consoling light across the square.

"It's the Chandler in me. Philip Marlowe got his important clients because he was always in his office when they called, and it was always late at night with the street ads flashing through his windows."

"Mrs MacPherson?"

"All right. I'm working on a report, actually. Don't worry, I've had enough." Peter closed the folder on the desk in front of him and tossed it into a drawer. "And if this girl hadn't been . . . I wouldn't have been here if my dinner date hadn't ended so early."

"Things didn't go well?"

"Women don't seem to take me seriously," Peter explained gloomily.

"Should they?" Shock seemed to have destroyed Phyllida's diffidence in favour of her actress's curiosity.

"Probably not. I didn't want my girlfriend to leave and I'm rather going through the motions."

"Poetry doesn't help like it used to?"

"Afraid not." But she had brought back his grin. "Anyway, these days it's verse if it's anything. Occasional. Weddings, funerals, graduations, adieus. You name it, Peter Piper will provide it. It's just a quirk of mind, like being able to do cryptic crosswords. Those lines of Brian Fletcher's," he went on smoothly. "He wouldn't have thought of anyone ever seeing them."

"No, of course not."

"Look. From what you've said it sounds as though Judith's friend's death was an accident. But I get the feeling you don't seem to think it was."

"I heard someone say you'd have to climb up on the balustrade before you could fall over it. And I know things the police don't know. Like Fiona worrying the rest of the Elite, perhaps even threatening their security."

"And you can imagine one, or two, or three of them deciding to put her out of their misery?"

"Having witnessed their grim single-mindedness, yes. On the other hand they looked dazed, and if they were guilty one would have expected them to look furtive. I saw the Art Master, Alan Williams, go up to Judith and she walked past him as if he wasn't there. She came away with us and just lay on the back seat of the car staring at the roof, I looked round at her a couple of times. Her father said how sorry he was, that he hadn't realised Fiona had been such a close friend. She didn't react to that, either."

"Mm. Brian Fletcher. You said he went missing during the supper interval."

"For longer than it would have taken to go to the loo unless there was a queue, which I don't imagine there often is in men's rooms."

"No. But he could have stopped to speak to someone on the way out or in, and with the full house you said there was, you didn't have to be able to see him for him to be in the supper-room."

"I know. I'm getting paranoid. And whether he was in the supper-room or out of it, there doesn't seem to be any reason why he should want to do away with Fiona

Jeffcoate. He seems to have had a motive of sorts for the murder of Ralph Unsworth, but unless he's a fantastic actor he was hardly aware of Fiona's existence before the police announcement of her death."

"Could it have been suicide?"

"It could have been technically, I suppose, and Fiona *was* taking the afternoon frustration a lot harder than the others. But I just can't see her as the sort of person who would take her own life. And she was already making up to Tim Rowland as a consolation prize . . ." A picture sharp in every detail flashed across her mind's eye. "Tim Rowland joined his pals out of a side corridor just before Fiona's body was discovered, looking as if he'd shed every care in the world."

"If he'd just pushed a girl to her death he'd hardly have looked like that."

"And his friends would hardly have patted him on the back, no. And it did seem consistent at the time with relief and congratulations at having simply managed to keep out of Fiona's way. He went scarlet, though, and hung his head when the police asked if Fiona's friends would make themselves known."

"And did he?"

"No. But that need only mean he doesn't consider himself to be one."

"And having successfully avoided her just before she died would have been quite enough to make him feel guilty. I mean, we British say sorry, don't we, when someone treads on our toe. Was there a big show of hands?"

"Just the Elite. Well, they had to, didn't they, everyone must have known them as a foursome with Fiona. And I suppose belonging to the Elite could have prevented her forming other friendships. Anyway, the other raised hands belonged to members of staff. The police said they'd

175

like to talk to those people there and then, together with anyone who'd seen Fiona during the interval, or noticed anything strange about her recent behaviour. Then they led the way to a makeshift interview room and the people who'd put their hands up followed them. I don't think any extra people went out, so it doesn't look as if anyone saw anything helpful. Judith didn't want to talk when she came out, but her father was persistent enough on the way home to get her to say that the moment she and her friends left the hall at the interval Fiona told them she was going to the loo and they didn't see her again."

"Didn't wonder where she was having her supper?"

"Judith said they assumed she'd been nobbled by a member of staff or a parent. Her own parents weren't there, thank God. Not on holiday like Ralph Unsworth's. Just doing other things. None of the Elite had supper in the dining-room, by the way. According to Judith she and a couple of friends ate in School House sixth form room; Gill's in School House. They apparently had the room to themselves, so there's only their word for it." Phyllida and Peter stared at one another. "The police only kept Judith a few minutes but they want to see her again in the morning." Phyllida glanced at her watch. "This morning. I suppose tonight was the facts and tomorrow will be the psychology."

"The police won't get much out of the Elite."

"If I know Judith, they'll get the suggestion from all three of them that Fiona was unstable and had begun to worry them. What won't worry them is giving a false impression of Fiona's character."

"It could just be the truth, Phyllida."

"Obviously, but that doesn't make me believe it. The police didn't offer any theories. When they left the hall for the interviews they asked the rest of us to give our names and addresses and go home." Phyllida drained her glass. "Would you say it was strange, Brian Fletcher apparently not knowing Fiona was one of his daughter's best friends?"

Peter looked thoughtful. "I'd say it could be part of an unnatural relationship, an attempt to blank out the schoolgirl side of her, maybe from conscience. I don't think it puts him in the frame. Which isn't to say of course that he isn't in it anyway."

"You're right. I really am starting to be silly."

"I don't think so, but have another drink. It isn't every night –" He stopped, the whisky bottle aloft.

"But it's more than one." Phyllida's laughter had an hysterical edge.

"It's not such a coincidence, when you think of it," Peter said when she had recovered. "You've been at two big Claire occasions in succession. The murderer obviously chose the first one because of so many people being about. If Fiona's death was a second murder the concert would have been chosen for the same reason. If it was suicide, Fiona could have been giving herself the final consolation of taking her life as dramatically as she could."

"That's the only reason I can imagine her doing it, and it's too far-fetched. Whatever, two violent deaths within weeks in the same school, the first one certainly murder. Won't that be enough to make the police suspicious about the second?"

"Of course it will. But I should say their inquiry's likely to be more productive if they keep it cool at this stage. They'll look for fingerprints on that balustrade, and on the door leading out to it, and if they find one clear one that isn't Fiona's, they'll have to fingerprint at least the staff and the students. And if there's no match there, they'll have to fingerprint everyone who was in the school during the first half of the concert who hasn't got a watertight alibi. Not that I think they'll find any fingerprints if it's murder. They didn't find any in the storeroom where Ralph Unsworth died."

"Which will save the world from the discovery that Jennifer Bond and Margaret Morrison make nonsense of forensic theory." Phyllida managed to stifle another desire to laugh immoderately.

"Yes, that's something. But seriously, Phyllida, if the surfaces in the area of the balustrade have been wiped clean, that'll mean Ralph Unsworth all over again and it'll do Claire one hell of a lot of harm."

"At least Margaret didn't leave the supper-room."

"You might have seen something if she had, but it's probably lucky that she didn't. With her hitting it off so well with Brian Fletcher we obviously want to keep her going. Can we extend her stay without making Fletcher think he's the reason?"

"She's told him her visit's open-ended."

"Wise woman. Now, you'll have been intending to sleep at home tonight, but it looks as though events at the concert have turned it into another night at the Golden Lion. To be able to take Fletcher's early morning apologetic phone call."

"Yes. I'd realised that before I left Claire." With what had already become the usual absurd pang of homesickness. But in a few hours' time the curtains at 8 Upland Road would have been drawn back anyway.

Brian Fletcher rang at nine next morning, when Phyllida had a tray across her knees and was finding it quite agreeable to be forced to have breakfast in bed in the line of duty.

"Margaret! Are you all right? I'm so sorry about last night."

"It wasn't your fault." *Was it, Brian?* "Don't worry, I'm fine. But what about Judith? How is she?"

178

She heard the sharp breath. "Quiet. But that's . . . I dropped her at school as usual, but I'll spend the morning expecting her to appear in the shop. When – the boy was killed, they closed the school the next day and all the day-students went home. I made her promise that if the school is closed again she'll come here before going anywhere else."

"She's talking to the police again first thing, isn't she?"

"Yes." His breathing was still audible.

"People were saying last night that you couldn't fall over that balustrade without first climbing up on it and I couldn't help wondering –"

He interrupted in a rush. "Judith thinks it was suicide. She knew Fiona, and apparently she wasn't the most stable of people."

"That's awful." Phyllida winked into the mirror at the foot of the bed. "And two deaths for whatever reasons won't do Claire much good, will they? I was listening to the news just now, and Claire was identified as the school where a prefect was recently murdered. People will think about connections even if there aren't any. I wonder if there are?" Such as both victims having been a nuisance to Judith. Phyllida surprised herself with a feeling of relief that she was unable to think of any way in which the second victim could have been a nuisance to Brian.

"I tried to ask Judith what she thought," he was saying hesitantly, "but she didn't want to talk about it. I don't envy the police, they've already started to get flak for not solving the murder. Look, we're obviously both going to be thinking about the wretched business. I'm not suggesting we should talk about it as well, but if you're free and feel like coming round to the shop at lunchtime one of my lads will bring in an extra sandwich. At least we'll understand each other's unsociability."

"I'd like to. But Judith . . ."

"If she's here you might help, I think in her own way she's upset and I can tell she likes you. Anyway, I expect she'll have gone off by lunchtime with her friends."

"Thank you, then. I can eat any kind of sandwich."

Phyllida was across the square by ten o'clock, reporting Brian's call to Peter and the other members of his staff. Steve and Jenny stood with awe-filled eyes at a noticeable remove from her before settling into Peter's most peripheral chairs, as if she really might be a magnet that attracted disaster.

But Jenny immediately leaned towards her. "You won't go on with Margaret Morrison now, will you, Miss Moon?"

"Of course she will!" Steve responded indignantly. "After all she's done to get the dame where she is!"

"Carrying on with Mrs Morrison is our justification for not reporting to Mrs MacPherson," Phyllida suggested. "And Judith isn't afraid of her the way she was of Jennifer Bond. Margaret isn't in any danger."

"Phyllida's got it right." Peter beamed his approval on her. His own desire unofficially to join the murder hunt about which he had so often dreamed and on which he actually had a head start was probably as strong as Steve's, but his conscience insisted on being stronger still, and he was grateful to Phyllida for appeasing it. "Have you made any plans for when you leave the ironworks?"

"If I come in between five and six?"

"I expect we'll all be here," Peter said.

When Margaret went through the ironworks gate at a quarter to one Brian Fletcher was on the forecourt, talking business with one of his assistants.

180

"Billy's gone for the sandwiches," he greeted her. "And Judith's moved on. Come inside."

She sat on one of the tall stools beside the counter, curling her feet round its iron legs. "So they've closed Claire again. How was she?"

"All right, I think." He opened his arms in a gesture of helplessness.

"Has she never confided in you?"

For a moment there was pain in his eyes so intense it cost Phyllida despite her suspicions a pang of pity. "I always hoped she confided in her mother, but somehow I never asked. Even as a child Judith was – private." He shook his head, tried to smile. "And teenage girls, of course . . ."

"Secretive. Yes." The pity had passed. "So you couldn't really tell if the police had upset her?"

"I don't think they had. I think she was already – well, numb. She did tell me Fiona Jeffcoate had been a close friend. If only she'd bring her friends home, Margaret."

But Brian Fletcher himself could have killed that possibility.

"It's sad she doesn't. Did she tell you what sort of things the police wanted to know?" He might not realize it, but one reason he had invited Margaret to lunch was to help him sort out his reactions. Which meant that he might welcome her questions as a solace rather than resent them as a catechism.

"Mostly about Fiona's recent state of mind, if she'd seemed different lately in any way. The police were questioning two of her other friends as well, apparently they went round in a foursome. Judith didn't think the others had been able to say anything helpful either. The Head Boy Tim Rowland turned up, even though he hadn't put his hand up last night. He told Judith he'd decided he ought to tell the police he was afraid Fiona might have had a crush on him and that he'd spent the interval keeping out of her way. Salving his conscience after a bad night, Judith said, in that put-down sort of way she has sometimes, but it occurred to me that he might have helped the police to understand the girl . . . It does rather look like suicide, doesn't it? Excuse me a moment. How can I help you, sir?"

Margaret wandered about the forecourt while Brian sold a weather vane, and when Billy came in with the sandwiches he took over at the counter and Brian made coffee which he and Margaret carried out with the sandwiches into the small garden behind the building.

"Suicide!" Margaret echoed belatedly as they sat down in the pale sunshine on wrought iron chairs.

"I know. It's awful. But what else?"

"I'm afraid I can't help thinking about the murder. The media will too. I mean, two violent deaths in one school in one week."

"Last night couldn't have any connection with the murder." Brian Fletcher had gone pale and his voice had sunk to a whisper.

"We can't know that. Are you all right?"

"Yes. Sorry. I have low blood pressure, sometimes it makes me feel faint." He drooped his head towards his knees.

"When you're worried."

"Not necessarily. Out of the blue . . ."

"But you're bound to be worried about Judith."

His head came up. "About Judith? Judith wasn't her friend's keeper!" The uncharacteristic protest had restored his colour and his voice. "I suppose I'm worried about her future at the school," he went on in his usual reasonable way. "Poor Claire, I wonder if its reputation is strong enough to get it through all this intact. It would be a very bad time for Judith to have to change teachers."

182

"Has she gone home?"

Brian shrugged. "She could have done. Sometimes when it seems to me she might be – upset – I find her writing or painting."

When love is murdered, it doesn't know how to die.

But Judith didn't write any more. And only painted threats.

"Or she could be with her friends," he persisted. "Getting through it together. Are the sandwiches all right?"

"Delicious. Like the coffee, and this blessed plot. If I were you I'd be out here every lunchtime." The garden reminded Phyllida of her own, a small secret extension of the building open to the sky.

"I usually am. But I don't at all mind going back inside. I've never quite got used to the miracle of working at what I like doing." But there was something forced in Brian Fletcher's enthusiasm, as if he was trying to convince himself that the good things outweighed the bad.

"I can imagine."

"Yes, I think you can." His sudden smile seemed to be spontaneous. She would have to resist the temptation to see a nuance merely because there was a chance it might be there.

That afternoon Phyllida was in luck. As Miss Pym walked into the Marigold the table she preferred was just being vacated. Grace served her with her usual disdain, and it was the sudden animation in the sullen face which alerted Phyllida to what after almost half an hour she was beginning to be afraid wasn't going to happen. Although the café was almost empty, Grace had flounced about in impatience as yet another page of Miss Pym's newspaper was turned. Her eyes drawn by the movement, Phyllida saw the mingling of wariness and excitement that took over from exasperation as Grace's eyes focused on the door.

On Gill and Becky wearing jeans and multi-coloured shirts and lagging their way to their accustomed seats.

It was the most she had hoped for, to satisfy her curiosity as to the extent of their loyalty to their leader.

At first, though, they didn't speak, they just sat with their elbows on the table and their heads drooped on their hands. It was only when Grace had interrupted them and disappeared into the kitchen after being told they were waiting that blonde Becky said, tossing back bright strands of hair, "She'd have to be last, wouldn't she?"

"It's an instinct," Gill said. "I envy it, actually. Isn't everything bloody?"

"I can't believe Fiona's dead. She was driving us mad because she was so alive, so much *there*."

"That was the trouble."

"Better not say things like that, Gill."

"Why not? It's true."

"I know. And you're getting more and more like Judith."

"I have to. So do you."

"Judith. Judith." If another of them went over the top it would be Becky.

"We wouldn't have had – what we've had – without Judith."

"We wouldn't be in trouble now."

"We're not in trouble. Come on, Becky." The severity of Gill's face lightened in concern, but whether it was for her friend or for her own security Phyllida couldn't tell.

"Yeah. Okay. I'm just upset. D'you think we'll ever get back to how it was last term?"

"We have to hope so. I should say that without Fiona there'll be more chance of it, although the police'll be all over the place again and doing all they can to put the deaths together."

The girls stared gravely into each other's faces. "Oh, Gill, how could she?" Becky eventually whispered.

"We don't know –"

Gill broke off as Judith entered the café, dressed tidily in crisp white blouse and a rather long emerald green skirt. She sat down in silence in her usual place, her eyes despite their blankness making the reflex survey of the room Phyllida expected. Grace reappeared.

"The usual, is it? What's with your school?"

"We've all turned into vampires and werewolves." Judith offered an unnerving flash of teeth. "Yes, the usual, please, Grace."

Grace stood still, her face struggling as she tried to decide whether or not she had been insulted.

"We don't know what's happening, Grace," Gill soothed swiftly. "We have to joke, it's so awful."

"Funny sense of humour," Grace commented, with a sniff. But her dilemma appeared to be resolved in favour of the *status quo*.

"Sorry, Judith," Gill said, as the waitress disappeared. "But Grace has no sense of humour at all."

"No. Look." Judith had moved on. "Why I told you to come. This isn't like Ralph Unsworth: we're connected with Fiona." It was not much more than a fierce whisper, and Phyllida had to concentrate. "Even though we've all told the police we believe she committed suicide we're in the spotlight and we've got to be squeaky clean."

"No chance of being anything else," commented Becky.

"You know what I mean." Judith concentrated her cold gaze. "Of course there's no chance. But we have to act as if there never was, never will be. We have to be absolutely what we seem. Try to think, if we can, that it's all been a dream."

185

"That won't be too difficult," Gill said.

"It will be very difficult," Judith corrected her sternly. "But it's what we have to do."

"Have you spoken –" Becky began.

"No!" Phyllida could see Judith's pale eyes, and the brief furtive look in them. She wondered if it explained the uncharacteristic violence of Judith's denial. "Of course I haven't. Now –"

"Three teas, three chocolate surprises." Grace dumped the tray on the table and slopped its contents around.

"I'm not hungry," Becky said when she had gone, poking at her chocolate surprise.

"Of course you're not," Judith said. "You're upset about Fiona."

"Yes, I am!"

"That's what I said." Judith was reading the signs of mutiny. "We all are. Naturally. But about coming here. This is a one-off, today, just to stiffen us up to being more careful than ever. We won't meet here again until things are back to normal. Which could be the new year, we have to face it. Becky. At Claire we'll have to go on doing what everyone's used to seeing us doing – going round together. We'll be expected to hang together more than ever now, if you think about it."

"So why can't we meet here as well?" Becky demanded.

"Because it encourages us to drop our guard, feel relaxed because we know there's no one to see or hear us." Judith's eyes as she spoke passed over Miss Pym as if she was no more than the chair she sat on.

"Judith's right," Gill said, after a short silence in which Becky played roughly with her hair. Phyllida decided there would be no situation where Judith was unable to rely on Gill, and that Gill would always keep Becky to heel.

"Of course I am." Judith looked at Gill with rare

186

approval. "We'll start from this moment acting as if it isn't any safer to talk here than it is in school."

Miss Pym sighed. Judith had been more right than she knew, ending access to the Elite's ambiguous crumbs.

Oh, Gill, how could she?

How could Fiona have committed suicide?

Phyllida couldn't believe Gill really thought Fiona had taken her own life.

So – how could Judith have done it for her?

Chapter Sixteen

Phyllida left Miss Pym at home and walked back into town, resisting the temptation to spend ten minutes tidying round the garden. Thinking of Judith and her certainties she called first at the Golden Lion to see if there was a note for Sharon and was handed a small white envelope, unstamped and addressed in a neat clear hand.

"I wonder if anyone could tell me anything about the person who delivered this?"

"Sorry." The girl pushed hair back from a gleaming forehead. "Tracy and I were both here but neither of us saw anyone, it was just there on the counter. We've had a bit of chaos, a party of Americans leaving, paying bills and so on, maybe it was one of them . . ."

Phyllida took the envelope unopened across the square. It was after six but Jenny was still typing and Steve was making coffee. Phyllida read the plea in their eyes, and sought and obtained Peter's permission for them to follow her into his office.

"A note for Sharon," she said as she reached for his paper knife. "I've just collected it." She slit the envelope and read the single sheet aloud. "'Sharon, Monday night at nine at the Café de Paris. Wear that red, white and green bandeau you had round your head in the Marigold. Sit down and order a drink and you'll be joined by someone who knows your name. If you don't come you don't come, no big deal. And that goes for the other side, too.' There's no signature or address or date," Phyllida said, looking up. "But it seems quite clear."

"You're not *going*?" Jenny asked, aghast.

"I have to go."

"The Governor and I will be going as well," Steve reassured Jenny, as he laid a protective hand on Phyllida's shoulder. "You'll be all right, Miss Moon."

"She'll be all right because she won't be going as Sharon," Peter said. "No need for heroics, she only has to recognise him." He and Phyllida exchanged looks. "Or not."

"She'll recognise him." Steve had recovered from his slight deflation. "Pimping'll be nothing to Brian Fletcher after what he's already done."

"We don't know what Brian Fletcher has done." But Steve's assumption had echoed Phyllida's fears.

"*He* won't recognise *her*," Jenny stated. "Will it be Miss Pym?"

"I don't know yet. Miss Pym has had her last bit of luck in the Marigold, by the way."

Phyllida reported the mood of the Elite and Judith's latest decision on their behalf, withholding the crux of the dialogue from the instant judgement of the young ones. Her move to leave with them when Peter decreed their departure was reluctant, and he saw it.

"I'm going to give Miss Moon a slug of my medicinal whisky," he told them. "I think she could do with one."

"I almost suggested it myself."

Steve had responded swiftly, confirming Phyllida's impression that his male ego was vulnerable to both real and imagined slights.

"You've earned it, Miss Moon." Jenny's smiling approval had to be confirmation that she had no personal interest in her boss.

189

"Thanks, Peter." Phyllida dropped back into her chair. "And thank you both for hanging on."

"Something more?" Peter suggested, as they heard the clunk of the outer door.

"Perhaps." She quoted Becky's lament.

"And you think she could have been referring to Judith?"

"I don't know, but it's hard to imagine her believing Fiona could have jumped. And I've already told you I suspect Judith of being capable of pushing her over."

"And the others could know, and be keeping quiet?"

"They could be afraid of Judith claiming they were involved if they shopped her. Or they could have been."

Neither pair of querying eyes was able to reassure the other.

"D'you think my imagination's running away with me?" Phyllida eventually asked.

"I'd like to, but I don't. At least it makes one feel a bit less queasy about withholding the evidence about Brian Fletcher from the police." Peter produced a bottle and glasses, and poured out. "So let's continue to remind ourselves that our policemen are wonderful and go on hoping for an arrest. Cheers and good luck."

"I've had it so far. And now there's Sharon's rendezvous."

"Which is enough in the mere planning to show that Judith isn't your average seventeen-year-old schoolgirl. D'you know the Café de Paris?"

"Some of the brighter sparks in the Independent Theatre Company used to sit around there between matinée and evening performance, sussing out the talent. I remember some tales of successful pick-ups. I went there a few times myself and rather enjoyed the way it spills out on to the pavement and people settle in for hours on end." The

190

memories were like the tiny distant view at the wrong end of a telescope.

"I think I'll go along myself on Monday night," Peter said casually. "And as I don't want to spoil Steve's fun on this one, there'll be two of us. You won't need us, you'll be protecting yourself, but one of us just might notice something."

"Yes. Oh, I'll be glad of that, Peter. And if it is Brian Fletcher," Phyllida forced herself to go on, "you'll see him at last."

"Actually" – Peter looked away from her as he lifted his glass – "I've seen him already. I went along to the ironworks late this afternoon, when I knew you'd have left, and had a look round. I didn't tell Jenny and Steve."

"Ah." Phyllida was out of breath. "You spoke to him?"

"Said I was thinking of gates but hadn't made up my mind. True in the end, because by the time I left I'd decided I had just the place . . . Sorry. Brian Fletcher. I thought he seemed a thoroughly nice chap. Not much else I can say, except that somehow that seemed to make it worse. I felt he was a touch nervy, but I didn't get any bad vibes from him."

"Mr Average."

"Well, yes. You get something more?" His eyes were down, looking into the whisky glass he was twirling.

"I could see a thoroughly nice chap," Phyllida said lightly. "If I didn't see a man who could be abusing his daughter."

"He made it a bit hard for me to remember that."

"Yes. I have to remind myself. I do it fairly successfully."

Peter had told her as she left not to come in the next day unless she couldn't keep away, and Phyllida spent the

191

morning in the garden. After ringing to tell him where she would be she spent the afternoon in the library. When she looked up towards the raised voice in the doorway she was astonished to see from the clock on the wall above it that it was almost five o'clock.

"Is there a Miss Moon in the room?" The young woman repeated herself with an embarrassed smile.

"Here!" As she threaded between the tables Phyllida smiled too, at the reflex word which had come with the memory of classroom assemblies. But by the time she reached the door her heart was bumping: she had given the library number to her father and Ken as well. "What is it?"

"A telephone call. Urgent, apparently." The young woman now looked slightly disapproving. "You'd better come behind the counter, Miss Moon."

"Sorry to interrupt," Peter said. "But Brian Fletcher's telephoned Margaret twice at the Golden Lion. John Bright's just been on to me."

"Oh, Peter!" The relief was enormous.

"Fletcher sounded agitated, according to John. Sorry, but you'd better get back to him."

"Of course. I'll go home. Margaret's there, if needed."

She was glad she had decided to give the car an outing. Her call had barely rung out when Brian was taking it.

"Yes?"

"This is Margaret Morrison. I've just got in and Reception told me –"

"Judith didn't come home last night, Margaret. She hasn't come home today. I haven't heard from her."

Phyllida tried to deplore the sense of excitement swamping her sense of concern. "Oh, Brian, what a worry! You've contacted the police, of course."

"No! No . . . Could I ask you to come over? Now?"

"Give me half an hour to change and tell Peter."

192

Brian opened his front door before she had rung the bell. Phyllida saw the light of hope die out of his eyes.

Or appear to. She had to remember there was an unidentified thespian at work.

"Come in," he said wearily. "Have a drink. I'm afraid I've had one already."

"Thanks." He was remembering she liked dry martini but his hands were unsteady and he was splashing it on to the tray that held bottles and glasses. "So you still haven't heard from her."

"No." He handed her the glass, turned away to pour for himself. "I haven't seen her since she left the works yesterday morning, before you came. When I got home last evening she wasn't here and that was a surprise, if not . . . Judith's very organised, you see. Very – tidy." It was a ridiculous word in the context, but Phyllida thought she understood it. "She always tells me when she's going to be out, even if it's only for a few hours. And anyway, at night-time she very rarely is. I mightn't see her all evening, she'll be upstairs writing or painting, but she'll be there. Oh, God . . ."

Brian Fletcher collapsed into a chair, slopping dark strings of his own drink across the pale arm as he slumped back and ran his free hand through his hair. Studying his portrayal of parental panic Phyllida had the unwelcome thought that he could know where Judith was, be using Mrs Morrison as an audience for the rehearsal of his performance of distraught father which he was preparing to present to the police.

But if he was what he seemed, twenty-four hours were a long time.

"Don't you think it's time you got in touch with the police?"

His beseeching eyes slid away from her face. "I've been in touch with one of her friends, Gill Jory. She saw Judith

193

in the café they go to yesterday afternoon, they split up at about five. She said – Judith was a bit dressed up. Not that that need mean anything, Judith was never sloppy, she was always . . ."

Brian Fletcher's voice tailed away, and he took a deep drink.

"So Judith did bring one of her friends home?"

"No, no." He was irritated, pulled himself upright. "I asked her about them after the concert and she told me their names. There was only one Jory in the phone book."

"The other one –"

"Gill said she'd get back to me if Becky knew anything. That was last night." He had put his glass down and was walking about the room, beating a fist into an open palm.

"Brian. One of Judith's best friends has just died a terrible death. She could have spent the night in shock on a park bench." Phyllida didn't believe it for a moment. "You must go to the police."

"The police . . ." Brian slumped back into the nearest chair and bowed his head to his knees. "Low blood pressure," he murmured.

"You told me. It has to be the police, Brian."

"I wouldn't want her . . . She'd think I was making a fool of her. She's as independent as a grown-up woman, Margaret." He raised his head and stared at her. "If Judith doesn't come home it's because she's decided not to."

"That's a strange thing to say. D'you know any reason why she might decide not to?"

"Of course not." The lie dyed his neck and face crimson. "It's just that I know Judith, she's always in charge."

"She's a schoolgirl," Margaret said gently, watching his colour ebb to pallor. "And even a grown-up woman

194

wouldn't be in charge of a car driven by someone else. I'm sorry, Brian, but –"

"If she'd been run over I'd have heard. She carries the pocket diary I give her each year in her bag and I fill in the personal details before I hand it over. So even if she couldn't speak . . . All right, I won't make it nine nine nine, but I'll ring the police."

"Good. Shall I leave you?"

"No." She thought he saw her for the first time since her arrival. "I'm glad you're here."

He looked up the number of the local station. While he was talking he mentioned Claire College, and the two detectives who had leaned against the college piano were there within minutes. They followed Brian into the sitting-room: tall, thin, cynical-faced Detective Superintendent Roberts, and pale, plump Detective Sergeant Atkinson.

"This is Mrs Morrison, Superintendent. A friend on holiday in Seaminster."

They hardly glanced at her and asked Brian if he would prefer to talk in private.

"No, no. I've done nothing since Mrs Morrison arrived except worry aloud about my daughter."

"You seem to have taken a long time to call us, sir. Is that because you know of some reason why she might not have wished to come home? A quarrel, for instance?"

"No!" The second question on the heels of the first had probably enabled Brian Fletcher to answer honestly. "We've never – needed to quarrel. If it seems a long time, that's because my daughter's so sensible, so mature for her age, so independent . . . I've hesitated to take steps that might upset her, make her think I'm being melodramatic . . ."

"Hardly very sensible or mature, sir, not at least to let you know she was intending to be absent. But then, she's just lost one of her best friends, hasn't she? She might not be thinking quite straight."

The Super's face was all concern, but Phyllida suspected a subtext.

"Yes," Brian agreed wretchedly.

"You've contacted her other friends, of course?"

"Yes. She left them yesterday afternoon following tea in a café without telling them what she was going to do."

"There's nowhere else you can think of where she might be? With another relative, for instance?"

"There aren't any."

"I see, sir. Is there anything at all you can tell us that might help us to find your daughter?"

"I'm afraid not." Phyllida wondered if the policemen were making anything of the flood of colour into Brian Fletcher's face.

"Have you been aware of any change in your daughter's recent mood or behaviour that could suggest a reason for her absence?" It was the Super's first question repeated, in more oblique and expansive form.

"None, Superintendent." Brian Fletcher answered it this time more calmly, but Phyllida saw him press his hands down on the arms of his chair to stop their trembling. "Judith is . . . she's a girl who keeps her own counsel, I'm afraid she doesn't confide in me how she's feeling, but I certainly haven't noticed any recent change. In her behaviour or her mood." His Adam's apple jerked up his throat, but this time he maintained his pallor. "It could be, though . . . As well as one of her best friends just dying so tragically, one of her fellow students was recently murdered. She was so outwardly controlled about them both, it could have caught up with her."

And if that was the truth, Brian Fletcher had got there first.

"I was just coming to that, sir," the Superintendent

countered quickly. "Did she know the murdered boy well, too?"

It was a rapier-thrust, but it appeared to miss its target. "I don't think so, Superintendent. As far as I know he was just a fellow sixth former." He should have sustained a scratch at least, but his ashen face hadn't coloured again or reacted in any other way. And if the police knew, or got to know, about Ralph Unsworth's infatuation, Brian Fletcher already had experience of pleading ignorance. Phyllida had to be sure, now, that he was an actor, if not the one she was looking for.

"I see, sir." Superintendent Roberts smiled with his mouth, his eyes remaining cool and appraising. He got to his feet, echoed by his sergeant. "Thank you for giving us as much to go on as you could."

As you were prepared to.

But she shouldn't be saddling the Super with a subtext just because he had the sort of face that has seen it all.

"Thank you for coming so promptly, Superintendent,' Brian was saying politely. "Where can I reach you if Judith comes home?"

The DS told him, and that they were contacting local hospitals.

"No news can be good news, Mr Fletcher," the Super said, as Brian led the way to the door after the policemen had remembered Mrs Morrison to the extent of wishing her good evening.

"Shall I go now?" Margaret asked, as he trailed back into the sitting-room. "You must be weary."

"I am, but don't go yet, I've got two chops, lots more drink. I'm not suggesting you share a vigil, but at least have dinner."

He poured her another drink and she followed him out to the kitchen. When he had got things under way they stayed there, perching on stools and talking in bursts about impersonal things and eating when the food was ready. Brian strewed more about his plate than he swallowed, but Phyllida was hungry and cleared hers, Margaret not being overtly involved in his anxiety. Not that he noticed. Several times during the meal he reacted as though he had heard a sound and sped to front or back door, reviving Phyllida's fear that she could be watching a performance.

When they had finished their coffee Margaret asked if she might see some of Judith's paintings.

He was hesitating.

"They're strange."

"I'm sorry, perhaps you'd rather not –"

"No, no, I didn't mean that. I can't think about anything but Judith, so I might as well talk about her. It's just . . ." He led the way upstairs, speaking over his shoulder as they climbed. "I find them a bit disturbing, actually, but her art master, Alan Williams, thinks quite highly of them. In here. I'd intended this room for her bedroom but she uses it as a studio."

It was a good-sized room, but the only furniture was a trestle table, a cupboard, and two unupholstered chairs. Some large canvases leaned against the skirting, their faces to the wall, and there were watercolours stacked neatly on the table. On an easel was a swirl of circles in violently coloured acrylic, which Phyllida found at the same time attractive and repellent. Brian pulled it forward to reveal a bright green garden under a violet-blue sky. The garden threatened as much chaos as the vortex already revealed.

"Strange, as I said." The arm that held the abstract forward was trembling.

"Yes. But powerful."

"Judith's strong." Brian Fletcher let the canvas fall back. "But she used to paint more delicate things. Mice, rabbits, still life with lots of detail."

198

"Not now?"

"When we first came here. Never now."

"People change. Young people develop." Margaret spoke lightly, turning to lead the way back downstairs. "I must go."

"I'll get a taxi," she said in the hall. "You have to stay here. Isn't there anyone you can call on? A good neighbour?"

Mrs MacPherson?

"Not just now."

Phyllida was pleased by the lack of reaction. But Brian Fletcher could have had up to three years' acting experience.

The taxi was there within minutes. "Ring me any time at all," Margaret said at the gate, as Brian peered into the shadows. "Whether or not there's news."

"Thank you."

"The Golden Lion," she told the driver.

Phyllida had secured herself another night away from home. There wasn't even the consolation of visiting Peter: as she got out of the taxi she saw that the office windows were dark.

Trying to be Pollyanna-glad his evening could be going well, she went reluctantly into the hotel.

The foyer bar was cheerful with people, but they seemed as remote to Phyllida as if she was seeing them in a film. The clerk in Reception told her there were no messages for Miss Moon or Mrs Morrison or Miss Lane, and she went to bed hoping she was wrong in her suspicion that, if Brian Fletcher really was ignorant of his daughter's whereabouts, he would prefer her to have had an accident than to attract the attention of the police and the social services by leaving home from choice.

Chapter Seventeen

When Brian Fletcher at last got to sleep in the early morning his waking nightmares about his daughter continued in more grotesque and surrealist form, and it was a relief when the sight of her body hanging in the stairwell exploded him back to consciousness.

He lay gasping, the nervous twitchings of his own body paralysed into stillness by the horror of his latest vision. When the telephone rang it was an effort to reach out for it.

"Brian, it's Margaret. Any news?"

"No." He had to cough to raise his voice above a whisper. "I eventually managed to knock myself out for a few hours with sleeping pills. That at least stopped me going downstairs every half hour to see if she'd dragged herself as far as the doorstep."

"What the police said last night, no news is good news. If she'd had an accident you'd certainly know by now."

"Yes." And if she'd had an accident (he was shocked to find himself thinking), they'd at least stay clear of the child-care department.

"Saturday," the Edinburgh voice was saying. "I've just drawn the curtains back and it's another fine day." All Phyllida could see was an oval of sky at the top of a well, but it was unclouded blue. "Will you be opening the shop?"

"I'll get on to Geoff, and he and Billy will. I expect

I'll look in at some point, when I can't stand it here any longer."

"Would you like me to come over this afternoon? If there's still no news."

"You're on holiday, for heaven's sake. I'm no company."

"Don't worry about that. Three o'clock?"

"Thank you."

Before getting up he rang the police station. Detective Sergeant Atkinson was already there, and said he was sorry, there wasn't anything as yet to report.

At nine Phyllida crossed the square. Jenny was at her desk.

"D'you always come in so early on a Saturday?"

"If I feel like it. I had rather a lot of typing . . ." Jenny collapsed into giggles under Phyllida's quizzical gaze. "All right, I wanted to know how you got on last night. And the Doctor's here, too."

"I'll tell you as I tell him. Steve?"

"Out on one of his standards. Looking for evidence of two-timing. That's rather taken over these days from looking for evidence to support a divorce case. He's back in his element."

Peter's tie was usually wrenched below the top button of his shirt in filmed Chandler style, but his appearance this morning gave Phyllida an impression of further slight disarray which she was unable to pinpoint.

"Did it go all right last night? When I got back to the Golden Lion I saw the dark window."

Peter rubbed a hand over his face. He had shaved, but had the air of a man who hadn't. "It went very well," he said bewilderedly. "Why did you stay at the Golden Lion?"

"Perhaps I might tell Jenny as well? The facts at least."

"Of course." Peter rang through and Jenny was instantly with them, leaving the door ajar on to her untended desk.

"Judith's father gives the impression he believes she's indestructible," Phyllida finished, "although he told me on the telephone just now that during the night he kept imagining her crawling home half dead. Which I suppose might be likely if he'd half killed her." The cynical comment was part of her new defence mechanism: the only way she could cope with Brian Fletcher, now, was by perpetually reminding herself of what he might have done. "Margaret's going to see him this afternoon. His anxieties might just prove burdensome enough for him to find himself offloading them on to her."

"No man would offload anxieties like his on to an attractive woman."

"If he had a choice. But I suspect Brian Fletcher is pretty near the edge. Anyway, even if he's no more than tempted it might tell me something."

Jenny had switched the telephone through and it rang on Peter's desk as he nodded his approval. Jenny's hand went out as well, but the receiver was nearer his.

"Mrs MacPherson," he mouthed sadly, drooping in his chair.

But as he listened to the animated squeak which was all Phyllida could hear he sat upright and his eyes brightened while his voice expressed distress and dismay.

"Disappeared? That's worrying . . . The police! That sounds drastic. Let's hope it means they've found her and are taking him . . ." He slumped again as the voice continued. "My inquiries? Nothing as yet, I'm afraid . . . Talk to the police?" His eyes rolled his alarm from Phyllida to Jenny. "No, I wouldn't advise it, Mrs MacPherson. I think in the circumstances it would be much fairer to say nothing. Particularly as I haven't been able to confirm your suspicions . . . Yes, I'll carry on with my inquiries, of course, but just at the moment . . . Yes, I thought you'd agree . . . Peter raised his thumb and a relieved smile. "Thank you very much for letting me know. I'll get back to you soon . . . You will? Thank you, Mrs MacPherson, that could be very helpful.

"The good lady's going to share any information she obtains about the Fletchers," Peter reported as he replaced the receiver. "We didn't put it into words, but Mrs M obviously shares our reluctance to relay suspicions about Brian Fletcher to the police just now, and she's quite prepared –"

"Doctor!" Jenny admonished. "Why did she ring?"

"Sorry. She rang to say that Fletcher was talking to her a moment ago at his gate, telling her about Judith's disappearance, when the police drove up. He asked them if they'd found her, and their answer was to ask him if he'd go with them to the station. Before they drove him off he got them to say in her hearing that they'd no evidence that anything dire had happened to Judith, so it must be that it's Fletcher himself they're interested in."

"And they'd hardly be inhumane enough to pick him up over income tax evasion at this particular moment."

"No." Peter looked thoughtful. "Go and ring Detective Sergeant Robinson, will you, Jenny? I've just remembered I owe him a pint and a pie."

They met at noon in the Eagle and Child. Dave said he'd have to make it snappy.

"Sure. I can imagine how the two Claire College deaths must be stirring things."

"Sure." Dave's baby face stretched in a smile of agreement.

Peter went to the counter, ordered sandwiches and collected two pints of draught bitter. He managed to

203

contain his question until Dave had picked up his last square of sandwich.

"How's the Claire College business going, then?"

"It isn't." But Dave's eyes had slid away from him.

"Look," Peter said. "For what it's worth I've got a friend who knows the Fletchers. And *you* know that I never reveal my sources."

The two men stared at one another.

"A letter arrived in this morning's post," Dave said at last. "Anonymous. The usual thing, individual letters cut out of newspaper headlines. It said that Brian Fletcher sleeps with his daughter." He paused to watch Peter through the motions of amazement. "Is that really a surprise, Peter?"

He had to offer something back. "The letter is. I've heard the rumour. I've no idea whether or not it's true. Have you?"

Dave shook his head. "He's been at the station this morning."

Peter waited, but Dave had drained his glass and was looking at his watch.

"I hear the Fletcher girl's gone missing," Peter said. He had, after all, just claimed to be a friend of a friend.

Dave didn't flinch, he could even be looking relieved. "Yes. Fletcher swears he doesn't know where she is. Or anything about the letter. He denies the allegation, of course."

"Of course. Is he being believed?"

Dave got to his feet. "It's too early to say. He's getting the third degree. And will get it again. It's all we can do to him at the moment." He turned away to look out of the window. "If you learn anything . . ."

"Of course," Peter said again, automatically. He was wondering if the letter would affect Phyllida's performance.

204

Brian Fletcher banged about his house, railing aloud against his daughter, feeling so mortally wounded he clutched his chest as he lurched around. He'd fulfilled his part of their bargain, how could she have done what she had? It had to be her, there was no one else who could have sent that letter, but it didn't make sense. When they caught up with her it would be one more thing to put her into the hands of the social services she had been so desperate to stay clear of. Did she really hate him so much?

But of course she'd deny it. In his mind's eye he could see her, the calm pale face, the wide steadfast eyes as she said she could only believe that her father must be ill . . .

The doorbell rang and he leaped across the hall. He was angry with her, he detested what she had done, but she was his dearly beloved daughter.

He wrenched his front door open, felt the hope dying out of his eyes as he saw Margaret Morrison. He'd forgotten she was coming. And wished that she hadn't, this serene Scotswoman on to whom he suddenly felt a longing to unload his anguish. And must not.

She was looking at him with compassion, not disconcerted by the disappointment he had made no attempt to hide.

"No news, Brian?"

"No news. Come in."

He lagged the way to the kitchen. "I'll make tea," he said, in the same toneless voice. He switched on the kettle and it began instantly to purr. In normal times he would have been amused at the discreet way she lifted it to make sure that it held enough water.

"You've been in touch with the police?"

"Oh, yes. I've got cake and biscuits."

"Just biscuits."

"Fine." He opened a tin and rolled some chocolate

biscuits out on to a plate. "The police called this morning and took me back with them to the station. Let's go into the sitting-room," he said as he poured boiling water. "I like seeing the garden."

"Fine," Margaret said in her turn. She followed him to the chairs by the open French window, waiting to speak until they were seated each side of the low table. "Why did the police do that, Brian?"

"They wanted to ask me about Fiona Jeffcoate, if she'd ever been here. I'm afraid I had to tell them I'd never met her."

Had he managed to persuade them that the letter was a lie? He'd told them Judith was adopted because he hadn't been able to bear the way they were looking at him, making sure they didn't touch him. At first that had made them even more contemptuous, they'd seen it as a feeble attempt to minimise what the letter claimed he was doing, but when he'd said he had chapter and verse at home they'd accepted he might just be human. But they'd still gone on and on. And promised him they'd go on again . . .

Margaret had closed the French window, making him aware that his legs had been cold.

"They didn't ask you anything about Judith?" She was pouring tea.

"Oh, yes. They thought it might help them to find her if they knew – what she's like."

"What did you tell them?" She asked so softly and gently he had no fear of her question.

"I told them she's always been reserved, undemonstrative. But that once upon a time she brought her friends home, talked about what she was doing, told me whether or not she was enjoying it. Then . . ." He stared down the garden, feeling himself frown. "She seemed to change overnight, the withdrawn secret side of her seemed to take

206

over." He paused again. "There was a phase before that when she seemed – excited. And then I lost her. That must sound ridiculously dramatic, but it's the only way I can describe how it felt. She just retreated into herself, shut me absolutely out. Upstairs every evening the moment dinner was over. Writing, reading, painting, working, staring into space, I don't know."

"You told the police all this?"

"I think so." Had he done? If he had, in the light of that letter it could only have increased their suspicions, and made him look a fool as well as . . . The interview had been so terrible he couldn't be sure what he'd told them. He only knew that he was telling things now to Margaret Morrison. That he wanted to tell her more and that he was having to struggle to hold it back.

A red-brown flash of fox took his eyes back to the garden. It was crossing a far corner of the lawn, a pair of vocally indignant crows hopping with spread wings each side of it.

"Judith used to call me when she saw foxes. Then it was only at dusk but nowadays they're less afraid . . . She only shows feelings these days with animals and birds. She's always cared about them, more than about people I've sometimes thought, although when our last cat died she said she didn't want another. I really must stop talking."

"It's all right, Brian. If it helps."

"It seems to. Margaret, I think Judith just doesn't want to live at home any more."

"Or go to school?"

"Oh, she wants to go to school. She's very ambitious, she wouldn't do anything to interrupt her education."

"Then she may be at school on Monday."

He shook his head. "Half term. The whole week."

207

"So she could be making a gesture which doesn't involve any sacrifice of her studies."

"I suppose so."

He was realising to his relief that he had told her enough to ease his craving for confession. He was so tired that when she got up to go he was almost glad.

Peter, Steve and Jenny had all announced their intention of being in the office at six, and when Phyllida arrived Steve and Jenny were playing poker and Peter was working on a report.

He invited them all into his room in what already felt to Phyllida like an age-old ritual.

"The difficulty is," she said, when she had told them the little she had learned, "he appears to be so worried about the disappearance of his daughter it's impossible to know how worried he is about the letter. We know he wasn't telling Margaret the truth about why the police wanted to question him, so there could be other lies as well. But his police interview must have been agonising and could account for his state of near collapse. It's half term at Claire next week, by the way, and he half agreed with me that Judith might be making a show of independence that didn't involve missing any school. Which he said she wouldn't want to do, she's too ambitious."

"If she's the third murder victim," Steve said, "at least she had time to arrange Sharon's rendezvous before being bumped off."

"Don't talk like that!" Jenny scolded

"Sharon's rendezvous," Phyllida repeated. "To wear, or not to wear, the red, white and green bandeau."

They stared at her. Jenny found her voice first.

"But you're not going as Sharon."

"Either as Sharon, or a Sharon type."

"No," Peter said.

208

"Yes. I've been thinking. Please all listen a minute. Argument for the bandeau: the two deaths at Claire will make Mr X wary whether or not he was responsible for one or both of them, and it could be that he'll do no more than come and see what he's missing. If he knows about Judith's disappearance – is responsible for it, even, and/or for the anonymous letter – that's even more likely. If he turns out to be someone I know, my seeing him will be enough. If I don't know him he'll see the girl Judith told him would be waiting, and give himself away in the moment of recognition."

"But you'd still be taking an unnecessary risk," Jenny protested. "I mean, if you're right and he doesn't approach Sharon" – she shuddered – "he'll leave when he's seen her, won't he? And you can hardly tear out after him."

"You could make a sign to me. Or the Governor," Steve added quickly. "One of us is going to be in the café and the other in the car parked nearby. Whether you know him or not we'll be after him."

Steve at least was with her so far. But it wasn't far enough. "Argument against the bandeau," Phyllida pursued. "If I don't wear it I don't think he'll be able to resist sitting down and waiting, and it will be a big bonus for me to be anonymous. If I know him it will be instructive, and if I don't he may still give himself away by his reactions." Phyllida paused. "And I'll be able to do something else, too."

"What?" Peter asked sharply.

"If he doesn't leave right away, sits down to wait for the bandeau, the Sharon-type can go up to him, commiserate with him for being stood up. He won't be wary of her, and she can –"

"Try to pick him up!" Steve completed.

"No!" protested Jenny.

Peter said, "And if she did, what then?"

209

"You follow him, as Steve suggested."

"If you picked him up," Jenny said, "it would be for . . ." Her eyes were huge with the mere idea. "You mustn't so much as *think* of picking him up, Miss Moon."

"I don't suppose I will. But if the opportunity was there and instinct suggested . . . Peter, you'd go along with it? You'll promise not to rescue me?"

"If an instinct were to tell me you needed rescuing, I'm afraid that's what I'd do. Before you left the café. I'm sorry, Phyllida."

"I should think so!" Jenny said. Steve offered Phyllida a despairing shrug.

"All right," Phyllida said. "But I'm still going to take option two. A Sharon-type. No bandeau."

"And the further option of leaving with him," Steve persisted.

"Stop it, Steve!"

"What I shan't be able to find out unless I go with him is Judith's role. Whether she's in charge or carrying out orders."

"The organ-grinder or the monkey," Steve amended. "That's the crux of it, isn't it?"

"That will be for the police to find out," Peter said severely. "If we're able to give them a lead."

But Phyllida wondered if the anxiety in his face might be a fear that his instincts would tell him to let her go if hers told her to try and pick up the man Judith Fletcher had provided, and she was successful.

Chapter Eighteen

Phyllida awoke on Sunday to wind-lashed rain and a view of the bay in which Great Hill had vanished behind an extended grey horizon. But inside her house she felt a calm as wary as the sun-flooded gardens of Judith Fletcher's paintings, awaiting the breakthrough of danger and revelation due on Monday night.

Phyllida grinned through a streaming window at her dramatic simile. Monday night could just as well be a damp squib bringing to an end her hopes of being able to help solve a murder or two.

She wanted the day to herself and ensured it by having Margaret ring Brian Fletcher and tell him she was struggling with a migraine but would do her best to get over to him if he was desperate for company. Considerate as ever over trivia, he told her, of course, not to dream of it, and she had to remind herself that she was not in fact leaving a friend in the lurch with a selfish white lie, she was merely declining to work on a Sunday.

By noon she had made good a week's neglect of the house, and had just sat down with her Sunday paper when the telephone rang.

The only work connection could be Peter, but her heart flew up into her throat.

"Yes?"

"Mrs Waterworth? It's Jackie Hart."

"I'm sorry?"

"The owner of Number Eight. How are you getting on?"

"Fine." A new alarm bell was ringing, far more clangingly than she could have anticipated. "I love it."

"You do?" On the far side of her unexpected fear, Phyllida found the voice pleasantly perky. "I'm sorry we didn't meet, but I'd had to leave quickly. You've got everything you need?"

"Oh, yes. It's a nice house, Mrs Hart." And hers until April, whatever Jackie Hart was about to say.

"You're saying all the right things. The thing is . . . I'm looking after my aunt in Eastbourne, as the estate agents may have told you. She's pretty ill, so I couldn't say when I'd be coming back to Seaminster. But she's just told me, Mrs Waterworth . . . She's leaving me her house. I'm ever so fond of Number Eight, but my aunt's house is something else again. Not size-wise, which I wouldn't want, but, well . . . I've friends in Eastbourne and the house is in a lovely position. So I reckon I'll just stay on. But that's in the future," Jackie Hart added hastily and on an audible intake of breath. "I'm only telling you . . . The thing is, I shall be selling Number Eight and before putting it on the market I wondered if you'd be interested in buying it."

It broke a law of Murphy, for something to happen at the height of one's desire for it. But Phyllida had to resist the dazzle streaming from the telephone receiver, secure a pause to think.

"I certainly would be interested, Mrs Hart. But –"

"But you've got to think about it. Of course. You can't just say off the top of your head."

"No. But if you could give me a week, say, before handing it to an estate agent . . . There's a very good chance I'll say yes at the end of a week."

212

"That's wonderful! Of course you can have a week. Two. Three. I can't do anything anyway until next spring, can I, with your lease running till then? If you do say yes I'll make arrangements so that I can come over. Nice to meet you, anyway."

"And you . . . I don't have to think about whether or not I want the house, it's whether or not I'll be staying in Seaminster."

"Which is a rather more important decision, I can see that."

"What are you thinking of asking?"

The question was academic: *A Policeman's Lot* would ensure she could meet it.

"I'm not. I mean, I'm afraid I've rung you as my first reaction to my aunt's announcement. I suppose in the region . . ." When Jackie Hart eventually came to a figure, Phyllida found it fair.

"If I buy, I'll be happy to give you that."

"Great! Let me give you my Eastbourne number."

They rang off with further expressions of hope for satisfactory outcomes all round. Phyllida found she had escaped Judith's baleful landscape, and leaped immediately upstairs to begin a tour of the house from the point of view of a prospective owner, although she knew it was unnecessary. As she had said to Mrs Hart, the question was whether or not she was going to stay long term in Seaminster.

The studio where *A Policeman's Lot* was to be made was south of London, she reminded herself at her bedroom window. And her salary would run to a hotel or even an intermittently rented small flat. And Number Eight Upland Road was her first real home since childhood.

The rain and wind hadn't slackened, but after forcing down a mug of coffee and a knob of cheese Phyllida put on a mac and whirled down to the satin-shiny promenade,

striding wet-lipped away from town. She walked round
the bay until the promenade petered out, then back again,
assessing the deserted seaside as she had just assessed the
house and discovering without surprise that she was not
a fair-weather friend, that she would love it at its greyest
and bleakest. She would have to struggle to keep off the
telephone to Mrs Hart at least long enough to appear
businesslike. Gerald wouldn't consider her businesslike.

When she turned into Upland Road she saw his car
outside her house, and discovered the real source of her
anxiety about telephone calls.

The car was facing towards the promenade, but until
she tapped on his window he didn't recognise her hooded,
hair-lashed face. His radio was too loud for where he was,
and she told him so as he wound down his window.

"Sorry, sorry!" He switched off without looking away
from her. "Was there a fire?"

"I fancied some exercise. Rain never hurt. I asked you
not to come, Gerald."

"I was about to go, you should have taken a longer
walk. But now you're here you can ask me in."

She was fascinated to be looking at him objectively;
it was so unfamiliar a viewpoint. She still saw his good
looks, of course, but also that his face was fattening at
the jawline and his eyes were bold and wary at the same
time. That, though, could be because of his temporary
situation.

"Of course. You've come far enough." It was an effort
to keep her reluctance out of her face. "I hope you've had
lunch, though, I've nothing in."

"I've had all the lunch I want. So these are your seaside
digs, darling."

"I rent the whole house," she said. Not rising to his
taunt was easier than opening her front door to him.

"Very nice," he said in the hall, before looking, as

214

she had known he would, into each downstairs room in turn.

"I don't think so," she told him, as he set foot on the stairs. Although she spoke quietly she knew her voice was confident and her eyes between strands of wet hair held his unwavering.

"OK," he said, letting go of the newel post. "Could I have a coffee?"

"Of course. Go through into the kitchen while I get my mac off."

Phyllida also tidied her hair, and saw in Gerald's face as she entered the kitchen the dawning of interest she had seen through the mirror in the Chelwood Hotel bedroom when she had had her first impulse to make more of her looks. This time, as she stared coolly back at him, the interest disappeared in a frown.

"A nice little house," he said, drawing a white chair out from the white kitchen table and dropping on to it. "But aren't you getting bored?"

"Not at all." The kettle purred right away, still warm from lunchtime. Phyllida spooned instant into two mugs. "I've a full-time job."

"Interesting, is it?"

"Very." She might have told him more, face to face, if her first assignment hadn't grown too serious to risk any mischief.

"So when are you coming home?"

"You mean to Wimbledon?" She wasn't trying to be unkind, it wasn't sufficiently important and her comment had been a reflex. But she saw the unkind effect of it in the jerk of his head. "I'm sorry, Gerald, but I never felt I really lived at The Cedars."

"You didn't give it a chance."

"Our circumstances didn't." She poured water on to the coffee grains, added milk to hers, put his in front of him.

"But I was there enough to know it would never feel like home."

"And your seaside nest does."

"Yes." Phyllida knew for sure as she spoke that she was going to buy Number Eight Upland Road. And that she would tell Gerald after she had done so.

"Because you're not sharing it with me?" He had looked away from her, and she realised on a pang of pity that the question was important to him.

"Partly," she said gently. "But I think, at the moment, mainly because I'm not sharing it with anyone."

"It's funny," he said, not looking in any way amused. "I never saw you as the self-sufficient type."

"Neither did I. Perhaps you did me a good turn."

"Please sit down, Phyl."

He held out his hand, and she took her coffee to the chair the far side of the table. They looked steadily at one another across it, and Phyllida saw that Gerald as well as Brian had an independent muscle under his eye. She had never noticed it before, nor the look of helplessness he was struggling to keep out of his face. But her second pang involved her no more than her first.

"D'you know yet how long this is going on?"

"It's only just begun." So much had happened, that sounded like a lie. And it wasn't the answer to his question.

"It feels like a long time." He spoke lightly, he might not even know what he was giving away. "And I still don't know what brought it all on."

If he had said that before she left him she might have told him, but already it was too much trouble. And there had been enough without the catalyst encounter at the theatre. "I think you do."

His eyes slid away. "I know we weren't getting on so well, but all marriages have bad patches."

216

"It was more than a bad patch, Gerald. You'd come to hate the sight of me."

"That's absurd." But his denial couldn't stand up to her steady gaze, and his eyes again veered away. "And you?" Slowly he brought them back to her.

"It wasn't doing me much good at all, and suddenly I'd had enough of it."

"And now?"

"I can answer you, Gerald, so I'd better do so. I shan't be coming back."

"I see."

This time he kept his eyes on hers. Willing them, she knew, to falter, to show that she didn't really mean what she had said. She kept them steady on his, mildly regretful that to do so she had to make them seem aggressive when all she felt was indifference. But perhaps indifference, the true flip side of love, would have been more devastating to Gerald than a belief that he still had power over her, if only to provoke hostility.

After a long moment he got to his feet. "You've become a stranger, Phyl," he said, looking down at her. "A cold, good-looking stranger."

"I'm sorry, Gerald." But she was glad the coldness was deterring him from reaching out for the good looks which she had no doubt would have been invisible to an objective eye. Gerald, in the end, was the one with illusions.

"We'll talk about divorce and so on another time," he said. The flicker of hope across his eyes died quickly in the face of her silence. "If you don't mind."

"Of course." She got up from the table, passed him to lead him to the front door without fear of being detained. The rain had stopped, and a pale sun rayed down through a hole in the clouds on to the freshly defined horizon. On the step Gerald put his hands for an instant on her shoulders, and when there was neither

217

response nor recoil he shrugged and walked off down the path.

"Goodbye, Gerald," she called when he reached the gate. He waved a hand without looking round, and as he disappeared behind her front hedge Phyllida closed the door.

The vacuum protecting the day had been breached and anyway, when she had poured the undrunk coffee down the sink, washed the mugs and put them away in an attempt to put away her uncomfortable thoughts, another concern was growing that she should spend the night at the Golden Lion. Brian Fletcher was bound to telephone in the morning, if not that night, to see if Margaret's migraine had left her.

After a couple of hours at the kitchen table, alternately making notes for the book and staring shocked down the garden at her detachment from the conclusion she had just wrought, Phyllida made and ate a snack, gathered her props and set off on foot along the promenade. She had provided the room at the Golden Lion with normal overnight needs, and all she had to carry was an airline bag containing the outward signs of Margaret Morrison in readiness for the unlikely event of a visit from Brian rather than a telephone call. It was no impediment to the solace of a now pastel-coloured sea and shore, which had her arriving in the square more cheerful than when she had set out.

At Reception she learned there were no messages or letters for herself or for any members of her cast, and came downstairs when she had deposited Margaret to order a whisky in the lobby bar, where she received a nod and a smile from a passing John Bright. By the time she had drained her glass she reckoned it would be dark and went outside to look across the square, reproving the intensity of her disappointment over the unlighted

218

windows announcing that there was nothing to keep her from the solitude of her dressing-room. But at least it was safe from Gerald, as Upland Road was safe from Brian.

Suddenly amused by her eccentric situation, Phyllida went light-footed upstairs, got quickly into bed, and switched on the television at the foot of it – in her few hours at the Golden Lion she had watched more television than in all her time at Upland Road.

The news was beginning, and although the customary sequence of tragedies and disasters was as distressing as ever Phyllida found herself growing irresistibly more relaxed. She was almost asleep when the words "Claire College" jerked her upright and she opened her eyes on to a picture of Judith's school. The police now had reason to believe, the newscaster told her, that the schoolgirl who had fallen from the roof had been murdered. Fiona smiled winsomely from the photograph into which Claire College had dissolved, and when she had switched the set off and eventually fallen asleep Phyllida had a dream of Judith's serious face breaking gradually into a smile so knowing it woke her sweating and she lay for what felt like hours trying to persuade herself that Judith was neither killer nor victim.

She must have slept again, because suddenly there was grey daylight in the well and a waiter was knocking with her breakfast tray. Brian Fletcher rang when she had finished her toast and was reading a small paragraph on page three of the *Telegraph* condensing the TV report on the death of Fiona Jeffcoate.

"How are you this morning, Margaret?"

"Better, thank you."

"Good. I'm sorry it's so early, but I've had a letter from Judith."

"Oh, Brian, I'm so glad! That means she's all right." The dream was still uncomfortably vivid.

219

"Yes . . . She and the postmark say she's in London. I'm not to worry or to look for her, and she'll be in touch again."

"What a wonderful relief."

"Yes."

"Does she give any sort of explanation? Or apology?"

"Neither. Margaret, I don't know if you've seen or heard the news, but the police are saying Judith's friend Fiona was murdered."

"I saw it on TV last night, and I've just read it in the paper." She could hardly wait to get across the square. "Look, shall I join you in the shop at lunchtime? I've a few things I want to do this morning, and I'm tied up tonight." Which she literally could be, maybe by the man she was speaking to, however grotesque the imagining.

"I'd like that. Thanks. If the police – want to speak to me again I'll leave a message with the lads."

The paper open on Peter's desk was a tabloid, but it didn't offer any more detail than Phyllida's *Telegraph*. Peter had, though, begun his working day with a telephone call to Detective Sergeant Robinson.

"The handle of the door out on to the roof balustrade had been wiped clean of fingerprints, and the middle edge of the door itself. Unless the Jeffcoate girl was killing herself in order to accuse someone of murder she would hardly have been responsible. There could be more questions now for Brian Fletcher. You said he left the supper party?"

"Yes. It's hard to say for how long. And it's hard to believe he spent the time taking or pursuing Fiona the height of Claire College. He'd have to have planned the ascent after a fashion at least and I just don't feel that he was a man that evening with a plan."

"One would have expected him to give something away. No second thoughts about tonight?" Anxiety took over the expressive face like a cloud across the sun.

220

"No. And I still want the best of two worlds. You letting me do something rash if my instincts tell me to, and keeping me in sight while I do it."

"If you do do it, we shan't be able to keep you in sight all the way. Where would you call a halt?"

"Where I still can, I hope. But I can't know in advance where that will be. You're going to give me my head, then?"

"I can't know in advance." They grinned at one another before anxiety settled back into Peter's face. "But I appear not to be such a stickler for my principles as I thought I was."

"Whoever it is may be just a simple punter," Phyllida encouraged. "We have to remember that the Elite weren't seen at all during the supper interval. And Judith's run away to London, her father just rang Margaret to say he's had a letter from her this morning telling him she's OK and not to look for her."

"But the police will," Peter said, after a long, drawn out whistle. "You know, I'm not really surprised, I knew that girl would surface in one piece, she's a survivor. Did she say why she'd gone, if and when she was coming back?"

"I gather not. Margaret's having lunch with Brian at the works. I expect the police will have taken the letter over by then, but he'll probably give her the details."

"Your confidence is surely not misplaced. About tonight. Sharon's rendezvous is for nine?"

"Yes. I'll be there by ten to."

"I'll be there, inside the café, at a quarter to. Steve will be strategically parked for access and a quick getaway."

"Thanks. Jenny?"

"I think not, but leave it to me. The letter from Judith should provide a distraction."

Peter had perhaps already prepared his ground: when

221

Phyllida arrived Jenny had been flushed and vigorously typing and when she left the situation was unchanged, with Jenny not looking up as she wished Phyllida luck and told her to be careful.

Phyllida crossed the square back to the Golden Lion, and at half-past twelve Margaret walked to the ironworks through cool pale sunshine.

"He's out back," one of the lads told her on the forecourt. The other was serving in the shop. Brian was in the armchair where Margaret had recovered from her dizzy spell, two mounds of unwrapped sandwiches on the table beside him.

"I gave the police Judith's letter," he said wearily as he got to his feet. "I looked out a postcard I had from her when she stayed with a friend last year and gave them that with it."

She took the armchair. "Did you have any doubts yourself that she'd written the letter?"

"No." He went over to the kettle. "While I was at the station they asked me my movements the night of the concert. I never thought I'd regret going to the loo." He was trying to make a joke of it.

"Most people will have gone, and the police now will have to question everyone who was at the concert."

"I suppose so. I had to tell them I had a companion who's staying at the Golden Lion. I'm sorry, Margaret."

So was she. Unlike Jennifer Bond, Margaret Morrison wasn't ready to check out.

Brian put two mugs of coffee on the table. "Let's eat, shall we?"

"Thank you." Phyllida waited until he had toyed with half a sandwich before speaking again. "Did the police ask you anything else about Judith?"

"Not really. But I told them I thought she'd be back the week after next for school, when half term's over."

"She's under age," Margaret said gently. "They'll still have to look for her."

"They told me that. They won't find her."

As she got up to go Phyllida heard herself say there was some doubt about her evening engagement. "I'll know by about six o'clock if it's on or not. If not, would you like to come to the hotel for dinner?" It was so shockingly simple a test she had only just thought of it.

"That's very kind of you, Margaret, but I think I'll try for an early night. See if I can get some sleep."

"Yes. Of course."

It didn't mean he was guilty, it only meant she hadn't proved his innocence.

And if the police took him into custody and no one came to see Sharon, that wouldn't mean he was guilty, either . . .

"I'll ring you tomorrow, Margaret."

Tomorrow seemed to be separated from today by more than the customary number of hours. Margaret walked back to the hotel, and Phyllida walked home. Then drove a wide semicircle beyond Seaminster, assessing it as she had assessed Seaminster itself and Number Eight Upland Road. It passed muster, and the exercise passed the time that had to be surmounted before she started her preparations for Sharon's date with the unknown. When she had forced herself to make and eat a very small meal, she packed Sharon into the airline bag and drove to the carpark behind the Golden Lion.

223

Chapter Nineteen

The oval of navy-blue sky above the well was high and clear, studded with constellations, and the air on Phyllida's cheek as she leaned through the narrow window was sharp and still. There wouldn't be tables on the pavement outside the Café de Paris, but there would be people strolling the promenade and deciding to stop for a drink at the tables inside.

It could have been just the lingering effect of her dream of Judith smiling, but Phyllida couldn't shake off a surrealist feeling that if Judith was free to do so she would somehow contrive to witness the encounter she had brokered, and decided it would be prudent to alter Sharon's appearance as well as remove her bandeau. And to change from streaked blonde to brilliant redhead was to offer Peter and Steve an easy marker if it turned out that they needed one.

When she was ready, and had overcome the moment of panic in which she wanted to spend the rest of her life in her spartan sanctuary, Phyllida left the Golden Lion by the back door John Bright had shown her and sped the short way to the promenade through deserted alleys. Beside the moonlit sea, where she slowed to a saunter, there were plenty of people, including a couple of men who tried to detain her but were quite easily deterred by a glance through the Sharon mask. It was good to see Peter's car parked where nothing could park in front of it and Steve looking alert at the wheel. Although she had rung the office to report the change in Sharon's appearance, Phyllida leaned for a moment against his open window and watched shock, lust and disappointed realisation flit across his sharp-featured face.

"Not bad," he murmured.

"Thank you."

She shimmied on, pleased to see that the café was as she had hoped to find it: a buzz at the entrance as customers came and went and passers-by peered in, and about half the tables occupied. She didn't have to search for Peter's fair head: the back of it was framed in one of the long windows next to the doors, so that he could see the whole art nouveau interior with scarcely a movement. She passed him with an exchange of glances and sat down at a small table against the wall, halfway down the café and from where she too could see every other customer and discover in a very few moments that there was no one at a table as yet whom she had seen before, or who seemed to be taking any sustained interest in her arrival. But there were a few more Sharon types to secure her a degree of anonymity and the prospect of her acrobatic heart returning to its proper place.

She would have liked whisky, but if she struck lucky there would be alcohol later. Otherwise she wasn't hungry or thirsty, but a waitress was approaching. There was a coffee pot on Peter's table so Phyllida ordered coffee. She left her bill on the table underneath what she owed plus a tip, in case she had to leave in a hurry.

Another thing she could see was the large round clock on the back wall in its elaborate silvery frame of floating-haired maidens and trailing plants and with what she thought at first were stationary black fingers. Her eyes had returned to it three times before she realised the fingers were moving, and by the time they reached two minutes to nine her whole day seemed to have been spent rigidly attached to a mauve-seated bentwood chair.

She didn't have to spend more than another few minutes of it there, of course: when the fingers of the clock had crawled to say nine-fifteen she could walk out to Peter's car and get into it having learned something – positive or negative – that she hadn't known when she arrived.

Phyllida played with the idea, wistfully as if it were out of her gift. Which it was, of course. If someone she knew, or identified by his actions, came into the Café de Paris she would have the chance to learn more. To learn, in Steve's all-encompassing phrase, whether Judith was the organ-grinder or the monkey. And if that chance was offered, she would not be completing her evening's assignment – in her own estimation at least – if she didn't take it . . .

She had learned something positive. She had recognised the figure standing just inside the café. Surveying the place in a leisurely way as if looking for no more than a vacant table, then sitting down the far side of the edge-to-edge glass doors, Gog to Peter's Magog. The hysterical laugh was bubbling again in Phyllida's throat.

When he was certain there was no red, white and green bandeau on any young female head he sat down and opened his evening paper, refolding it loosely on the table for ease of reading. But before he looked down at it he caught the eye of a waitress and ordered a double scotch, and when he started to read he interrupted himself to look up whenever anyone passed his table, and again to make regular surveys of the interior of the café and imagine what he might do with the young women who could appropriately have been wearing the signal Judith had given him.

A pity he couldn't claim the bandeau, if and when it

appeared. He'd enjoyed the other two prostitutes Judith had procured for him. But now the police knew the death of her close friend hadn't been an accident it would be too risky, even with the house to himself. And the fact that Judith had become the object of a police search made it utterly impossible.

Thinking about Judith's disappearance made him smile down at his newspaper. But when he had mastered the smile and looked up again, the big art nouveau clock showed five past nine and he felt himself frowning. If she was coming she should come in time.

He should be relieved, of course, to be spared the tantalisation of seeing her and not being able to do anything about it. If she looked as good as the other two had turned out he would have found it very difficult to resist the temptation . . .

But if the girl did appear, he would at least have the satisfaction of knowing that Judith was still mentally to heel. If she didn't, it could just be that Judith had been playing a different sort of game with him, taking a nasty little revenge because she wasn't enough for him these days on her own. As he looked round the bandeau-less café he began to feel himself a victim. He could be wrong, of course, but he could be right, and when he got back he'd make sure he found out which.

Nine-fifteen, and he ordered another scotch. She was unlikely to come now so he might as well enjoy looking at the others while his drink lasted, not waste a pleasantly titillating situation being angry with Judith, particularly when it just might not be her fault. She'd make it hard for him to find out whether it was or not, and he'd have to be careful because he mustn't kill her until she'd written at least one more letter from London . . . The post at least had been kind to him, arriving so promptly – Monday posts could be tricky.

One of the girls was miming at him, looking at the clock as he supposed he had been looking at it, then shrugging her shoulders and ruefully smiling. His first reaction was disdain, that she could equate her squalid situation with his, but then he saw that she was attractive and began to feel flattered. And there was only a coffee pot on her table, it was unlikely to be drink priming her.

His response was minimal – the slightest widening of the lips and the eyes, lifting of the shoulders – but she was getting lazily to her feet and it could be that it had been enough to bring her over.

Unless it was just that she had had enough of waiting, she was making her way to the cash desk, paying her bill. Moving, automatically provocative, towards the door.

Veering at the last second to seat herself on the chair the other side of his table.

"You been stood up too, ducky?" She must really like the look of him, to risk the embarrassment of discovering she was propositioning a gay, or a born again. That would be why her eyes were defensive and her smile a bit nervous, making it friendly rather than sexually inviting. "Murmur 'Get lost', and I'll be on my way. It's just that my friend hasn't shown, either, and two lonely evenings could add up to one well spent."

Phyllida waited, watching the wariness intensify, sharpen the smooth outline.

"Okay, okay. I'm on my way." She would swear to herself ever after that there was no relief in her disappointment. She started to get to her feet.

"Okay, okay," he mimicked. Reverting to the self she knew yet of course didn't know at all, relaxing, smiling. "Sit down."

His skull could have been glass, she could see his brain dismissing risk and switching to the prospect of pleasure, finding amusement in his unexpected good fortune.

"What's it to be?" he asked her.

"Scotch? Just a single."

"Sure. But we'll make it a double."

"I'll be persuaded."

The waitress was there right away, he was that kind of man. He ordered two double whiskies, not asking if she wanted hers diluted.

"So tell me about yourself. Your name, for instance."

"My name's Marilyn."

"Of course."

She could have warmed her hands at his smile. "And I'm the sort that tends to strike lucky."

"Me, too."

"Well, good."

It went on like that until the whisky came, while they were drinking it. She was asking her instincts how long she should hang on when he drained his glass and leaned across the table. "Shall we go, Marilyn?"

"If you give me a name I can call you."

"Rex. Okay?"

"Okay, Rex." Marilyn grinned, letting out Phyllida's contemptuous amusement. She stayed at the table while he went to pay, facing Peter across the doorway so that it was easy to meet his eyes. The shake of his head was feeble, and she grinned again.

"On our way, then." He was back, and putting a hand lightly under her elbow to steer her outside. It was a touch so much too far that Phyllida had to force herself not to move clear of it as she realised to her relief that there were things her instincts were not going to allow her to do.

Voluntarily.

So she ought to stop now.

"My car's not far."

Farther than Peter's. Phyllida stared expressionlessly

into Steve's excited eyes as she strolled past. When she stopped for a moment to adjust her shoestrap, steadying herself with the support of a shoulder that burned her hand, she saw Peter getting into the front passenger seat.

"All right, Marilyn?" He unlocked his passenger door, assisted her inside. The door closing brought a moment of panic regret that it wasn't Peter's, but he and Steve wouldn't, couldn't, be far behind.

"Nice perfume, Marilyn."

"A lady I worked for gave it me." Gerald had given it last Christmas, probably something he had grabbed at the latest moment before the shops shut, expensive but not right for Phyllida Moon. She had put it among her props.

The people round them on the promenade could be on another planet, they seemed so far away. They drove the length of it, passing the ironworks without a glance from either of them, and then he took the next road inland and they began to climb away from the town.

As far as a familiar pair of gateposts.

Between them.

"All right?" he asked. She could feel his tension returning. But even at half term a school was a school. "We're almost there."

He drove past the unlighted Gothic row and parked round the side of the farthest house. St Jude's. Was Jude a form of Judas?

"Hey! What are we doing at Claire College? I thought we were stopping in the park. You kinky or something?"

"I'm a teacher here, and it's half term," he said as he switched off. "Better than the back seat of the car."

He was out of the car, beside her door, opening it. "There won't be anyone around," he said, "but we won't hang about."

"I'm not sure . . ."

230

"Out you get! I've told you, it's all right."

Already it was a different contact with her arm. A grip rather than a touch, which she was grateful to the whisky for softening.

"All right, all right, I'm coming." Experimentally she shook her arm, and he let it go. They took the steps at a canter and his key was ready for the lock.

He shut the heavy door before feeling for a light. So far as Phyllida could remember, the stark, darkly defined hall was identical to the hall of St Bride's.

"All right, Marilyn." Radiantly he smiled at her. Relaxing again, holding her shoulders between his hands. Turning her towards the stairs . . .

No, turning her towards the kitchen, the grip on her arm painfully tight as she instinctively resisted, bruising her flesh instead of making it crawl.

"Come along." The continuing smile, the bright empty eyes, were in chilling contrast to the pinching hand. Which he relaxed again as they entered the embrasure that hid the door to the cellar. He had another key in his hand, he was unlocking the door.

Miss Turner had been going to say something about the cellars to Jennifer Bond, but then her assistant had come screaming the news about Ralph Unsworth's body. The scream echoed in Phyllida's head the length of the steep downward flight.

"In here."

Two doors at right angles. He took a key from a hook to open the larger one. It was heavy and metallic, the door to a strongroom.

Perhaps containing something Phyllida was suddenly as terrified of facing as her own immediate future. If Judith was the monkey rather than the organ-grinder she too could be dead.

Or worse.

231

"In you go!"

He pushed her, so that she stumbled forward into the vast dim space. It took a few moments to make out the enormous bed jutting into the centre, and then to see that the darker shape lying on it was a body.

As Phyllida ran towards it the room was brilliantly illumined and she saw that the body was manacled to the bed by an ankle and a wrist.

And that Judith was blinking, and drowsily smiling.

"Christ almighty!" Marilyn turned on him, eyes blazing. "When I asked if you was kinky you said you were a teacher. You should have said kinky teacher. I'm off!"

He barred her way, of course, gripped her arm again. "When we've had our fun."

"That isn't her," Judith said, feeble but distinct. "That isn't Sharon, Alan."

"I know it isn't Sharon." The smile was a sheer baring of the teeth as, still holding Marilyn's arm, he bent over the bed. "Sharon didn't come, did she?"

"She said she would. Honestly, Alan. But so long as you've found someone who'll do –"

"She'll do." He put his hands on Phyllida's shoulders, pushed the wide low neck of her blouse down her arms. Above the door, a bell-shaped piece of metal began to vibrate and emit a deep regular clang. The smile disappeared. "Who the hell . . ."

Tightening his grip on Phyllida's arms he wrenched her round to the other side of the bed and pushed her down. She didn't see the second pair of manacles until he had snapped them on her. The bed was so large there was room for two or three more people between her and Judith.

Gill, Becky, Fiona . . .

The door confirmed its strength by the sound it made as he went out. He had left the fluorescent tubes alight and Phyllida could see from the high pillow that the long wall opposite the bed was covered with painting. A vast stretch of green lawn with a fountain under a cloudless blue sky, balefully precise. Fading each side into a rage of bombarding missiles, arrows, wedges, circles, flashes in aggressive primary colours.

Except that at the inner end, extending a couple of feet or so, there was a delicate and affectionate country scene with animals and birds.

Judith wriggled and gave a contented sigh. "That was the front door," she murmured. "Alan will get whoever it is to go away, and then he'll come back."

If Peter and Steve hadn't been close enough to see which saint had swallowed her up . . . There was a grating high up on the wall opposite the door. And a gentle whirring sound. She tried to shout "Help!" and managed a croak.

"Nobody can hear," Judith said dreamily. "But we don't want them to."

"Why does Alan keep you prisoner, Judith?" She could manage a whisper, too.

"Because it's a game, of course. The best game in the world, even when the others played too. Alan taught us. He taught us lots of things. At first when I lost . . . when things changed . . . I didn't like it, and I'm glad I've got him to myself again, now. All to myself." Not yet, but on the way. *Oh, Gill, how could she?* One down, two to go. "Like at the beginning."

"Judith, Alan killed Ralph Unsworth."

It was worth a try, because with enormous effort Phyllida had managed to turn her head far enough to be able to watch Judith's calm profile.

It didn't change.

"And your friend Fiona."

All to myself . . . Phyllida was less certain Alan Williams

233

had killed twice, but Judith murmured, "I know," and smiled at the flaking yellow ceiling. "I told him, you see. I told him what a danger both of them were to him. Ralph tailing me all day – he almost caught me once on the way down here, it had to be a matter of time – and Fiona getting more and more hysterical. They were as dangerous as each other, they could have destroyed him and I couldn't let that happen, I had to warn him. When you love someone . . ."

When Judith Fletcher loved someone the love, however abused, didn't know how to die. Steve's sharp voice quoting from the remains of Judith's diary seemed to come from a world Phyllida hadn't inhabited for a very long time. And Judith was so far away from it, if she were to die now in place of her love she would scarcely notice.

Phyllida, though, would notice death, she had never more desperately wanted to live. To play the sister in *A Policeman's Lot.*

"That grille must lead to the outside."

"To the bank at the back of the houses." Judith nestled into the bed. She had got used to the extent of her bondage: since Phyllida had been laid beside her all her movement had been inside it, not testing it. And Phyllida wasn't testing hers, because of being paralysed by fear. "We tried it out, of course, we couldn't take any risks. It's okay for ventilation but it cuts out sound. The person outside has to have an ear to it and the person inside has to shout her head off for the faintest sound . . . So we reckoned we were safe."

"Can you hear anything from inside the house?"

"Not a sound," Judith murmured. "Not even at the foot of the stairs."

But Phyllida found herself trying another shout. Still a

croak, so she tried again. She tried harder and harder until her lungs burst on a gush of screaming which made way for more and then more, against Judith's eventual lazy protestations. The answering shout came simultaneously with the unlocking of the door.

Chapter Twenty

"You could have saved your breath," Peter told her in the Golden Lion, when she was lying on another bed at a man's insistence.

"You could have told me you had the police on standby," she reproved him.

"I was afraid it would make you bold." Peter looked severely at Steve, who decided to sit on the floor rather than the one small armchair. "As you were bold anyway I needn't have worried. But even with the police waiting I could and should have stopped you. I'm sorry, Phyllida."

"I'm not, he could have gone back and killed Judith sooner rather than later. And I was on the warpath, I would have been furious. I had to find out who was the boss. Why did the police let you take Sharon/Marilyn away with you without even asking her name?"

Peter grinned. "I told them through my Detective Sergeant before I told them anything else that you were a member of my staff and they'd have to leave you out if you delivered the goods. If Williams hadn't appeared I'd have aborted and they wouldn't have been any the wiser. So you're still anonymous." He pulled a face as they heard the knock on the door. "It's only the drinks. Get them, will you, Steve."

"You look quite interesting," Steve said when he had found a place for the tray, cocking his head like a sparrow. "A tramp with ladylike Miss Moon sort of showing through."

She had shed the wig and vaguely wiped her face. "Oh, never let it be said that Miss Moon is ladylike, Steve." The hysterical laugh was on its way up again, and she let it out.

"Sleep for you, I think," Peter said, when she had done. "After you've had this." He handed her the brandy. "It's bedtime, anyway."

Phyllida sat up and wiped her face again, turning the tissue into an artist's palette. "It's just reaction. Alan Williams must have opened the door to the police, I didn't see any evidence of break-in when they brought us out."

"He did open it. And they tried St Jude's first because of where his car was parked. They wouldn't let us keep close enough to see where you went in, in case he bolted with you."

"He pulled a knife when he saw the police," Steve took up. He was sitting against the small severe dressing-table unit, his beer glass in the acute angle of his spread legs. "I think he was just hoping to get to his car and away by waving it around, which was pretty moronic. They got it off him quite easily, and then he sort of made a gesture like a host and they followed him in."

"You were there?"

"We were stuck behind the shrubbery," Steve said in disgust. "But I left the car to have a shufti. It seemed like ages before anything happened, I suppose he was trying to put them off. They brought him out before they brought you."

"It was a long hard wait," Peter said. "Until one of them brought Steve back to the car and told us you and Judith were okay."

"Judith was drugged," Phyllida said. "I suppose they've

237

taken her to hospital." Her mind was back at work. "Brian's bound to be on the phone early to tell Margaret about it. Judith seemed to like her, I'll suggest a visit from her might be helpful."

"You're a real pro, Miss Moon," Steve said approvingly, raising white-rimmed lips from his half pint of mild. "And she knows what I mean," he told Peter, shielding himself with an arm in mock terror of reproof.

But Peter only said, "So do I," and leaned towards Phyllida so that he could touch her glass with his.

Morning was an anticlimax. Phyllida stayed in her room because of not wanting to miss Brian's telephone call, but by lunchtime he still hadn't rung. She could have gone downstairs, but he might come in person and she couldn't summon the energy to produce Margaret before she was forced to. It would have helped to talk to Peter, but when she rang across the square Jenny – no longer sulking, and all scolding and affectionate relief – told her he was with the police, and Steve reluctantly on another job. So all Phyllida could do was tell herself that Peter had to maximise and minimise the role of his anonymous operator simultaneously, which would take time as well as ingenuity, and ask Jenny to ring the Golden Lion as soon as he got back.

Brian's call came as she was picking self-pityingly at a chicken sandwich with her narrow sash window open on to the well. He had spent the morning beside Judith's hospital bed.

"The tragedy is," he said, when he had told Phyllida most of what she already knew, "she still seems to care about him. She didn't really tell me anything – what I've learned I've learned from the police – she just kept saying, I know you understand, Daddy. But I don't, how could I?"

"How could you?" Margaret agreed.

238

"I think she was glad I was there, though. She held my hand and I could see it in her face." Phyllida waited through the pause. "Look, would you consider seeing if Judith will talk to *you*? I know she liked you, and as showing she likes someone is a rare thing with Judith there might just be a chance."

"Of course."

"You're very good. I have to tell you, though . . ." She heard the sob. "The devil was doping her. Just Valium, it seems, but she isn't clear of it yet."

"Clear enough for me to see her today?" Phyllida had realised her anxiety for Margaret to be free to disappear.

"They say so. I'm afraid I asked the doctor if I might bring someone this afternoon."

"That's all right."

"Thank you. I'll come for you, then. How soon –"

"Give me an hour. I'll be at the door."

So she couldn't do more with Peter's call when it came than arrange to go straight to the office when she left the hospital.

"Hello, Judith."

"You're Mrs Morrison." Judith was less comfortable than she had been in the cellars of St Jude's. There was sweat and a frown on her forehead and her hands were pulling at the sheet.

"Yes. How do you feel?"

Judith's gaze became an angry stare. "I want to see Alan."

"I'm afraid Alan's in police custody. You know why, don't you?"

"Of course I know why. He killed Ralph Unsworth and Fiona. Because they were threatening him. I warned him. I told him Ralph wouldn't leave me alone and almost caught me once opening the door to my house cellar. The cellars are connected underground which was how we got into St Jude's. If Ralph had got to know that it would have been the end of things, the end of everything for Alan, so he had to stop him. Fiona couldn't handle it, she was as dangerous as Ralph so Alan had to deal with her as well. He's told the police," Judith said impatiently, "he hasn't tried to hide anything. Is my father still here?"

"Of course. D'you want to see him?"

"I shall do. Although he doesn't understand. You might. Alan was looking after me. He wouldn't have hurt me. He never did anything I didn't want when the time came."

Because he had always made sure that the time was ripe. Phyllida shivered in the overheated room as she decided to exploit the ending of Judith's lifelong reticence. "What was it you and your friends did with Alan, Judith?"

"Played games. Games like plays. At first I didn't . . . At first it was just Alan and me. No games. Just – what you dream." Even Judith Fletcher. "That was all I ever wanted, but Alan . . . Alan got tired of that." A shudder went the length of the white coverlet. "So I had to do something else for him. He gave me an idea, and there were Gill and Becky. And Fiona." Scorn flickered in Judith's face. "That was a mistake, but once she knew . . . Gill and Becky thought I'd killed her."

And in a sense they had been right. "Judith?"

"I didn't spend the whole of the supper interval with them, you see. Everyone else thought she'd killed herself, but she hadn't the guts or the single-mindedness, she was already making up to Tim Rowland. I was the only one who knew it was Alan. I told him. I said I ought to go to the police but I wouldn't have done." Of course not, but even Judith couldn't resist a show of power in so unequal a relationship. "That's when we went back to being on our own. Just him and me. No one else. No Becky, no Gill."

240

"Sharon?"

It was a gamble; drug-free, in charge of herself, Judith would have questioned Mrs Morrison's knowledge of Sharon. But she was still living exclusively in her mind.

"Sharon was nothing," Judith said scornfully. "Alan had had another idea so I'd got two girls like Sharon for him for times when I – we – couldn't be there. Nights. Slumming, he called it. I never saw him with them, but he always told me everything they did." Judith's legs were moving restlessly about the bed and her hands were still plucking at the sheet. "Then this time he thought . . . Sharon with him and me . . ." Judith stared at Phyllida, the pain of the latest betrayal in her eyes.

"Alan could have killed you as well, Judith." But that was something Phyllida suspected Judith had half been courting, and wasn't surprised that she didn't answer the charge.

"I was glad when Alan said I should write to my father, I didn't want him to be worried. I was glad when he told me to write to Gill and Becky, too. Otherwise they might have said something, especially if they were afraid I might be with Alan . . . Alan was away the next morning, he went to London to post the letters."

"He left you on the bed?"

"If I wanted. He said he didn't believe in games for one, even though he had to leave me to play patience." Judith's exquisite lips widened to a rictus rather than a smile. "And he knew I'd need to go behind the screen. There's a sink there, and a camper's loo."

"Ah." That aspect of things might be comparatively trivial, but it was good to be able to discard the range of images it had offered. The policeman behind the screen by the door scraped a shoe on the polished floor, and Phyllida coughed and copied him. On a reflex, she was sure now that all Judith was aware of outside her head was

241

the presence of a listener. "What about the bed, Judith? And the paintings?"

The smile was brief, and disappeared in a look of sadness Phyllida found disturbing in Judith's face. "I started the painting at the beginning. When it was just Alan and me. I saw all the boring wall from the bed . . . The bed had belonged to St Jude's first housemaster, it'd taken up a whole room and when the owner retired it was shunted down to the strongroom. When Alan and I realised how we felt he took me down there. It was safe and private, no one else ever went near it. I started the painting the next afternoon, you don't have to play games at Claire, I mean games like hockey and lacrosse." Judith stared unsmiling at Margaret, confirming Phyllida's instinct that she lacked a sense of humour. "And if you don't you have what they call a quiet hour, in the library or your house, the staff too, so most weekday afternoons we managed to get down there . . . We dressed the bed up and Alan found some rugs."

And Judith started thinking about happiness ever after. There couldn't be more than fifteen years between them, and there wasn't a wife. The murals had begun as the equivalent of gloss and eggshell in a new home. Phyllida's sudden sharp picture of Judith painting, smiling to herself, turning to greet the love of her life, was making tears prick behind her eyes.

"I didn't stop painting until the wall was full. Even when things – changed, and the others . . . All you have to do in all three houses is go into the kitchen and disappear. Gill would come to me from School House and we'd go down together, Becky went from her house, and Fiona was there already. Not that that meant she and Alan ever . . . on their own . . . he didn't want *that*." Judith tossed from side to side of the bed, pushing hair off her forehead with both trembling hands. "And I didn't want the others

242

at first, but Alan made it all right . . . And then when Ralph was dead we couldn't, we daren't, with the police about. Will you please get my father?"

"Of course. In a minute. Judith, the police received an anonymous letter."

"What about?" A languid surprise.

"About you and your father. What you were doing together." She had to force it out.

For a moment Judith lay motionless, a frantic appeal in her wide eyes. Then, as Margaret stared comfortlessly back at her, she slowly pulled herself upright, shrinking against the iron bed-frame as she tried to back away from what she had just learned. "Alan . . . It could only be Alan . . . No one else . . ."

"Yes, it was Alan, he's admitted it. Because of Alan the police know what your father's been doing to you." Phyllida chose Margaret's words with reluctant care.

"My father? My father hasn't been doing anything to me. It was me!"

"Judith?"

"Me, me, me!" Judith's angry sense of justice had temporarily eclipsed even Phyllida's revelation. "When Alan . . . When he didn't want just me any more, when we started the games . . . Daddy isn't my blood father and he's the only other person I love, so I tried to make him, I tried to make poor Daddy . . . So that I could pretend it was Alan and me like we were at the beginning."

"Oh, Judith." The relief was so great she had to hold herself back from seizing one of the fluttering hands.

"I suppose I always knew that Daddy never would. Poor Daddy. In the end he was locking his bedroom door against me. But I told Alan I'd done it, that I'd seduced my father. I thought it would be the sort of thing – he'd like to hear. I didn't tell anyone else because it wasn't true. So Alan . . ." Judith shrank back again, and Phyllida watched the ugly process of her love at last discovering how to die. "Alan – did – that. Alan – could – do – that. To Daddy. To me. To *anyone*." The love had encouraged and surmounted two murders, but not a casually selfish destruction of living people. Phyllida wondered if Judith's mouth could recover from the disgust into which it had twisted. "He's vile, I hate him; I wish they still had hanging. Get my father to come, will you?"

"All right, Judith. You'll leave him in peace, now?"

"Of course!" Judith said impatiently. "Anyway, I don't want anything to do with men – like that – ever again."

The extravagant reaction was the first sign of youth Phyllida had seen in Judith. Perhaps there was a chance of recovery. She moved away from the bed, and the policeman met her at the door.

"Mr Fletcher told me about the anonymous letter," she lied to him.

"Of course, Mrs Morrison. And thank you. You'll find Mr Fletcher outside. Perhaps you'll ask him to come in. When you've had a word."

Brian Fletcher was pacing the corridor.

"She's all right," Margaret told him. "She's over Alan Williams and she's waiting for you."

His arms were round her. "I shall never be able to thank you for all your help. Although I'll try."

As the pressure intensified Phyllida drew away.

"I've been glad to do what I could, Brian. Goodbye."

"You can say goodbye to Mrs Morrison any time you like," Peter said. "The police won't want to see her again, they know she's one of my operators."

"The same one?" Phyllida asked, through wild laughter.

"I didn't quite say . . . Better have a medicinal glass, Phyllida. Sit down."

"Thanks. And sorry. It's just reaction. It was all so sad." She seemed to be crying, too. "I think I'd rather have coffee."

"They'll make it. Better get them in here, anyway." Peter swung heavy-footed to the door and opened it noisily, giving Steve time to retreat as far as Jenny's desk. "Come on in," he said, "with a tray of coffee."

"How did you get Margaret off the hook, as well?" Phyllida asked while they were waiting.

"With the anonymous letter having done the dirty on Fletcher I was able to tell the police we'd been asked to investigate his relationship with his daughter. After last night it wasn't too hard for them to accept my story that a member of my staff had become a family friend as part of the investigation." Peter leaned across his desk, his eyes shining. "Thanks to you, Phyllida, I think we're about to enjoy a special relationship with the local constabulary."

"And I'm going to retain my anonymity?"

"Of course. Come in!"

Steve held the door for Jenny and the coffee tray.

"You've been very clever, Peter," Phyllida said. "Tell me what you learned this morning."

"We none of us know," Jenny said. "We were waiting for you."

"Thanks to Miss Moon again, I learned a lot more than my tame Detective Sergeant would have told me if the firm hadn't handed the police their murderer." Peter sat back in his chair and put his fingertips together. "It looks as though it was his double life that gave Williams his buzz. All charm and respectability in public, and in private seducing his students and depraving them." Phyllida found the severity of Peter's moral judgement rather comforting. "To say nothing of killing the two people who threatened his cosy set-up. The police have been lucky, he seems to feel now that by flaunting what he's done he can cut his losses. And he's doing his best to get Judith to share the guilt with him, saying she kept on at him to silence them."

"She kept on telling him how dangerous they were. I learned that in the cellar when Judith was really drugged. She told him Ralph Unsworth was on the point of learning the unique geography of the houses because of following her everywhere. And that Fiona couldn't cope. Judith's lifestyle was at risk as well."

"Fiona started cutting up rough in the concert interval," Peter resumed after a pause, "to use Williams's words as quoted by my DS. So he suggested they go upstairs and have a few moments to themselves."

Jenny gave a choked cry, and Peter paused again until Steve had returned to his seat after crossing the room to pat her shoulder.

"Judith's disappearance. She told Williams she knew he'd done both the killings and that she might go to the police, so he enticed her down to the cellar with the promise that she could spend the half-term week with him and pretend to be in London. She was to have him all to herself, which was enough to ensure her total cooperation, down to the wording of the letters he virtually dictated to her father and her two friends. He told her she was to go home at the end of the week, but he didn't tell her to write that to her father and her friends, because she wasn't." They stared round at one another in silence. "The anonymous letter was the other half of his scheme," Peter eventually resumed, "suggested by Judith's boast that she'd seduced her father. It offered a reason for her leaving home which conveniently put the blame on Brian Fletcher. Not for killing her, of course, because Williams wanted it thought she had disappeared of her own accord into the bottomless pit of London like so many other young people." He hesitated. "Williams has told the police he was planning to dispatch her in time to dispose of her body before school reassembled. He was thinking of another letter from London in the meantime."

"And more games," Steve said.

Phyllida was glad to see him recoil the instant he had spoken. "What was his attitude to her lie about her relationship with her father?"

"Amusement."

"Poor Judith. She thought he'd be impressed. Is he a psychopath?"

Peter shrugged. "It's possible. He hasn't any form, but psychopaths can have bags of charm and be very clever at keeping their distance from the mayhem they create. If he is one, though, it means he always has been, at least potentially, and to have kept his nose squeaky clean for thirty-two years in that condition is a bit unlikely. I'm more inclined to think of his trouble as the John F. Kennedy syndrome. But he hasn't got Kennedy's legion of minders, so that when he was threatened he did his dirty work himself. An underdeveloped moral sense, at the very least." Peter crossed to a window and pulled up the sash. "Phyllida?"

She told them about her visit to the hospital. "I couldn't have imagined being sorry for Judith Fletcher, but I was. I suspect she's never been a 'nice' girl, I think she's been cold, self-centred and calculating since she was a child, but she fell in love and became as vulnerable as the sweetest girl next door. All she wanted, I should say, was a straightforward exclusive relationship. And she got Alan Williams." *I couldn't let that happen, I had to warn him.* "She was a match for him, though. He'll be shut away and she'll stay free, but I think they're both guilty.

"So far as Brian Fletcher is concerned, my guess is that

247

most of his misery came from his fear that because Judith was capable of one monstrosity – trying to seduce her father – she might be capable of another – murder. And I don't suppose he knows the history of her genes."

"Let's hope he recovers." Peter's eyes were on Phyllida's face. "I must say it'll be a pleasure to give Mrs MacPherson the good news. Judith must have been taking the initiative when Mrs M saw them. And what she heard in the garden would have sounded much more likely the way she interpreted it. Now, I've got other things for you to think about in the morning, but tonight I'm taking everyone out for a celebration dinner. So I suggest you all go home and titivate. Phyllida, remember you came into town this time by car."

"Thanks, I'd forgotten." It seemed a very long time ago.

"I'll pick you up at home, at seven. All right?"

"Fine."

Back in her room at the Golden Lion to dispatch Margaret, Phyllida sat down in the little armchair and stared out at the well. She sat there for a long time before swivelling the chair round to the dressing-table unit and taking some hotel stationery out of its only drawer. Margaret told Brian Fletcher she was about to leave Seaminster, and would have left earlier if she hadn't wanted to try and be of help to him and Judith. Now she could no longer delay her departure, and events had fallen out so that she was unlikely to return. She sent him and Judith her sincerest good wishes, and no other address.

Phyllida posted the letter in the Golden Lion postbox, then drove home. When she had put her car away she walked back to the promenade and leaned on the rail. The day was fine, but sky and sea were delicately pale and the tap of cool air on her cheek was a herald of winter.

248

Winter . . . What would she be doing then? Still working for Peter, she hoped, and still looking forward to her TV debut. Which needn't mean the end of her career as a private eye. In fact, if Peter was willing she could combine them, work for him when she wasn't filming. And when filming came to an end, if she didn't want – or couldn't manage – to go back to the stage . . .

As she stared at the thin grey line of the horizon Phyllida's pensiveness faded into an awareness of being alive and well, and thoughts of the telephone call she was about to make to the owner of Number Eight Upland Road.

Anyway, she wasn't ready for a man so much in need of healing. And if she ever was . . . The gate leading from the front to the back of what would soon be Phyllida Moon's property was in need of replacement, and a view of the garden through handmade wrought-iron would add considerably to its attraction.

ST. LOUIS COUNTY LIBRARY

INFORMATION

RECREATION

EDUCATION

E-18